PRAISE FOR *THE L*

D1633450

*"**The Last Laugh** is just what I like in a story—funny, mystical, original, deep. If you like adventures of the heart and spirit, you'll really enjoy Arjuna Ardagh's story of an awakening journey like none other."*

— Gay Hendricks, Ph.D., author of *Conscious Loving* and *The First Rule of Ten: A Tenzing Norbu Mystery*

*"This moving story of one man's journey from profound darkness to the light powerfully illuminates the central struggle of modern times to find a new way forward. **The Last Laugh** is chock full of wit and wisdom but also that rarest of qualities in modern fiction: hope."*

— Lynne McTaggart, international best-selling author of *The Field, The Intention Experiment,* and *The Bond*

"This is a great book. Arjuna is a wordsmith of the highest order, and this is brilliantly written. I laughed out loud many times, and loved the way the deep insights are also entertaining. Highly recommended."

— John Gray, Ph.D., author of *Men Are from Mars, Women Are from Venus*

"A rich and feisty tale, beautifully told, of people who live out of the box while they make the world a better place. This is spirited spiritual literature of a new order and is highly recommended."

— Jean Houston, Ph.D., author of *Jump Time* and *A Passion for the Possible*

*"Arjuna awakens us to the joy and humor of life ever-evolving! His brilliant wit, perception of reality, and love make **The Last Laugh** a real journey into the divine."*

— Barbara Marx Hubbard, president of the Foundation for Conscious Evolution

*"**The Last Laugh** is a delightful adventure in consciousness, and will uplift the soul, and lead to transformation in the most marvelous way."*

— Sonia Choquette, *New York Times* best-selling author of *The Answer Is Simple . . . Love Yourself, Live Your Spirit!*

*"**The Last Laugh** is simply a tour de force. I want everyone to read it. With compelling power, grace and wit, it presents the great teaching that your small contracted self is not the true or full you, it is simply a case of mistaken identity. The book has clarity, love, and the power of a direct transmission of an awakened state. And it is wildly funny. I laughed out loud many, many times, I found ancient perennial wisdom presented in fresh and original ways, and I fell in love with the characters. This is a book I never wanted to end. Essential reading—truly one of the great 'visionary' novels."*

— Marc Gafni, Ph.D., author of *Your Unique Self: The Radical Path to Personal Enlightenment* and founder of the Center for World Spirituality

"This has to be one of my top ten reads of all time. What can I say? Everything important about being human is in this book . . . and it is funny, too! Everyone should have a copy."

— Marci Shimoff, author of *Happy for No Reason* and *Love for No Reason*

*"**The Last Laugh** is funny, it offers deep insight, and it is so well written that you will not want to put it down till you are done. I highly recommend everyone buy this book and pass it on to your friends. I promise you will not regret it."*

— Hale Dwoskin, author of the *New York Times* bestseller *The Sedona Method*

*"Arjuna's novel **The Last Laugh** points us back to the things that are really important in life, in a style that is heartfelt; well written; and very, very funny!"*

— Janet Bray Attwood, *New York Times* best-selling author of *The Passion Test*

"This is an amazing and funny book that will bring enlightenment and laughter into your life."

— Yakov Smirnoff, Russian comedian, actor, and author of *Smirnoff for the Soul*

*"**The Last Laugh** is an outstanding novel! It presents all of the wisdom of the ages in a story that you can't stop reading. If you want to become wise without having to study over it, read this book. I am buying a bunch of these novels to give to my friends."*

— Brad Blanton, author of *Radical Honesty*

*"This new book by my good friend Arjuna Ardagh is a Zen Koan come alive. He manages to capture the paradox, the ecstatic highs and the great falls from grace, and the humor of the authentic spiritual Path of us Human Beings. **The Last Laugh** takes us on a journey that is authentic, compelling, and very funny. I highly recommend it!"*

— Genpo Merzel Roshi, American Zen Master, creator of The Big Mind

*"**The Last Laugh** is, simply put, a wonderful book! Arjuna Ardagh's writing puts you squarely in the middle of every scene, and he weaves a story with such skill that you want to keep turning pages. This novel speaks clearly about who the author is: bright, funny, articulate, and compelling. You will feel brighter and better for having read this wonderful book."*

— Mary Morrissey, founder of Life SOULutions

*"While many, many books have been written about the concept of enlightenment, **The Last Laugh** is a well-written, totally engaging, wise, and modern story of what the transformational process looks like, sounds like, tastes like, and feels like. Just as a picture is worth a thousand words, a book like this is worth a hundred preachy tutorials."*

— Steve Bhaerman, a.k.a. Swami Beyondananda, co-author of *Spontaneous Evolution: Our Positive Future and a Way to Get There from Here*

"At last . . . a spiritual novel with guts and depth."

— Peter Russell, author of *From Science to God* and *The Global Brain*

"This book guides you through a spiritual journey full of surprises, triumphs, defeats, and belly laughs that will open your heart and your mind."

— Deborah Rozman, Ph.D., CEO, HeartMath, Inc.

"We're lucky that Arjuna is such a good writer because he's managed to take timeless spiritual wisdom and turn it into a thoroughly entertaining story. While reading **The Last Laugh**, I loved how the lessons in the novel were in alignment with my own life, helping me be inspired to take the next step in my own evolution."

— Jonathan Robinson, author of *The Complete Idiot's Guide to Awakening Your Spirituality* and *Communication Miracles for Couples*

"Hilarious and refreshing! Arjuna elegantly reminds us, laughter is transcendence. This book is fun to the core, wise, and a must-read for any spiritual seeker."

— Rob McNamara, author of *The Elegant Self* and *Strength to Awaken* and president of Performance Integral

"Sometimes we get stuck in a web of thoughts, desires, fears, stress, and not knowing about the future. And I mean stuck. BUT . . . we can free ourselves, really free ourselves. This sweet, powerful book shows you how."

— Martin Rutte, founder of ProjectHeavenonEarth.com and co-author of *Chicken Soup for the Soul at Work*

"I love Arjuna Ardagh! **The Last Laugh** shines with humor, heart, authenticity, and depth. It will cause you to question reality, reminding you of what's really important in life. Full of wisdom . . . read it if you dare!"

— Kute Blackson, inspirational speaker and author of *Love.Now.*

"**The Last Laugh** is a funny, moving, passionate exploration of what it means to be fully alive. Filled with entertaining, inspirational, daily life lessons that every reader can put into immediate practice. And it's a fun read!"

— Matt Weinstein, founder of Playfair and author of *Managing to Have Fun*

"The writing is lyrical, sensual, and rich in details, and the characters are wonderfully drawn. All that alone is a fine achievement, but what was really inspiring is how effective this story is in conveying the journey of Awakening. I loved the way it conveyed the almost magical quality of first induction and breakthrough, the collapse into ego self-protection, the displacement of the energy onto the external anima and the understanding of bringing it home. I can feel the richness of Arjuna's own experience in what he portrayed and it mirrors much of my own."

— Richard Moss, author of *The Black Butterfly*

"Delightful. A compelling real-life journey that caught and held my attention immediately while providing a unique glimpse at the real-life pain and cloaked divinity that surrounds us all the time. Some books are fun while others are important; this one is both."

— Eric Edmeades, CEO, Kerner Studios

"In my profession, filmmaking, it's all about story. To make a good movie is to tell a good story. A skilled storyteller uses words like colors to paint a world that can be seen and felt. Arjuna Ardagh's words are so vibrant with necessary detail and poetic charm that it's hard not to get sucked down the rabbit hole. The Last Laugh enlightens as it entertains! Reading it left me deeply aware that this is a writer who has lived the full spectrum of life, and as a result deeply understands the mythologies that are the foundation of our human experience."

— Mikki Willis, founder of Elevate Films

"This book offers us the best in visionary fiction. The Last Laugh frequently takes us by surprise, and it's subtly insightful, touching, and laugh-out-loud funny. I did not want it to end."

— Barnet Bain, producer of *What Dreams May Come* and *The Celestine Prophecy*

"The Last Laugh takes you on Matt's thrilling journey from profound human despair to awakened hope, then into authentic freedom. Arjuna Ardagh's brilliant new novel will thoroughly entice and captivate you, then awaken and introduce you to your own personal freedom. Read this brilliantly developed and wonderfully written novel for inspiring entertainment, then find yourself automatically transformed and awakened to your own exciting potential. A 'Wow!' Book!"

— Bill Bauman, Ph.D., founder of the Center for Soulful Living, author of *Soul Vision* and *Oz Power*, and originator of The Ultimate Human

"This gem of a novel leads us on a journey of spiritual awakening, with art, humor, and unblinking honesty. Buy it!"

— Stephen Josephs, Leadership Development Expert and author of *Leadership Agility* and *Dragons at Work*

"Arjuna Ardagh is a masterful storyteller. From the moment I began reading The Last Laugh, I felt immediately engaged and a part of this enriching journey. Through Arjuna's rich and textural writing style, mixed with his steeped understanding of spiritual awakening, I've witnessed moments of deeper insight, compassion, and clearer vision in my life choices, bringing a richer awakening of freedom and love throughout my daily experience."

— Carl Studna, photographer, author of *CLICK!: Choosing Love One Frame at a Time*, and founder of the LuminEssence Method

"Arjuna has written a profound page-turner with deep insight into reality that anyone who has been through any crises in life can easily relate to. I thoroughly enjoyed it."

— Isaac Shapiro, Spiritual Teacher and author of *Outbreak of Peace*

"The Last Laugh smashes the same mold most spiritual stories drearily recycle through. Finally an enlightened story that is funny, uplifting, and unpredictable. Great read!"

— Steve D'Annunzio, author of *The Prosperity Paradigm* and founder of The Soul Purpose Institute

"Both laugh-out-loud funny and deeply touching, **The Last Laugh** offers an entertaining and realistic glimpse of one man's awakening. An added bonus is Arjuna's deep understanding of consciousness-in-action, which gifts readers with rich reminders and insights to apply to everyday life."

— Vickie Falcone, author of *Buddha Never Raised Kids and Jesus Didn't Drive Carpool: Seven Principles for Parenting with Soul*

"**The Last Laugh** is a charming, postmodern fable about the awakenings and transformations we can go through when life takes us to the bottom and won't let us up—and we suddenly access resources both in others and in ourselves that we couldn't possibly have imagined in advance."

— Saniel Bonder, author of *Waking Down: Beyond Hypermasculine Dharmas, Great Relief,* and *The Tantra of Trust*

"I highly recommend this entertaining novel of the spiritual path home for its humor, insight, and sheer exuberance. It's a real page-turner!"

— Paul John Roach, Senior Minister, Unity Church of Fort Worth

"This is a wonderful read—I stayed up all night to finish it, and the story returns often in my daily life. . . "

— Haines Ely, Host, KVMR Radio

"Arjuna is a great storyteller. He creates a wonderful mix of mysticism and action with his first novel, **The Last Laugh**. It's a masterpiece."

— Nik Colyer, author of *Channeling Biker Bob*

"Sometimes when I finish a book I don't want the book's world to end—I want to stay in it a little longer. This is a lovely book showing the span from despair to ecstasy and the everyday life that occurs in between. Ultimately, I think it's the book's lightheartedness that moved me to tears in the last chapter."

— Anne Anderson, Institute for Noetic Science

THE
LAST
LAUGH

ALSO BY ARJUNA ARDAGH

The Last Laugh

ARJUNA ARDAGH

VISIONS

HAY HOUSE, INC.
Carlsbad, California • New York City
London • Sydney • Johannesburg
Vancouver • Hong Kong • New Delhi

Copyright © 2013 by Arjuna Ardagh

Published and distributed in the United States by: Hay House, Inc.: www.hayhouse.com®
• *Published and distributed in Australia by:* Hay House Australia Pty. Ltd.: www.hayhouse.
com.au • *Published and distributed in the United Kingdom by:* Hay House UK, Ltd.: www.
hayhouse.co.uk • *Published and distributed in the Republic of South Africa by:* Hay House
SA (Pty), Ltd.: www.hayhouse.co.za • *Distributed in Canada by:* Raincoast: www.raincoast.
com • *Published in India by:* Hay House Publishers India: www.hayhouse.co.in

Cover Design: Amy Rose Grigoriou • *Interior Design:* Jenny Richards

All rights reserved. No part of this book may be reproduced by any mechanical, photo-
graphic, or electronic process, or in the form of a phonographic recording; nor may it be
stored in a retrieval system, transmitted, or otherwise be copied for public or private use—
other than for "fair use" as brief quotations embodied in articles and reviews—without
prior written permission of the publisher.

This is a work of fiction. Names, characters, places, and incidents are the product
of the author's imagination or are used fictitiously. Any resemblance to actual events or
locales, or persons living or deceased, is strictly coincidental.

Cataloging-in-Publication Data is on file at the Library of Congress

Tradepaper ISBN: 978-1-4019-4232-8

16   15   14   13   4   3   2   1
1st edition, May 2013

CONTENTS

CHAPTER 1

THE BRIDGE

They say when a body hits water from a great height, it's like hitting concrete.

I looked down into the freezing Pacific.

Only if the impact is purely perpendicular, is there any chance to survive. Then comes the swim, and the coldness. The swim to what? To another dead end.

I stood on the bridge just before midnight, the wind from the ocean arriving in violent blasts, as if saying under its breath, "Jump, mother-fucker, jump." The occasional passing car sent another small wash of air, adding an additional vote for my extinction.

This was the last of a string of attempted departures, most orches-trated in my tired mind. Hours spent in Long's Drugs looking at little bottles and wondering what dosages were lethal. Painful walks on the train tracks by the park, punctuated by the carefree laughter of children on the swings. Children. Always a bitter reminder of all that had been lost and destroyed by my foolishness.

The horn of a truck on the bridge shocked me back to the cold and isolation of the night. And to the decision. How could the end bring with it such concern for consequence? The longing for annihilation tugged against the quivering fear of retribution. A gull swooped down, and shat on the iron of the bridge. Nausea. Everything brought on nausea, as if I were allergic to all of life. Everything was out of control.

The descent had been gradual. I had vague memories, like images out of focus, of a time of optimism. The wedding. That was a time of lingering dinners, of best wishes, of shiny new kitchen gadgets that would whisk up a lifetime of security. Their built-in obsolescence was brightly overlooked. Her eyes were so adoring then, everyone was a friend; everyone wanted to be close. The world was made of good smells.

We had built the perfect life. I had my own radio show on KYQD, "Beyond Belief." It was an eclectic forum for anything beyond the ordinary. Over the years, I talked to John Bradshaw, Ram Dass, even the Dalai Lama once. We had environmentalists on the show, authors, New-Age gurus, you name it.

We lived on the east side of town, Rebecca, me, and the kids. We had the best of everything, a beautiful house, two cars, an apparently idyllic marriage, and good friends. Becca was a graphic artist and had a few clients without having to worry. We had a good life, not extravagant but very comfortable. We preferred camping over hotels, barbecues at home over eating out.

"Once I led the life of a rich man . . ." Clapton's voice came out of the darkness from a passing car radio, and was gone. The glare of headlights from a truck, another harsh lunge at one already stumbling. Give me time, give me time. I looked away from the glare, the rust on the metal bridge tower. Another wave of nausea.

Back to the endless tightrope between this hell and another. Papers were blowing randomly on the quay nearby. My thoughts flew out of control. Sarah's birth, four years ago, the whole world was full of blessing then. Such promise, a new daughter, my career going so well. Dom's first day at school. He cried when I left, and I hid for an hour in the bushes outside to be sure he was all right.

All gone now.

The stink of reality, the faint smell of the river below, the even fainter hints of food cooking beyond the quay: Indian, Italian, American smells, it made no difference. It all made me want to throw up into the beckoning and horror of the December water below.

Another demon lunged, appearing from who knows where to join in the endless chaos of mania and indecision. Dominic's voice on the phone last week, "I love you, Daddy. When can I see you, Daddy?" Words which only months ago had brought such riches, now drove the knife deeper into the wound beneath the ribs. There was no way to explain to him my confusion, my mumblings, it just added to his conviction that it was he who had done something terribly wrong. Each time my children's voices came into the discordant medley, the water below became more horrifying. Without them, the jump could be so perfect, final, free of consequence.

Harmer. Dave Harmer. The only man I knew I could kill with my bare hands, and enjoy it completely. On the show, he was so cocky, talking about his new invention, a bike powered by the sun. Tiny cells between the spokes and on the frame picked up the sun's rays, stored them in a patented lightweight battery inside the frame, which could then propel the bike up hills. Like a moped, but so light you could put it on top of your car. He talked about the environmental benefits, how many more people would ride a bike if the hard work was taken out of it.

Afterward, over drinks, he told me how Costco and Pepsi were both endorsing the bike in national sweepstakes, that the military had a stake in it, that he had offers from all over the world. And . . . he was short $125,000 to complete his last essential safety tests before the bike was ready for national marketing.

I kicked the railing of the bridge. Bastard. How could I have been such a fool?

There were reasons he was not at liberty to reveal, why he had to borrow the money from a very special, very lucky private party. People were fighting for the chance to be that special one, but he had turned them all down for "karmic reasons." He kept in touch, calling me from hotel rooms all over the world with stories of great potential success. He never asked me directly for the loan, just told me that he would make the right person a very special offer: lend him the money for six months, and he would then return it with 100 percent interest.

I bit.

We had good equity in our house, and I had great credit. A mixture of greed and environmental exuberance led me to do something I later came to bitterly regret. I took out a second mortgage on the house, effectively leaving no equity in it at all, and took out a line of credit at the bank. I lent him the money. Sure, I had an iron-clad contract; I even had my attorney check it. Everything seemed above board and reliable.

I felt a stare, like a grip on the back of my neck. I glanced over my shoulder. An old man was standing by the next tower. Probably homeless. Whichever way I angled myself away from him, I could still feel the intrusion of his look. I wanted to be left alone. Even in this despair there was no peace.

A police car drove slowly over the bridge, slowing almost to a stop as it came close to me. Time was running out. Time to jump and be done forever, or walk away. Another flash of Dominic and then of Sarah, sweeping out of the darkness at me. What had these innocents done to deserve a father's suicide?

The old man was still staring, as though challenging me to make a clean decision. Jump or move. The police car was coming closer. I started to walk to the other side of the bridge, as if pushing my body through treacle. I glanced at the police car, and averted my eyes as I passed the hobo, his look still piercing.

I walked into the pre-Christmas bustle of the city at night.

CHAPTER 2

A Visit from Venus

The neon sign said: "Open till 2 A.M.," a spider's web luring passing drunks and insomniacs. I stepped inside to old cracked linoleum on the floor, small booths around the outside wall, a few sad lost souls sipping black coffee at the bar. "Idiot Wind" was playing on the jukebox. I looked for the table with least exposure. Safety. Above all I had to protect my wounds.

I sank down into the dirty upholstery of the booth, patched together with gray duct tape. Cold, defeated, I did my best to avoid the accusing stares of lonely people.

A woman walked out from the kitchen into the serving area behind the bar. Wavy blond hair was pulled back into an ornate clip on top of her head. Even from this distance, I could see penetrating blue eyes. She looked as if she could be in her 30s, past the naïve exuberance of youth, but still fresh, still open. She picked up the decaf flask to fill a patron's cup, with the elegance of a Roman goddess. Shy and retiring, yet without fear. She had the strength and presence of royalty. Venus—suddenly it was clear. She could be the model Botticelli used for his Birth of Venus. She turned to the glass-fronted display case to take out a lemon meringue pie. She lifted it like a holy sacrament. She placed the pie on the counter and sank a knife into its heart. In that cut, I was also slain. She placed the pie on a plate, and without any change of her demure expression, she offered it up to her midnight guest. I was in a fairy story with kings and dragons and princesses. This was a woman of royal blood.

Memory came crashing back in. I looked away. My jeans were frayed and smelled of many days and nights of use. My jacket, once a prized object, was torn and stained. The sneakers, only months before my passport to distinction at the city's most exclusive health club, were now old and dirty, and had holes in the sides. My eyes, when I dared look in a mirror, peered out of darkness and confusion.

She came over to my table. My stomach turned. She had the body of a dancer or an athlete. From under her white uniform I could see perfectly toned legs. Her arms were strong and brown.

"Can I get you something?" she asked.

I looked at her with hunger. A few clever and flirtatious answers flew across the screen to respond to her. But then that sinking feeling returned. She softened her composure, and laid one slender hand gently on the vinyl of the table.

"A cup of tea and toast," was all I could say. "Please."

The moment of tenderness which had opened between us suddenly snapped shut like a mousetrap. She stiffened. Her lips tightened. She wrote on a little pad that she pulled from her hip pocket.

"Whole wheat, rye, or sourdough?"

I chose rye, mechanically looking at the table.

"I'll be back shortly," she said with a perfunctory smile, and returned to her sanctuary behind the counter.

I pulled out pen and paper, an old habit which had started in cafés in Europe, more than 20 years before. My leather-bound notebook then was full of optimism, of witty things to say and futures to live. Now I used the back of an unpaid utility bill, sent to a house I no longer owned. As I had done so many times over the last months, I played the game of retracing my steps. Maybe I could undo the damage if I could only understand what went wrong.

"March, 2000," I wrote. "The Crash." I had prided myself on providing a safe haven for my lovelies. Where did I start to go wrong? Where exactly was my big mistake? The bike had a design flaw. The battery worked fine for about 16 hours, then refused to take any more charge. The deals with Costco and Pepsi were never properly signed. Within months of having given Harmer the money, the whole thing went belly up. Harmer disappeared completely—turned out in retrospect he was something of a professional con man.

Who knows? Maybe I could have weathered the storm, were it not for the change of management at the station. KYQD has been privately owned since the '30s. Will Thurston took it over from his father in the '70s. Now Will wanted to retire, so he hired a younger man to manage the station, fresh out of business school, a man named Bruce Pushar. What a jerk. He had a whole new campaign to increase listeners and to attract more advertising money. This meant, as he put it, "more zap, less yap." Which also meant less of me. I resigned before they had a chance to fire me. They wanted me to slot rock music and commercials into talks with environmentalists and visionaries. It just wasn't my idea of radio.

A man looking as sad and crazy as I was feeling stood up from the bar. A cigarette hanging from his lower lip, he tripped on the step, in a haze of alcohol and nicotine. He stumbled over to the now silent jukebox and flipped a coin into its open lips. After a few seconds came the voice of Neil Young singing "Oh Lonesome Me," once the accompaniment to my lovemaking and painting in Paris. I returned to my envelope, also in search of the elusive end to my troubles.

"April," I continued. "Becca's fury." I'd never told my wife about the second mortgage, or the line of credit at the bank. I knew she wouldn't approve, and I wanted to surprise her with our huge profit when it came in. Besides, I was ashamed of myself, the money we had had in the house all came from her family. Finally, after it was clear that the money was gone for good, I made up my mind to confess and begged her forgiveness.

She went through the roof. Italian blood, very fiery. When she called her parents in hysterics, her father finally got his way, persuading her that she had married a spineless wimp. "He's not a real man, hon. You deserve better than that." I overheard his booming voice as I paced the living room. "Now come on home with the kids, where you belong, and we'll look after you good, honey." She was very torn, but her anger at me and a lifetime's habit of privilege finally won the decision.

"May. Abandonment." Within a month, she took the kids to Chicago. At first it was just for a visit, while I sorted things out, tried to find a job, but after that it all went downhill. I couldn't make the house payments or car payments; everything was falling apart. Even renting the house couldn't have saved me at that point. What could I have done differently? Should I have begged more thoroughly for her forgiveness?

My analysis was interrupted by the return of Venus. She bent slightly to put the teapot and cup before me, revealing the lace at the top of her bra. I winced and looked away from this greater intimacy.

She returned a few moments later with my toast. The entire operation was like a ballet. As I looked up, our eyes met for a few seconds, long enough to transport me back into a world of laughter and bright colors. There was something in those eyes. They soothed me from behind her cool exterior.

"How's everything?" she asked.

Lost for a moment in confusion, I answered her more literally than she had probably expected. "Things have never been worse in my life . . . " My throat tightened, my chest felt explosive, and I looked back to my notes on the envelope, waiting for her to leave.

She didn't leave. She stayed. "I'm sorry," she finally whispered. This was really not what I wanted. I felt humiliated, yet pulled at the same time to tell her everything, to rest my head in her lap and go to sleep.

"Well, thank you for your sympathy. I'm just going through a hard time lately, that's all. And thanks for the tea; it's nice and hot . . . " I forced a smile. She took my change of subject as a dismissal. She returned to the kitchen, and I to my chronology of failures.

"June/July. Falling apart." I had just spiraled down into a state of terror and apathy. At first I tried to get other work. I had a good track record in broadcasting. Will had gone away to Hawaii with his wife after Bruce took over managing the station. I tried to reach him to get a reference, but he was out of contact. Will always liked me. I had been with him for more than ten years. I got a few jobs subbing on talk shows, but I'd lost my knack and my nerve. On one show I couldn't think of anything to say at all. I had a guest on the air talking about affirmations and creating a great life, people were calling in, but I was just frozen in a numb blankness. Soon word spread that I was a "has-been." It got harder and harder to get jobs.

"September. War." Rebecca's father hired an attorney to press for exorbitant child support. He based his attack on my previous earnings and came up with a huge monthly figure I had to pay. The pressure was overwhelming, and each day I had less strength to meet it.

"October. Homeless." The bank repossessed the house; I had next to nothing. I put my stuff in storage, and my friend Paul let me stay in the attic room of the apartment building he managed. Things just went from bad to worse, and every day I woke up with even less motivation and self-respect. I lost so much weight that my pants wouldn't stay up without a belt. I spent hours trying to sleep at night, and then I'd wake up before dawn in a panic. Every joint in my body began to ache, like I had the feeling of constant flu. I had no appetite or desire for anything. I tried to call the kids as often as I could, but Becca wouldn't even come to the phone. She was sore as hell. As far as she was concerned, I had ruined a perfectly good life for four people, and there was no way she was going to forgive me or even talk to me. I couldn't really say that I blamed her.

"November. Drifting." I tried a few odd jobs after the radio stopped working for me, but mostly I just wandered around the town, sitting in coffee shops or on cold park benches, waiting for something to change. I thought of killing myself. A lot. Even sorting through the bureaucracy of claiming unemployment benefits seemed like too much of an effort. I was living in total shame and hiding.

The same drunk stumbled over to the jukebox, and fed it more coins. Leonard Cohen's voice growled out of the darkness, reminding us that it was four in the morning, the end of December. What's with this place? Do they only offer funeral dirges? I'd already spent my whole day wallowing. Paul had insisted I go to a shrink. He was right; I was totally depressed.

So where did that leave me? "December. Today." I finally went to the outpatient department of the university hospital. My medical insurance had run out, so I was a freebie. I had to sit for hours in a waiting room with people who had overdosed on every kind of chemical, and every kind of misery. Finally I was ushered in to see the shrink. He was with me for about ten minutes. He looked like he had read every book known to man on psychology. He wore a dapper little polka-dot bow tie and looked at me over the top of his bifocals. I told him my whole story while he listened and made notes. He looked some stuff up in a big book, and then proudly announced that I had "acutely isolating depression." There was a moment of relief . . . I was not a failure, the destroyer of my kids' lives; now I had a "condition." He gave me some pills, and told me they wouldn't do much for a couple weeks, till they started to inhibit uptake of some chemical in my brain. And that was it.

When I left the hospital, it was dark and cold and drizzling. As I walked to the bus stop, I realized I'd left my key in my room. Paul worked the late shift at his job, so I was obliged to wander the streets till he got home, after midnight. No one else in the building even knew I was officially there. After all, I was paying no rent.

Christmas can be the most tender or bitter time of year, depending on your condition. As I traversed the city, each happy family out buying gifts was another knife between the ribs. Small voices called out, "Daddy, will you carry me?" How many times had I refused that request in tired self-importance? I would give up a limb to carry them even one block now.

I passed old men, mumbling into beards, left out of the warmth of family and comfort in the cold and derangement of the mind. I saw my own pain and regret stumbling before me. I felt hopeless.

I passed well-dressed executives, wearing just the right shoes and tie and designer brand overcoat, life hurried along by cell phone, appointments, and the next giddy achievement. I grieved over my wasted years of busy self-absorption.

And I passed old men and women, struggling to hold onto their last remnants of dignity, with hardly the energy left to hide the pain of another Christmas alone with canned food and the TV. I grew weak at the inevitability of my own doomed future.

So, as the evening turned into night, I ended up on the bridge, freezing cold, and absolutely, irreversibly alone.

I caught the waitress's eye for the check. She glided over almost immediately, and placed the ticket on my table. She lightly touched my wrist. "Listen, I don't want to pry," she said, "but I have written a number on the back of your check. I can't explain now, but I really suggest that you call. You won't be sorry." With that she smiled and evaporated back into the kitchen again. I left a few dollars for the toast and stepped out into the crisp winter night.

My walk home was brisk and determined. It was starting to drizzle; I wrapped my arms over my chest and made a beeline for my attic. After a couple of blocks I stopped in panic. I had left her no tip. I turned back, walking into the cold wind. She'll think I'm crazy, going back again. I'll go back another time and tip her double. I turned again. The nausea. I'll just go home.

Luckily, Paul answered his buzzer and let me in right away.

Paul has never made any attempt to meet the world half way. With his shock of wild red hair and matching beard, his huge burly body crammed into baggy jeans and a faded T-shirt, and his size 14 skater shoes, he had clearly long ago abandoned any attempt to be inconspicuous. His apartment displayed the same long-standing habit of relaxing into anarchy. The furniture was all unmatched and worn; even the most desperate thrift store would politely refuse it. Books were stacked in piles on the floor, in piles on the shelves, sharing space with abundant dirty coffee cups and assorted bric-a-brac collected from the far corners of the globe. A confusing assortment of electronics was scattered amidst the chaos. A computer, derobed of its plastic case, spread its intestines into the room. Various cables led to all kinds of black boxes, many of them homemade, as though the computer was now on complete life support. And video. Every remaining square inch was taken up by videos, of a variety of different formats: some of those tiny ones hardly bigger than a matchbox, and some the same size you would put into a VHS player. They all sported labels adorned with Paul's spidery illegible writing: "Bali from the air"; "Bullfighting accident in Madrid"; "Bombay slums #3"; "New Jersey pollution scenes." They had been shot over almost 20 years.

Paul is a filmmaker. Inspired, while we were both in college, by Francis Ford Coppola's *Koyaanisqatsi,* he had devoted the intervening years to what he called visual poetry. He had been creating a full-length feature film, shot mostly on a video camera, with no story or language, only Paul's quirky touch for startling and unusual images. Various incomplete grant proposals sat on his table, which continued to be in various stages of incompletion since I had known him.

"Hey, Matt, what's with you getting home at one o'clock in the morning?"

"I forgot my key. You weren't asleep, were you?" I tried to look upbeat, but probably failed.

Paul and I had grown up together in North Carolina and moved to the big city in the same pickup truck after college. I got the job at the KYQD, starting in the mailroom, fresh out of school with a journalism major. Paul got his job at the TV station and had worked his way up to being a production assistant. He was working half the time at the studio and on his opus the rest of the time, hence he was living in this small apartment where he also acted as a manager for the building.

Paul's lack of orderliness was perfectly balanced by his extraordinary heart and kindness. He once stayed an extra month on a trip to India to nurse a fellow traveler back from hepatitis, someone he had met briefly on a train. When Rebecca left, his offer of the garret at the top of the building was without a moment's forethought. Devoid of any interest in religion or philosophy, his was a kindness like his dress sense: entirely uncultivated and purely intuitive.

I told him about the long wait, the shrink, and the pills, but omitted the moment of flunked suicide on the bridge. He had given me all he could these last months; I did not want to add to his concern. So I skipped ahead to the waitress and the mysterious number on the back of the check.

"There you go," he grinned. "That's what you need. Call her in the morning and ask her out. Sounds like just the ticket for a stud like you."

Why is it that the friends who have sidestepped sex most thoroughly end up being the ones who think it will cure everything?

"No, Paul, I don't think it was her number. It's probably some kind of support group, depressives anonymous or something. I doubt it's anything worthwhile."

"Well, don't dismiss it too quickly."

A loyal connoisseur of French cinema, he sees life as a well-orchestrated movie plot, where each small detail is somehow contributing to the unfolding of a perfect ending. He even acts faithfully on the advice in fortune cookies and the horoscope predictions in tabloids.

"I'll see, let me sleep on it. Thanks for everything."

I climbed the five flights to my attic room, and collapsed immediately into the sleeping bag on my foam mattress and the welcome oblivion of sleep.

CHAPTER 3

NEW DIRECTIONS

As always, I woke at five in the morning, my heart pounding. My room was more of a storage area for the apartment building than a real home. In addition to my single foam mattress on the floor, there were piled boxes of repair materials for the building, a roll of carpet, and some pieces of wood leaning against the wall. The floor was just bare boards. My suitcase and duffel bag in the corner contained only long overdue laundry.

Above my head was a skylight, and there was one other window looking out toward the ocean. This window was my only source of grace. In the darkness I lay still, half awake, half caught in a dream that had come during the night.

In the dream, I was in a damp dark cellar with Rebecca and the two children. Water had collected on the floor. The walls were shiny with moisture. We were all freezing cold, dressed in dirty rags, like slum dwellers in a developing country. A rat ran across the cellar floor, and both children screamed. Rebecca pulled them to her.

I felt so isolated. All I could see in their eyes was cold accusation. "I'm sorry," I told them. "I'm so, so very sorry." But they just stared back at me, the villain in their movie. I felt rage rising in my chest, a rage at myself, a rage that this prison even existed, that my family had to experience any of this. I lunged at the wall of the cellar, wanting to beat the cold damp stone with my bare hands.

As my fist met the wall, I ripped a tear in it. It was made only of the thinnest fabric. I pulled on each side of the tear with my hands, and it opened a hole large enough to walk through. It exposed a garden, rich with daffodils, the sound of birds, the smell of the spring. Further off I could see a pond, a cluster of trees, and a waterfall. I stepped through the tear into the garden and looked back through the ripped fabric into the dark damp cellar. I called out to my precious ones to follow me, but they stayed huddled together, their eyes still betraying their distrust. And so I stood, poised between the allure of this brand new paradise and the pull of family responsibility. It was in this dilemma that I awoke.

Lying on my mattress, I closed my eyes again and curled into a ball, yearning to go back there, anywhere but here. I rocked myself back and forth. This was always the worst time for missing the children. They had been my all, my everything. They trusted me completely. I lay in the darkness re-creating Christmases, remembering gifts. Last year it was a bicycle for Dom. We had played games for weeks, Dom asking me for one with 15 gears, me saying it was way too expensive, while all the time I had the prize already locked away for him in the garden shed. His ecstasy was explosive when he discovered my deceit. A dollhouse for Sarah. We bought it at Thanksgiving and then spent weeks making our own improvements. Rebecca sewed endless minute curtains, sheets, and tiny comforters for the beds. I built a garden fence out of balsa wood. We delighted together in creating her dream.

My attention came back with a thud to the cold attic room. My chest winced. My intestines tightened so forcibly, I thought I would retch. The room was cold and smelled of mold and dust.

I sensed a pleading deep within me: "Oh, please, what have I done? What must I do? I will do anything—just for relief from this pain I will do anything." I had never been religious. God and all related deities always seemed more of a concept to me, an opiate for the people, Karl Marx called it. I think this was the first attempt at prayer I had ever allowed.

I looked up through my only window. The sky was lightening up. I wanted so much to feel that the pink early clouds would listen to the depth of my begging. I found myself involuntarily calling out loud to the sky, to those clouds, to an invisible deity, to the memory of my parents' love, "Oh, please! Mother, Father, God, please hear me! I know I have been a fool, please show me how to repair all I have done." For the first time in many months, I cried.

"Please," I silently screamed, again to some unknown but faintly felt benefactor. A cloud shifted a little to the left, the sun rose a little more, and I was bathed in its morning glory.

I closed my eyes.

I faintly sensed an upswing, like music coming from so far away that you cannot quite tell if it's real or imagined.

I had interviewed a hundred teachers on the radio about God and Grace and prayer and divinity, and I thought I understood it all. But this little flicker of hope was beyond any understanding, this was something hinted at in my body, not in thought. Like a man released from prison after decades, I sensed a clumsy desire to move, to dance. I felt hungry again.

Breakfast, I thought. Then I remembered the number on the restaurant check.

It was still too early in the morning; I had to wait. An urgency burned in my chest, making it hard to stay inside. I pulled on some clothes and descended the five flights of stairs from my room to the street below. I offered a rain check to the strong urge to scrub my body from head to foot, as the only shower was in Paul's apartment. I started to walk, in company with the early morning crowd, the other half of humanity from last night's café patrons. This was the hour of the joggers, muscular, determined people who meant business and played hard. I used to do that, too.

I also started to jog, turning from the street to the entrance into the park. My feet hit the tarmac of the park's running track. I was breathing. In. Out. In. Out. The awakened energy in my lower belly crept down into my thighs. I ran harder and faster. In. Out. In. Out. I passed retired ladies walking their dogs. Bizarre, how the body of the dog is a miniaturized version of its owner. I passed women with hair tied back, in the latest designer sweats. I savored the skin imagined beneath. In. Out. In. Out. I passed young men whose physiques exposed diligent hours spent at the gym. I said hello, brightly. Even though they all ignored me, I felt alive. The stronger the return to life, the stronger the need for action. In. Out. In. Out. I felt a pain in my side. Keep going. "Take a step toward God, he will take a hundred toward you," my mother once told me. In. Out. Breathe through the pain.

There again was the muffled plea within my heart, Please help me, please help me . . .

My hunger grew, as I ran to the far end of the park and out onto Grant Avenue. Some shops were already open; cars were passing taking their drivers from the security of home to the duties of the day. My appetite for breakfast amplified my determination to participate in all of this again, to pick up the instruments of war and go back to battle.

There was a family diner on the corner. Grand Slam, $4.99. That would do. I ran over and sat at the counter, panting. A previous patron had left behind a newspaper and a half-full glass of orange juice. I grabbed the glass, emptied it, and slapped the counter.

The waitress ran out to me, almost tripping in her urgency to get me my own menu. I ordered the special. Eggs, hash browns, toast, coffee, and orange juice. She smiled at me nervously, flustered by my lust for her bargain menu. I picked up the paper and randomly devoured news stories. Bush had just stolen the election from Al Gore. Everyone had something to say. I even pored over sports results of teams I did not know, jumping to the next story before finishing the first. It didn't take long to reduce the Grand Slam to a smeared plate, and still there was the desire for more, for more of anything. My whole body was trembling. The inside of my head felt overcharged with electricity.

I sat in the now-crowded restaurant watching the clock on the wall, drumming my fingers on the table, rereading news results and reports of business I did not understand. I had decided that 9 A.M. was the earliest I could call. Each successive minute the clock went into an even slower cycle. Time was slowing down, stretching like elastic to tease my impatience.

At five to nine, I finally abandoned all restraint and walked to the pay phone. I tried to slow my gait to a respectable walk, but inside I was running, to what or away from what I did not know. I pulled the crumpled stub of the night before from my pocket, standing trembling outside the doors to the toilets. The pay phone looked dirty and unforgiving. It would do me no favors. Graffiti offered me a number for the best head in town with Jeannie, and triumphantly declared that Joe loves Cindy forever. Good for them, but I was on my own.

I dialed the digits with shaking hands. The phone rang, once, twice, and my stomach muscles tightened. I had not realized how badly I needed to piss. Why was this so important? Wasn't I just getting into a frenzy, setting myself up for more foolishness and pain? Three rings, four, five, and my bladder was about to burst. *Hang up and go home, stupid fool,* a voice said from within me, with a vicious lunge on the word *fool*. By now it was maybe eight rings, and my bladder would wait no more. I took the phone from my ear to replace it in its dirty cradle. As I simultaneously started to turn toward the men's room door, I heard a real voice bellowing into the air between my ear and the pay phone: "Goood mooorning!" Just like Robin Williams in that Vietnam movie Rebecca and I must have rented five times.

So this was it. I brought the phone back to my ear again.

"Hello," I quivered.

"Hi! Goooood morning!" the voice repeated with evangelical triumph.

Oh God. That's it. Some born-again outfit, or a weird religious organization with an imported leader that makes you shave your head and vow lifelong allegiance. Hang up now, hang up before it's too late.

"Uh, good morning," I offered tentatively. "I was in a café late last night, and the waitress . . . " I paused, realizing I'd never even asked her name. "She suggested that I give you a call."

"Fantastic, great," enthused the voice. "So you met the beautiful Samantha. That's great! So, do you want to come over tonight?"

I had no idea if I wanted to come over tonight or not. My bladder was voicing a loud vote for forgetting the whole thing completely, as were many other unidentified voices vying for attention.

"Well," I stammered. "I really have no idea who you are or what it is that you do." I was not really being honest here. If I had passed the phone to my thumping heart instead of putting suspicion on the line, it would have just said, Yes, yes, yes, whatever you do, the look in that waitress's eyes is enough, I'm coming.

The voice laughed. "So Sam didn't tell you anything?"

"She told me I should call." I looked around to see if anyone was listening and lowered my voice to a conspiratorial whisper. "And that it would help me."

"Okay, so come tonight and meet Joey. She is right; you won't regret coming, at least no one has regretted it so far. Come at 7:30 P.M., the address is 627 West Broad Street. Do you know where that is?"

"Yes, I think so, it's in the university district, isn't it?"

"Right. Okay, what's your name, I'll be there myself."

"Matt, my name is Matt Thomson. No P."

"Good Matt, great. We will see you tonight. Have a grrreaaaat day." The phone went dead. Obscene, to have that much zest for life before nine o'clock in the morning. I won't go, forget it. Insane.

I bolted for the bathroom.

I walked home, alternating every 60 seconds or so between I'm absolutely definitely not going near any place where they actually say "have a great day," and I have to go; it's my only chance; my whole life depends on it.

I woke Paul from what would otherwise have been his usual morning in bed. He stumbled around in his red tartan bathrobe—like everything else he owned, he bought it for a song with all stylistic caution thrown to the winds. I told him what had happened on the phone. He peered at me, scratching his scraggly red beard, and started to boil water in a saucepan with almost none of its original white porcelain coating left. Every other dish, cup, saucepan, and utensil that he owned was piled in the kitchen sink.

"Matt, you're nuts, man. Don't even think about it. I know it's hard with Becca and the kids gone and all, but you've got to build things up again, there's no sense in joining a cult. Have you started taking the pills yet?"

He offered me at least a dozen more scary explanations about what I might be getting into. I would have listened to him more carefully, but the look in the eyes of my Botticelli waitress kept haunting me. I took a long shower and changed into the cleanest clothes I could find, before we sat on his tattered brown couch to watch hours of footage of funerals he had shot in the Indonesian archipelago.

We microwaved a precooked chicken casserole and washed it down with cup after cup of tea with powdered milk. One body after another went up in smoke—some in colorful houses specially constructed for the job, and some au naturel, naked wrinkled bodies which looked uncannily like our chicken pieces, turned to smoke released into the sky. Anything to pass the time until I discovered what happened at 627 West Broad Street.

CHAPTER 4

THE MEETING

This couldn't be right. All I could find was a hippie-style café, the kind that sells precooked food from a limited menu. Chickpea casserole, vegan pizza, Indian chai with almond milk. Ask for white sugar and you risk getting lynched, or voodooed, more likely.

I looked around. This was the bohemian area of town, home to bookstores, bike shops, even a Tibetan imports store. I checked for a number again, perhaps it was all a joke. I cursed my stupidity, chasing after another dead end after so many disappointments already. I shivered; the air was chilly, and I was underdressed.

I turned away, back to the bus ride, back to my lonely attic. Back to no future at all. Then I noticed a door at least ten feet from the street, at the end of a dark alley. There was the number, 627. I walked up and knocked, my heart pounding. What if this was some ghastly soul-bearing support group where everyone got deep and honest? Or an Eastern cult, with exotic names and incense? I'm not selling anything at the airport—there I draw the line. Then I thought of the long bus ride home. What the hell? I knocked again. And . . . nothing, no one came. I banged a third time, with my fist this time; again, unwelcoming silence.

What a waste of time. I spun around to the street and collided with great force with someone coming the other way.

"Are you Matt?" beamed my assailant. He was in his mid-40s, with balding blond hair tied back into a ponytail. About my height, he was plump, and wearing a ridiculous grin. This guy was definitely all granola and incense, the embodiment of "It's all so beautiful I could cry." I nodded, and sure enough he hugged me and looked very emotional.

"Great you came," he beamed. "You are in the right place." I was not so sure.

I separated myself from his embrace. He was wearing jeans and some kind of ethnic jacket from South America or India. Probably made from organic hemp. He kept beaming. I was sure I could have punched the guy full force in the belly, and he would have hugged me and told me he loved me. Just behind him was a woman with long hair almost to her waist, dark and streaked with gray. She was also adorned in imported clothing, a maroon skirt with little mirrors sewn into it and a velvety blouse over her full breasts. If her Earth Mother role was not already clear, I saw that she was wearing the kind of sandals that mold themselves to your feet. In December. Welcome to Looneyville. I stepped back a couple paces to safeguard myself from further hugging.

"I'm Alan, and this is my wife, June," declared my new friend. He spoke in a British accent, obviously softened by a few years away from the Queen's empire. "Well, let's go, he's expecting you." He pushed past me to open the door. "Next time, just go on up. The door is always open." A flight of stairs was flanked on each side by a dirty wall. I wondered if his instructions for a next time would prove necessary. The carpet on the stairs was worn, so much so that it had gone completely white in places. The whole place was ominously silent.

I followed Alan up the stairs with June in tow behind me. At the top was a small hallway, with three doors leading off of it—one straight ahead, one to the left, and one to the right. Outside the door to the right were about a dozen pairs of shoes, of every possible description: sandals sat next to brown leather business shoes, walking shoes had been cast off next to high heels. There were hiking boots, old sneakers, and more of those molded sandals. Alan motioned to me. I followed his cue and added my shoes to the collection. I had holes in my socks, and they were not clean that day; I hoped this would not prove to be a disqualification for whatever was to follow. Alan motioned briefly with his fingers to his lips, as though we might wake a baby, and opened the door, ushering me to follow him inside.

The silence swept over me, as if someone had switched off a TV I had not even noticed was on. There were 12 or 15 people in the room, all sitting or leaning against the walls with their eyes closed. Immediately, I spotted my waitress from the night before, now out of uniform. She still had her hair tied back, and she sat quite still. The room was almost completely unfurnished, except for an oat-colored carpet on the floor and a pile of cushions in the corner. Each of the inhabitants had a similar cushion, some had two or three. No one was speaking, but they weren't tense, more as if they were actively listening to something I couldn't hear.

I looked around the room, restless. I wanted to run away, or jump up and down, or engage someone in some kind of an exchange or animated debate. Since there were clearly no willing volunteers, I involved myself in a game of "match the shoes."

At the start it was easy. The lady in the business suit and the hair up in a tight bun on top of her head, early 50s, wearing pince-nez glasses with great precision; she must go with the high heels. Next to her, the man with the thin wispy beard, oversized sweater, and baggy jeans? Older tennis shoes or sandals. Next to him was a dead cinch; the gray-haired man in the brown tweed jacket and khaki pants, a discreet tie over his pale blue shirt; without doubt he came in the lace-up brown business shoes. An eccentric-looking man, who could have been a professor or an inventor, eluded me; I decided to come back to him later and give him whichever pair was left over.

I would have kept going much longer in this way, but my eyes came to rest on the only person in the room not sitting on a cushion. A lean old man was sitting almost completely upright in an equally upright armchair. His eyes were open, but he could easily have been a waxwork. His gaze was not on anything at all; it seemed as though he was looking into something behind his own eyes. His absolute nobility of posture and calm of face made the unkempt goatee and shoulder length snow-white ringlets irrelevant. As I stared at this statue of a man, his gaze slowly shifted, moving in a way that included everything in its path. Then he was looking back into me. Now I could see his eyes were completely blue, almost electric in their blueness. Panic gripped my chest, as though I had been running wildly on a path and suddenly came to the stark edge of a cliff. I felt I might fall into him. I closed my eyes. My heart was beating wildly.

After some time I could sense the shifting of bodies. Then the inventor-type started talking. I couldn't understand a word. It was as though he were speaking Chinese, with frequent use of terms like *fullness, emptiness,* and *the witness.* I'd heard the lingo before, but my brain could not register the meaning. Every time the old man seemed engrossed in the talk, I snuck another look at him, and every time I did, he would look back almost right away, raising one eyebrow at me, laughing without moving his mouth at all. As soon as our eyes met I had to avert my eyes. It was not like looking at a man at all, more like I was looking through him into . . . I cannot say what. I was facing an abyss.

Finally, when other talk was done, which could well have been ten minutes or a couple of hours, he looked at me and would not look away. The rest of the room shifted its attention to me, too. The business suit lady stiffened her posture and was sitting more erect, my Goddess waitress opened her eyes and smiled demurely, and Alan beamed even more exuberantly, like a sports fan settling down to cheer his favorite team. Everyone, including me, was waiting, as those clear blue eyes continued to greet me. Finally, the eyes wrinkled a little at the edges, the corners of the mouth curled slightly, and now the face was smiling at me.

"I have been waiting for you," he said. His voice was a deep growl, which seemed more like it was coming from the room itself, like the air was speaking. It shuddered normal thought back into motion, and I realized that throughout this gazing I had been out of time, suspended in stasis. The room giggled, and bodies shifted as though in anticipation of slapstick or a shoot-out.

"Yes," I stammered. The waitress must have told him she gave me the number, or my hugging host might have tipped him off.

"I'm sorry I'm late," I added. "Couldn't find the place, you know." The room burst out laughing. I felt uncomfortable. Was I missing some private joke here? Even my waitress was shyly giggling, all the while staring resolutely at the floor.

"You are not late," retorted the voice, still speaking more from the air itself through this elderly wiry body than from a person in the normal way. "You are right on time," he continued. "Everything always is. And I have been waiting for you . . . forever."

His gaze was like a hawk circling a small mouse in a field. My mind was racing now with excuses of how to leave, how to get out of this.

"Your heart will not let you run away any more," said the voice. This was becoming seriously scary. "Something has brought you to this moment; there is nowhere left for you to run."

I felt a surge in my chest as he spoke these words. I looked in his eyes. I was running from, and was somehow attracted to, a tenderness and a relief that I had run from and longed for forever. Then I was sobbing. It came out of nowhere, but it felt strangely pleasurable, a relief. A long forgotten sense of relaxation was pouring over me, but I did not fully trust it or even want to let it have its way.

I found myself babbling, out of all control. "It is true . . . I feel like I've been running forever. I don't know to what or from what." It all came pouring out: the loss of my job, the money, the house, Rebecca and the kids. I told him about the shrink at the hospital the previous afternoon, I even told him about the dream and the sunlight in the morning. During the whole confession a voice was telling me I was insane; I did not know these people from Adam. Throughout my torrent he was unmoving—his eyes were still and open; I felt as though they absorbed and dissolved all of it. I kept going for several minutes. No one interrupted me. Finally he spoke.

"You are very fortunate. This is a rare blessing." All his words came in a slow measured flow, with no more emphasis on one word than another. He looked directly into my eyes, without wavering or pausing for consideration. It was as though he were reciting lines he knew by heart and had no need to think of what to say next. "Everything must fall apart for the new to be born. You have reached the end of the road in the life you are used to."

At this point he paused and let his gaze fall to his hands, which were gently resting on one another. His left palm was upturned, and his right hand was resting on it with the palm turned down. These were the hands of a pianist, hands of refinement and reflection. They were ridged with heavy blue veins.

"All your old habits have led you to this dead end. It is truly time to die now, as you have been, but it is a deeper death than a physical one. It is time to rip through the fabric of the trance you have been living in."

How could he talk of being fortunate? Had he ever been abandoned, separated from his family, penniless? Had he even known what it was like to want to kill yourself—and then to flunk even that? Involuntarily, something else spoke from within me. I heard it speak more than said it. "Show me how . . ." I wanted to withdraw the words as soon as they were said, like a suicidal chess move. Too late. I'd taken my hand off the piece and had to face what came.

As though waiting for this invitation, his eyes locked onto mine, and all else disappeared. I couldn't think straight, colors grew vivid and bright, the smells became stronger. A cauldron was brewing in my lower belly, like being turned on, but without a hard-on. In the vacuum I heard him ask a question: "Through all this story of my life, my wife, my money, my children, my house, my pain, my problems, even my death and my suicide, who is this 'I' you refer to? Look now, and find this person who is in trouble."

It was very hard to focus. I had no idea at all what he was talking about. I felt a gravity, a pull to close my eyes and forget about everything.

"I am Matt," I answered. It felt so weak.

"Okay, that's a name, isn't it? And to whom does that name refer? See this?" he asked, tapping the face of his nautical-looking, very old watch.

"Yes, it's a watch," I replied. What was happening to me? His questions were so stupid and annoying, but I was feeling pulled by an unfamiliar force that I could not understand.

"Watch. That's a word, isn't it? And there is an object, a thing, to which the word is pointing."

"Right, that's your watch," I said, hoping to raise a laugh from the room, but sadly disappointed.

"And do you see this?" he asked, raising a glass of water from the table next to his chair. I noticed that on the table was a single red rose in a vase and a very small picture in a frame.

"That's a glass of water," I replied. I looked across and noticed that my waitress had a Band-Aid on her left little finger. What a beautiful finger.

"Good, name and form, name and form. Each word has an object or a thing it is pointing to. Words are signposts to that which exists."

He held up an empty fist. "Now. Can you see this screwdriver?"

"There is no screwdriver," I replied.

"You are good at this," he grinned at me. They all laughed. I felt like an idiot.

"Now, do you need to think to see the glass of water?"

"No." I said the word, afterward realizing it was true.

"Does it take time to see it?"

"No time." Simple, thoughtless. A split second later came thoughts about the speed of light and brain chemistry.

"Do you have to think to see my watch?"

The more he went on, the more still and luminous everything was becoming. I was being slowly seduced into something I was resisting. I just stared at him. It was getting harder to speak.

"And time?"

I shook my head. I didn't even really understand what he was saying.

"Do you have to think to see the screwdriver?" he asked, again holding up an empty hand.

"There is no screwdriver."

"But to see one there, would you need to think?"

"I would need to imagine one there, yes."

"Good, you need to imagine, to activate thought to see that which does not exist. Now, in this same way, look directly for this 'I' who has come here today with all these problems."

I looked. Things were getting very shaky. "I am a talk show host on the radio, I am a man, I am a failure," I offered.

"Are you still a talk show host?"

"No," I admitted.

"So is it true?"

"Not now, no."

"If you do not look at the body, are you a man?"

"Yes," I argued. He was not going to rob me of that. "This was certainly a male body the last time I looked at it."

"Very good, you look at the body and say *man*. Now, who is looking at the body?" This would be a lot easier if he weren't looking into my eyes with such intensity. I was unable to respond coherently, disarmed before the battle.

"I am," was all I could say to him in reply.

"Good, 'I am.' Now, with the same innocence that you looked at the watch, just as you looked at the glass of water, look now for this 'I.' Try to find it."

All I could find to reply to his question was "I am me," which seemed immediately ridiculous.

"Good, and who is this 'I', this 'me'?"

I feebly tried to answer his question. "I am American." Totally not true. I cannot be defined by a passport. "I am . . . I am a father to two children." Ah, yes! I locked onto that and squeezed it for sentiment, but it was also drawn away by the vacuum in his eyes. I was struggling, wobbling, overcome by a kind of insanity. Finally words came, through my lips but now from a source unknown.

"I don't know. I don't know who I am."

"Yes, that is an honest answer," came his reply. "And who is experiencing this moment?" He emphasized the word *this* with great force. "Ask the question of yourself now, 'Who am I?'"

I asked myself.

There is no way to describe what happened then. I still cannot recall it or think about it or understand it. It is as though there is a gap in the whole event. As though it were a movie, and for a short time, it could have been a fraction of a second or even a few minutes, someone switched off the projector. Blank screen. White. Nothing. No limits. Terrifying and indescribably familiar at the same time.

My body filled with an energy that was almost unbearable. It went from pelvis to skull, and sent jerks and spasms of movement up my spine. It was both ecstatic and painful, but mostly just too much. My body was incapable of coping with this much raw life.

Then a small thought passed. A lost, small thought, a bemused thought, a tourist separated from the rest of the party, wandering alone through the vast halls of emptiness. This small thought wondered to itself if this was the same stuff that the Dalai Lama had talked about to me, Nirvana. With that, the regular world came back into focus.

Slowly there were his eyes again, then the rest of his face reformed, then his body, then the room. The people were here again, but as though they were made of nothing. Although there were thoughts and noises, everything was dancing in the silence that was now so clearly omnipresent. A bus passed on the street outside. It was also passing through silence. The sounds were brushstrokes in silence. All was still; all was indescribably perfect.

He was smiling at me. Suddenly, like an amnesiac in recovery, I found him very familiar, as if I had known him forever.

"Who are you?" I asked him out of the silence. The voice was familiar and habitual, but no longer could it be called "mine." His eyes looked back, the familiarity deepened, a trap door opened to an even more mysterious place of meeting.

"Who do you see here?" came the reply. "Look not at this old body, but through it, and find out now who is looking back at you."

The looking happened. There were no limits again, like looking into the sky. And then I had the strangest experience. I was not ready for it at all. The rest of his face went out of focus, so I could only see his eyes, and I became convinced that I was looking into my own eyes. As though he were a mirror. I tried to shake it off, to get him back again, but now his face was like a mask. I recognized myself hidden behind the veneer.

"Myself," I whispered, afraid I would be thought insane.

"Look around you," came another instruction through the old body. "See who is here."

My body turned and met the eyes of the lady in the business suit. I had the same feeling, the same myself looking back at me. I blinked a few times, not quite sure if I liked it. The woman in a blue suit was just packaging now; it made no difference if she was wearing a bikini or a bowler hat, it was just a thin disguise. She sat very still with me, very present. She was clearly sharing the recognition. She nodded soberly, her eyes unmoving.

I looked around the circle. One by one, it was the same. I met the eyes of the eccentric-looking professor. I could feel he was shy and reserved by nature; right away I could feel it as my own. I could feel what he was feeling, an intimacy for which I was not prepared.

Next in the circle came Alan. He was still looking exuberant, and I had the body sensation of liking him. It was a softening in my chest, my body opened a little, and I knew he could feel it. The whole room laughed. They too could feel it. I found myself laughing too. I could not hide. I hated it and loved it. My gaze passed from body to body, the shock never lessening as I saw myself in disguise again and again. Each person was entirely different. There was no code of dress or behavior in this gathering; all that we shared in common was a simple recognition of something that was by now unavoidable and completely obvious.

My eyes finally came to rest on my waitress from the previous night. This time the recognition was accompanied by a rush of energy in my lower belly. I felt transparent, naked. She smiled at me modestly. I knew she knew. I wanted to say something, thank her for bringing me here, but I saw now how deeply shy she was. She held my gaze for just a few seconds, then reddened and looked to the floor. Finally, I came full circle to the old man.

He laughed, obviously delighting in the show that was unfolding. "Yes, Matt, you are absolutely alone. There is no other anywhere.

Welcome home, welcome home. I have been waiting for you." He reached out his hand to me, and pulled me to him. As I moved toward him I had the feeling that this body was moving through the real me. I was much bigger than I was used to. I extended even beyond the walls of the room itself.

After some time, I found my own spot against the wall. Someone handed me two cushions. I sat between Alan and his wife, who both reached out to me and took each of my hands in one of theirs.

I did not pull away.

I closed my eyes, and fell into a very comfortable resting, a happiness that felt like being massaged in the sunshine. There were periods of silence and of talking in the room, but again the words seemed foreign. The silence was so much more real and important. The slightest movement of activity or energy in the room stirred a wave of pleasure in my body. I could only move very slowly. A thought briefly tried to grab my attention, asking me if I had been drugged, but the thought had nothing to land on or grab onto, so it evaporated into thin air.

Someone addressed the old man as Joey, and I remembered that Alan had used this name on the phone in the morning. As I listened, Joey changed his manner abruptly from one questioner to another, sometimes laughing uproariously, sometimes being very stern and serious, sometimes just grunting in response to a well-articulated and thought-out question and giving no reply at all. The whole evening was like a movie playing in another room. I could hear everything, but I was absorbed in an immensely funny joke that I did not understand, nor even need to.

After a while there was a long silence. I opened my eyes to see what was happening. Joey was looking right into me with a beam of warmth. It took me deeper into a place of not knowing.

"Now, tell me again of all your troubles, because we don't have much time and all your issues must be resolved to your satisfaction." He spoke sternly, then looked at Alan, and they both burst into laughter. "You came with so many problems, and now is the time to deal with them. Hurry up please, I don't wish to miss the ten o'clock news." Again everyone laughed, even me.

I tried to recapture the filing system of my heavy misfortune, only to find the office had been ransacked. "I have lost all my money." The words sounded empty and contrived.

"Is it true?" he asked.

It was a strange question, for in terms of the story of my life it was absolutely true, yet in this meeting and with this intoxicated feeling even the word *money* had little meaning.

"In a sense it is true, yes. But it doesn't feel the same now."

"Are you lacking anything just now?" he asked.

There was a long pause.

"Just now, no," came my reply.

"So what are you going to do now?"

If I listened to the thought pool, I had no idea, and that created a big problem. If I just remained present with him in the room I still had no idea, but there was no problem at all.

"I have no idea," I said.

"Well," he demanded, "don't you have any problems left for us to solve here? Come on, boy, speak up."

"No," I had to admit. It seemed absurd. I grinned sheepishly and wanted to close my eyes. The inside of my body felt so much more pleasurable than all this talk.

"How did you solve so many problems in such a short time?" Although he was obviously playing with me, his eyes emanated a soothing balm, which made me want to stay silent.

"I don't know," I stammered.

"Tell me," he went on. "What is to prevent you from resting in this way of seeing things? Are you under any obligation to return to your misery that you came with tonight?"

I had nothing to say. I felt confused. "It is good. It is good," beamed Joey. Then he looked over at my waitress. "I like your new boyfriend very much," he chuckled. "You always bring me the best catches. . . . "

Sam's eyes opened wide. She turned bright red and tried to protest, "Oh, no, Joey, he's not my boyfr—," but he cut her off.

"You have done very well to harvest such a ripe prize, and now you will have to take good care of him."

She seemed visibly annoyed, but returned her gaze to the floor. Joey looked around the room. He inhaled slowly, as though savoring the smell of great food. He pressed down hard on the arms of his chair, elevating himself to a standing position. He stood there for a moment in his luminous white shirt and black pants. He could have been an aging musketeer.

"KYSH," he said, grinning. "KYSH."

With that enigmatic closing comment he picked up the rose from the vase on the table and was walking, or better to say, floating to the door of the room. He shot me one last glance of amused affection, threw the rose in my lap, and was gone.

The room immediately coagulated into clusters of twos and threes. Everyone here knew each other fairly well, for there was a relaxed atmosphere, like a family gathering. I felt pulled to my waitress. She met my eyes with an awkward and tense smile.

The man I had pegged as a professor came to introduce himself; he was actually named Roy, and owned an artsy cinema, also in the university district. The woman in the business suit was Swiss German, her name was Maryanne, a clinical psychologist. And the man in the suit next to her was Jack. He owned a company on the outskirts of town that manufactured parts for laser printers. The young bearded man with the long hair, Sundance, had a voice so soft and etheric it hardly moved the air as he spoke. They all seemed extraordinarily sober after this bizarre evening.

I looked back over for my waitress, anticipation growing in my belly, but she was gone.

Alan and June surrounded me, like protective parents.

"Why did he say KYSH as he left tonight?" I asked them. It was the name of the rival station to the one I used to work for. "Does he have corporate sponsors?"

They laughed. "No, it's not the radio station!" Alan replied. "It means Kiss Your Sweet Hearts. He used to always say that, but now he abbreviates it to KYSH."

Alan helped me to my feet. I was giddy and lightheaded.

"It's great that you came, really great," he exuded as we moved toward the door. "You can come here every night at the same time, except Wednesdays and Sundays. You are always welcome."

I stepped out into the hallway to find that mine were among the last remaining shoes to be collected. As I pulled them on, I heard Joey's voice from the door to my left call out, "Eh, Alan." My British host brushed past me through the other door, and popped his head out again after no more than 30 seconds.

"He wants to see you," he said, and then immediately bounded down the stairs back to the street.

I stepped through the door, rose still in hand. Joey was in a high-backed chair, in a sparsely furnished room. There was another older-looking leather chair, a carpet on the floor, and a table with some more small framed photographs including, surprisingly, an autographed picture of Joey with J.F.K.

Joey was looking at me with a warm smile.

"I am very happy with you," he said. "You got the point right away." I felt empty and quiet.

"I am very grateful to you," I replied. "For the first time in months I feel like myself again. I feel I have the courage and energy now to put my life back together."

I thought he would be happy with this little endorsement, but instead he scowled at me. When he did reply, it was with a fierce intensity.

"Do not fool yourself, kid. Do not fool yourself. The life you know has been completely predetermined by old habits, both your triumphs and your failures. There is one way out, to exercise the only free choice that an individual ever has, and that is to choose freedom. If you are really at the end of your rope, these habits will drop away, and you will be free of the chains that have bound you."

"That could take a very long time," I replied, daunted at the task of unraveling every twist of my dark subconscious mind.

"The time it takes depends on you. If you are really ready to die, as you have been, and if you are as intelligent as you seem, it can take almost no time at all. You seem to be ready. But we will find out.

"You have run on automatic, each event sparking a reaction in you, which in turn caused a new event, which caused another reaction. If you return to those old habits, it will not take long before you find yourself again on that bridge. But, if you truly understand what has been running you, you can be free. That is your birthright, to enter a life beyond your old desire and fear, and to discover real blessedness.

"I give you ten days, starting today. I will show you all you need to see. It is up to you. Come back tomorrow."

CHAPTER 5

FLEETING HEAVEN

I stepped back into the short alley, then into the street. The light drizzle, lit up by passing headlights, fell to the earth like millions of tiny diamonds. The sidewalk glistened under my feet as the tickle in my lower belly spread throughout my body. I was invigorated, consumed with lust for it all: the people, the food, the jeweled, luminous moisture. The city smells of cooking caressed my body. Chinese, Indian, Italian—all fed my insatiable lust for raw experience, for life itself. Finally I was pulled, bursting with appetite, into the magic world of Taco Bell.

I looked around at the shiny small tables, the illuminated pictures of the kitchen's offerings, the abundance of small packets of hot sauce, and I knew: The world was infused with a divine and benevolent intelligence. The short journey from the door to the counter felt liquid. I was swimming through myself, through an ocean of living presence.

I was received at the counter, still holding my rose, by the divine mother. I wanted to fall at her feet in adoration, but instead opened my arms wide in a greeting of recognition. She was black and huge, more than 200 pounds of pure divinity. Her hair was braided into hundreds of little multicolored beaded ropes. Her eyes were enormous saucers of infinite love, absolutely still in their capacity to embrace the suffering of all humanity.

"Next," spoke the goddess of all creation. I get it; she's undercover, pretending to be a poor and uneducated woman working for minimum wage. She's good, really good. She's probably fooled most of her customers, but she doesn't fool me. I looked back into those deep pools of compassion with a devotion I could not suppress.

"A super burrito, please," I asked, trying not to blow her cover, and then, unable to fully hide that I saw her, I added, "Your eyes contain galaxies." She looked a little startled, and peered at me.

"Excuse me?" she asked.

"Your eyes are very, very beautiful," I said, standing my ground.

"Uh . . . thanks. Want anything to drink?" The divine mother cares only for her children, thinks constantly of their every need.

"Sprite," I replied. She took my money, keyed some codes into her cash register, and turned her back on me to take a foil-wrapped offering from the display. Turning back, she dropped her disguise for a moment. She beamed. Every cell of her body was smiling heavenly love.

"You have a nice day now." The Mother had blessed me. I kissed the rose, and offered it to her. She did not refuse it. A sign.

As I continued down the counter, I saw another incarnation of divinity, a young man of 20 or so, sporting a goatee and a musketeer mustache. A gold hoop dangled from one ear, and his oiled hair lay in ringlets on his shoulders. His eyes were bright, laserlike. As they fixed onto me for a moment, a spark of fierce energy ignited between us. Mother had brought Shiva along to help with the tacos.

"Need anything more, man?" asked Shiva, jutting his jaw toward me in a gesture nudging me further into the cosmic void.

"Nothing more than this," I beamed. "It's all perfect. It's all utterly perfect. We are blessed." I could feel the tears welling up in my eyes as we shared this brief moment of rapture.

"Cool. Thanks for choosing Taco Bell," replied Shiva, obviously also undercover. I winked at him, and took my sanctified foil-wrapped prize to a vacant table. I wished I had a second rose.

As I unwrapped the burrito, I was flooded with gratitude—such care and love had gone into the creation of this miracle. Rice and beans were cradled together in a cheesy sauce. I sank my teeth into the sacrament, acutely aware of the food passing through my mouth and down into the belly. The bliss intensified. I had no idea that nectar such as this could be served under such humble cover. I was making hot, wet, sticky love to all of it. As I sipped my Sprite, I tasted rose petals and sacred fragrant herbs from the Himalayas.

The entire staff were celestial beings. Their eyes completely blew their thin disguises, no matter how bored or unhappy they pretended to be. Shiva came out from behind the counter and began wiping off the little stand where more packets of hot sauce were made available for devotees. He was so close to my table now that we could talk without being overheard. He leaned toward me.

"Hey man, what are you on?" he asked. It must have been a divine riddle.

"It has no name, but one drop of this has destroyed all that is not love," I replied. Surely he would follow my coded language.

"Hey, man, got any more?"

"It is infinite; it is everywhere, once you know where to look."

"Could you get me some of what you took?" Shiva was serious. Although full of Grace, he was longing to drink yet again at the fountain of eternity. I reached into my jacket pocket and found the check Sam had written on the night before. I copied the number for Shiva.

"Hey, thanks man. Cool." He reached out his hand. "Carlos." I shook the hand, and winked at him as though to say, "I'll call you Carlos, but I know who you really are," and returned to my blessed burrito.

As I stepped out again into the night drizzle, I noticed the invasion of divinity was not restricted to the fast food restaurant. God was everywhere in many disguises: waiting at bus stops, walking along hand in hand, even playing at being a street person. Each and every person I saw became immediately fascinating to me. I had to restrain myself from rushing up to people randomly to ask if they would like to have a drink, share intimate secrets, let our hair down, and go really deep and get real.

As I turned from West Broad Street onto Moulton to catch the bus, a wave of doubt came over me like a visitor from nowhere. Thoughts began to coagulate again: Am I just fooling myself? Has anything really happened? Am I just projecting all this divinity onto ordinary people?

Then I saw the sign, a direct communication from the intelligence that protected me completely. Across the street was an enormous billboard blaring the slogan: Your Search Ends Here. I knew it was meant for me, a direct confirmation that what had been found was real and true. I stopped dead in my tracks and held my hands to my chest. "Oh, yes!" I called out aloud. "Yes, it is over, the search is truly over!" I stood there, gazing in awe. A couple, walking arm in arm down the street toward me, stepped aside to avoid me, looking embarrassed and intrigued.

"I can't believe how emotional people get about a search engine," I heard the man say to his companion. "The Internet is taking over our lives."

I floated along the remaining few blocks to the bus stop in unwavering contentment. The light drizzle made my hair and face damp, but even that and the cold of the night mysteriously added to the sense of unconditional pleasure. Nothing was out of place anywhere. Nothing was resisted; nothing needed to be different than it was.

The bus arrived at the stop at exactly the same moment as I did. Perfect, just perfect, it's all part of the great plan. I recognized the driver—riding the bus for the last several months I had come to know every driver on this route. But tonight I realized I had seen only a face. Now I could feel the real man. I was getting the picture. Everyone was undercover, pretending to be small and suffering. Almost everyone had persuaded themselves to believe their own disguise. The driver must have been in his mid-50s, with graying hair brushed back and a lined face with pockmarked skin. His whole presence smelled of fatigue, of a life lived oblivious to any passion. His eyes flickered, betraying a fear he might be suddenly accused of wasting precious human birth.

"Howyerdoin," he grunted to me.

"Very, very good," I replied, in a voice that also said, "It could not get any better than this." I could not lie. I had been living a lie for too long. He peered at me through the decades of habit. Something deeper than words or even thought was calling out to be rescued from the damp cellar.

"Well, you have a good night," came the driver's response, still speaking in automatic transmission, while his eyes said: "I desperately want to dance and love and laugh and scream. I want to make love all night. I want fifth gear."

I took my seat in the bus and looked around me. The world was fresh, new, and interesting. I felt I had just arrived on a flight from Pluto. Suddenly the world was in 3-D, where it had been flat before. There were only a few other passengers. As I looked into each one, I saw an exquisite mystery trapped inside a personal soap opera. I wanted to jump up and pull the emergency cord and shout, Listen, none of this is necessary! You are not what you think! You can shake off your habits of self-restraint with one finger snap and be free. But a sign above the cord warned of huge fines for improper use, so I restrained myself, exploding with urgent love.

The bus stopped across the street from the apartment building that had become home. Paul's light was already on. He must have come home early. It was hard to leave the bus. I really wanted to invite them all in for massage and food and wild fun. I let myself into the building and went straight to Paul's door.

"That you, Matt?" he called from the sofa. He was watching more of his endless video footage: Brazilian prostitutes were tonight's entertainment. "Well, did you go, what happened?" Paul switched off the TV and sat in avid anticipation.

Now that I had a captive audience with whom to share my secret, no words were coming. I sat on the sofa with him, looking into his eyes and grinning.

"You okay, man? Did you smoke a joint or something?"

"Not a joint, no," I answered. "I got high without touching any drug at all."

"Well, c'mon, Matt. Spill the beans. Did you go out with your beautiful waitress? You have the look of a man in love."

"Yes, she was there, but that's not the point, Paul. Something has totally changed. I just keep seeing God everywhere." Even as I said the words they sounded wrong. Paul knitted his brow. This was going to be harder to talk about than I had thought. Paul reached for a cigarette.

"What do you mean, seeing God?" he asked quickly, leaning forward and lighting his cigarette. He took a long drag and sat back in the sofa, stretching out his legs. "What does he look like, anyway?" The filmmaker in Paul was obviously getting intrigued.

I told him the sequence of events as best I could. I even tried to recapitulate my talk with Joey. "It has become really clear that I am not what I was pretending to be," I concluded. "And neither are you." The more words I used, the more uneasy Paul looked. "I feel so good." I was trying to make it better now. "Everything is perfect. Everything. Losing the money, Rebecca leaving, all of it. It's all the way it's supposed to be." Now Paul looked more than confused; he looked angry.

"Are you taking those pills from the shrink, Matt? You really need to get things together, you know. You can't go on like this." There was a pregnant pause. We looked away from each other.

So I lied. I told him I was taking the pills, although I had not even opened the bottle yet. Paul switched the TV back on. He abandoned Rio nightlife and flipped to the cable channels. We sat together in awkward silence, trying to be amused by a late night stand-up comic. I bid him goodnight and climbed the stairs to my attic.

I dropped off to sleep caught between two opposing realities. Paul's cynicism was cozy and safe, like a mad relative to whom I felt uneasy loyalty. The ability to doubt intelligently was familiar; it had held all of my friendships in place. It was the very quality that allowed me to excel as a journalist, and it had put food on my family's table. I had worked hard to earn a reputation as the champion of reason held up to all this spiritual jargon. But it had led me to a dead end. Doubt had enclosed me in a world devoid of hope, devoid of faith.

Beyond this small harbor of logical understanding lay the open waters of an unfamiliar freedom—something new, as yet unnamed, perhaps unnamable, which my aching heart longed to embrace. To enter the universe Joey had unveiled meant leaving my old world behind on the quay, and braving the uncharted waters alone.

CHAPTER 6

DOING LAUNDRY

As always, I awoke before dawn. At first it seemed the pain was gone, just stillness and heavy ease in the body. Then, as I reached down with morbid interest again, I found the familiar black hole in my chest. My gut tightened. The previous night's events seemed to have opened something bigger, something which contained the pain and was not affected by it. I was only half hurting, I was also just here, just watching.

Laying on the foam pad in my sleeping bag, I surveyed my kingdom. There were piles of dirty clothes both in and all around my suitcase and the duffel bag. The window that looked out onto the mountains was layered with dust and grime. A roll of carpet leaned against the wall in the corner, despite the fact that I was living on bare boards. My universe was crying out for the action I had been avoiding.

I jumped up from the pad and attacked piles of laundry. Every last stitch I owned was to be found here—all of it dirty. Each garment reminded me of some memory of family life, but I was learning now not to dwell there. They were just dirty clothes on bare boards.

I threw on a sweater, socks, and my gray sweatpants, a gift from Becca two years before; I headed back down the five flights of stairs to the park, claiming again my membership among the ranks of the committed. As I ran through the park at dawn, everything damp and cold, the air so crisp it seemed to burn a little, it was actually impossible to make sense of anything from the night before. A sense of space remained, an alive excitement; there was no way to make logic from it all.

On my return, it was clear the laundry would not tolerate more indecision. I sorted it into piles, like my mother had shown me as a child. What would she say if she could see me now? She died when I had hardly begun to shave, and with her died the simplicity of whites, colors, and delicates. Stay here, stay now. The machines in the basement of the building demanded quarters for their service. By plundering the pockets of every available garment, I raised the ransom. And so it was that the morning after my first meeting with Joey, I had all three machines frothily rotating. It was the token start of the great cleansing.

I found a broom in the basement, and brought it up to my turret. The room looked empty without its laundry pile, stark even. I emptied what little remained into the hallway, and swept the floor. All the time, Mother, Dom, Becca, old movies, and everything else fought with the simplicity of sweep, sweep, sweep. I took the roll of carpet from the corner and uncurled it on the floor. A perfect fit. In the corner of the room where the roof slanted down was an opening in the wall, only a few feet tall. In the dim light, I became aware of all kinds of old stuff in there.

I knocked on Paul's door. He was still asleep. I made us coffee and used his shower. Nothing felt more important now than to be clean. I scrubbed under my toenails, and washed my hair, rubbing deeply into the scalp. Soon, Paul was wandering around in his bathrobe. He eyed me suspiciously as he sipped his coffee, as though my newfound cleanliness might be an infectious disease. Common sense told me not to mention God or any related topics.

"I took the roll of carpet in the attic and put it on the floor," I confessed.

"No problem." He paused, and peered at me again, still cautious. I decided not to mention that I was into my second shift of laundry.

"There's a bunch of stuff in the attic under the roof. Does it belong to anyone?"

"No, it's been there for years. Help yourself." He turned away, and scratched his crotch thoughtfully.

We had breakfast, Paul glancing at me now and then, noticing something different, but unsure if I had had a haircut, or shaved off some facial hair he could no longer remember. Finally, he left for the studio, and I finished my laundry.

I scavenged through Paul's magnificent collection of flashlights. When I found one that actually worked, I took it upstairs.

Further exploration of the storage area yielded a table, a lampshade for my bare bulb, and a magnificent collection of *National Geographic* magazines, to add a splash of color. Soon the room was transformed. By midmorning I had my clothes folded on makeshift shelves, a clean window, and a variety of views of the Grand Canyon and sites in Peru pinned on the walls.

But the need to clean, to restore, would not give in. Midday, I began tentative inroads into Paul's world, trying not to disturb the private version of order known only to himself. There must have been 12 years of accumulated grime and mold in his fridge. I emptied and scrubbed it, washed all the piled dishes in the sink, washed every surface in the bathroom, and then took another shower. Every time I stopped, there it was again. The same anxiety, the soreness in the chest like the feeling just before you need to cry, and underneath it, like a watchful parent, an ocean of something still.

While wiping the shelves underneath Paul's bric-a-brac, I found a video he had shot in our house, years before. Becca had put up with Paul as a relic from my past, just as one might accept an old and drooling dog as a part of the package with a new roommate. She never truly liked him, but she tolerated him as a gesture to me. I slid the video into the VHS player. The kids had dressed up as fairies. Paul filmed them through filters of colored liquid gel. I watched my beauties transformed through Paul's artistry into psychedelic apparitions. Sarah was only two then, skipping around after Dom, imitating his every move. I was lost in the unmapped wilderness somewhere between laughter and longing. Impulsively, I picked up the phone and dialed the Chicago number, my family's kidnappers.

Becca answered the phone. I was not ready for this.

"Hello?" That voice still melted my belly, even after all these years.

"It's me, Becca. It's me. It's Matt."

"Hey . . ." I could feel her collision of conflicting moods. After so many years, just the rise or the fall of a word speaks volumes. "What are you doing?"

"I've been cleaning. But listen, Becca, things are changing. I'm going to pull things around."

"Is that him?" A voice boomed from the distance. My father-in-law. "Ask him if he's got a job, Becca. Ask him if he's making any damned money yet."

"Matt, I can't talk now. Let me put the kids on the line."

"Daddy, where are you?" came Dom's voice. My son, my very own son. My chest exploded to hear his voice.

"I'm at Paul's, Dom. Hey Dom, I just saw that film of you and Sarah, remember, with the fairy wings?" My voice was cracking up. I was choking.

"Yeah," his voice trailed. I could see him looking at the ceiling, thinking his father was just as wacko as everyone was telling him. "Why can't you come here for Christmas?"

"I can't, Dom. Not this year."

"Are you still going to give me the Connect-it set you promised?"

"I'll have to give you that later, Dom. I sent you something else." It was a book. A small and short book.

"Dad, Grandpa says you're a loser. He says you lost all our money, and that's why we have to live with him and Granmama. Are you a loser, Dad?"

I wished I hadn't called.

"No, Dom. It will be okay."

"I wanted the Connect-it set," his own voice began to crack. There was a silence. He had no other way to express his rage and confusion. The restoration of his universe was distilled down to a set of colored plastic pieces.

Next came Sarah on the line.

"Daddy," she yelled. "Daddy, Grandpa bought me another doll-house, and a pink tee vee, and lots and lots of moovies." We had never had a TV. Waldorf education discouraged it. "Daddy, Grandpa says he will take us to Disneyland and we can stay here as long as we like."

"I love you, Sarah," was all I could say.

"I'm going to watch more TV now."

In a few short minutes the call was over. My heart was heavy, my body aching. I was no closer to resolving my mistakes. All that had really changed so far was that my best friend now had a cleaner kitchen.

Despair and failure led me to arrive early, too early to go up those fateful stairs, so I wandered into the café. Alan was behind the counter making an avocado, cheese, and sprouted millet sandwich. The distance between the bottom slice and the top was about the same as the width of the sandwich. As he triumphantly set it before his patron, he saw me.

"Matt!" he exclaimed. "How wonderful to see you. Are you hungry? Let me make you a sandwich you'll never forget." Alan was starting to grow on me. I sat down at a vacant table. A few minutes later he brought me an offering even more magnificent than the last, and refused any payment. He sat down with me.

"Is this your café?" I asked.

"June and I have had this place for years. I took it over when I first came to the States, back in the late seventies."

"So is the upstairs yours, too?"

"We own the whole building. June and I usually live up there, except when Joey's in town. Then we stay in a little room behind the café."

"You mean Joey's not here all the time?"

"My God, no! Joey's the most elusive man you'll ever meet. Here today . . . gone tomorrow. There's no rhyme or reason to his movements. He started a community a couple hours out of town near Idlewood. But he's not even there very much anymore. He goes where the wind blows him."

"So how long will he be here in town?"

"Until he's gone. That's all I can tell you. He usually jokes and says that when there's more than fifteen people, it smells like a crowd . . . and that's when he takes off. How many were we last night? I think I counted twelve. Three more to go, and that's it."

"Oh my God!" I said. "I gave out the number to someone in Taco Bell last night. I didn't realize these seats were so precious. "

"Yeah," he laughed. "A lad named Carlos. He called me this morning wanting to buy some drugs. I told him to come tonight. Joey will love him." He leaned toward me over the table. "But how are you, Matt? How was your day?"

"Not so great," I said. "I felt fantastic last night, but then I got home and talked to my roommate, and I got very confused. Then today I had a lot of energy again. I was feeling great until I talked to my estranged wife in Chicago."

Alan laughed. "That will do it."

"Yes, but how can you stop this from going away?"

"Keep your questions for the old man; he'll sort you out. Never failed yet!"

I drowned my sorrows in the sandwich Alan had given me and waited till it was time to go upstairs. When I did climb the stairs to the apartment, I was only the third person there. Maryanne, the therapist, and Jack in the business suit were already sitting silently with their eyes closed. I took a cushion and closed my eyes, too. My body felt heavy. I was still replaying the phone call in my head. I think I must have dropped off, because the next thing I remember was the sound of laughter. I opened my eyes abruptly. The room was full. There was the beautiful Sam, as well as the same faces from the night before. Carlos was sitting in front of me, and to my left, Joey was just taking his seat. He grinned at me, placed his two palms together at the level of his lips, smiled at the assembled friends in the room, and closed his eyes. We all followed suit. The whole room fell extremely quiet.

My mind was still racing with thoughts of having blown the previous night's attainment. I was wondering if I could ever get it back. Then there was Carlos. He seemed to be making some kind of clicking noises at the back of his throat. Every time I opened my eyes to see what was happening, he was fidgeting and looking nervously around the room. I felt responsible for him being there, and his clicking completely obsessed me.

Finally, I heard Joey's murmur . . . "I kiss your sweet hearts. Welcome, welcome."

With that, Joey raised one eyebrow and looked with a curious and amused expression at Carlos sitting before him.

"I understand that you're a close colleague of our friend Matt," smiled Joey.

"Hey no, man. Just met him last night," Carlos bubbled, obviously relieved to be talking again.

"So what can I do for you?" asked Joey.

"Well, man, like this guy comes to Taco Bell last night, man, where I work, see, looking real high. Told me if I call the number on the paper, I could get me some too. So that's why I'm here, man."

"Very good." Joey smiled and paused for a moment, "man." The room laughed. "I suppose you wouldn't believe it if I told you I'd been waiting for you forever, would you?"

"Sure, man. Anything."

Joey again paused for a long time. He stared at Carlos with a grin and said, "Cool."

Now the room erupted in laughter. Joey continued, "So you want to be high."

"Sure, man, doesn't everybody?"

"Tell me," said Joey. "What kind of high would you like? Would you like a high that goes away again? Or would you like a high that keeps going?"

"Well, like, you know, I don't know if my body is up to that, man. You mean, like, just stay high all the time?"

"You don't worry about the body. The body will be okay. Are you ready to pay the price?"

"Does this stuff cost a lot?"

"What have you got?"

"Well, maybe fifty bucks, but I need some of that, man."

"I need more than that!" laughed Joey.

"Whoa! Slow down here, amigo. Well, hey man, like, what kind of shit is this, anyway?"

"Here's what I need," said Joey. "I need you to give me your mind." Carlos looked around the room with a wild expression on his face, then looked back at Joey.

"Come again?"

Joey repeated himself very clearly. "I need you to give me your mind and you will be high forever." Carlos looked caught between conflicting emotions, like he was choosing between pulling a knife to defend himself and running away crying to his mother.

"So you're saying that if I give you my mind, you'll make me high forever?"

"Does that sound like a deal?" beamed Joey, triumphantly.

Carlos braced himself in sudden resolve, like a prizefighter about to enter the ring. "Sure man, I'll try it." Then he paused and frowned. "How do I give you my mind?"

"Look for it," said Joey. "Look for it, find it, and give it to me." At that moment, Joey's eyes heightened in their intensity. The life force that was already shining through them suddenly became radically brighter. Carlos looked right back into Joey's eyes. Everything stopped. Then he fell face forward to the carpet, and his body began to shake uncontrollably.

After several minutes he looked up again, straight into Joey's eyes as though mesmerized, and kept repeating, "Whoa man, this is something else! Whoa man, what is this?" Joey was smiling magnificently; the rest of the room erupted into laughter.

"How do you do that, man?" Carlos asked, finally.

"I assure you, I didn't do anything," replied Joey. "I am quite innocent."

"Do you guys do this kind of thing often?" asked Carlos.

Joey replied enigmatically, "You can come as often as you like. And besides, your friend Matt will be a great help." This seemed like a cue to pour my troubles at Joey's feet. Joey looked over to me with an inquiring expression. "Any problem now?" he asked.

"Well," I replied, "I feel like I blew it." I told him the story of getting home to Paul. The feeling of a crash landing, the renewed energy in the morning, the pain of talking to Rebecca and the kids. I felt like a sorrowful creature, sitting before him. He paused a while, like a puppet president waiting for the answer to be relayed to him in a concealed earpiece. Finally he spoke slowly.

"Okay," said Joey. "So like I told you last night, there are many old habits that must be seen and must drop away for things to be complete. It's all old habits. If you want a blue sky, you simply need a strong wind to blow away the clouds. Now, when you got home last night, what did you want from your friend?"

"I didn't want anything," I replied. "I just wanted to share with him the joy I was feeling."

"If you didn't want anything from him," replied Joey, "then why the hurt and disappointment?"

I hadn't considered this. "I suppose I wanted him to feel good, too."

"And what would that give you, if he felt good, too?" asked Joey.

I had to pause to consider. "It would allow me to feel close to him."

"And if you felt close to him," asked Joey, "what would that give you?" This sounded redundant.

"I'd feel more relaxed and comfortable with him."

"And what is in the way of feeling relaxed and comfortable with him, just as it is?"

"Well, he's given me a place to stay for quite a while now, and I feel kind of indebted to him. I feel like he disapproves of my coming here."

"That's right, so you want his approval, right?"

"I guess I do."

"And, aside from what happened last night, does your friend Paul like you or dislike you?"

"Of course he likes me. We're best friends."

"Does he basically approve or disapprove of you?"

"We're buddies."

"So would you rather run around in circles to try to get his approval or just recognize the approval that is already there?"

I didn't answer.

"Can you want approval and feel approval at the same time?"

I had never considered this. I felt something drop inside me, like a stone into a deep well.

"Could you let go of wanting approval and just have what is already here?"

"Yes," I said, back in last night's mode, where I was more listening to my responses than speaking.

"Very good. And is it all right for Paul to not understand what occurred for you here?"

Each time, I had to check and feel to be able to answer him, as if I were a patient describing my symptoms to a doctor.

"It's okay."

"Is it okay for him to not like what occurred for you here?"

"Well . . ."

"Is it okay for him to have no interest in what occurred for you here?"

"I guess so."

"Then what remains?"

"He's my friend."

"Very good. What problem is there now?"

"I love my children."

"Is that a problem?" He raised one eyebrow, keeping the other unmoving. I made a mental note to see if I could do the same thing, alone with a mirror. If I could, the kids would love it.

"When I talk to my wife and kids, I still feel the agony of the separation from them."

"Does your wife love you?" asked Joey.

The question stopped me in my tracks. The events of the previous months had been so contentious and difficult that my immediate answer wanted to be "No." But as I started to mouth that single syllable it felt like a lie. "My wife, Rebecca, does love me," I had to admit.

"Good. And how about your children?"

"Yes, my children love me, too."

"Good."

Joey put both his hands behind his back. "In my left hand," he smiled, "there is peace. There is a peace that doesn't care what happens in the external world. There's a peace that comes from who you are, not what's happening to you. And in my right hand," he continued, "there's looking for love. There is a lack of love. There is the constant fear of rejection and abandonment." He brought both his fists out and placed them before me side by side. "Which hand do you choose?"

I said nothing, which he took as an answer anyway.

"Can you have both at the same time?"

I had never looked at things like this before. "No," I had to admit. I was getting back to the same brainless state of the night before. I was answering these questions spontaneously and only afterward trying to figure out what I had said.

"Could you let go of this?" he said, holding up his right hand, "to have this?" holding up his left hand.

Silence. My mind's admission of defeat.

He paused, and then dropped both his hands. "What problem remains?"

"Right now, none. But I miss my children."

"Good," said Joey. "Do your children love you?"

"Yes," I said.

"Do you love your children?"

"Yes, I do," I said.

"Would you rather miss your children? Or enjoy love?"

"But today they sounded so distant, so cold. My daughter was more interested in her new television than in talking to me."

"Which comes first?" asked Joey. "A feeling of missing? Or the external reality of estrangement? Before you phoned them, what were you feeling?"

"I was missing them."

"Exactly," said Joey. "You phoned them in a state of lack. Now once again . . . if you could choose in this moment between being the love or missing the love, which would you choose?"

"Love," I admitted reluctantly, looking at the ground.

"And how about now?"

"I choose love." I tried on Californian-style enthusiasm for size and was surprised to find it felt quite acceptable.

"And now?"

"I choose love." The more I said these words, the more they became a sensation in my chest. I wanted to burst into song, and I half-expected that the room would join me in a chorus if I did, perhaps even tap dancing.

"Keep choosing love over missing and then tell me what happens." He smiled and closed his eyes for what seemed like the longest time. When he opened them again, he said: "Don't worry, you can relax. The blessings of thousands of angels are hovering over you. All will be well."

With that, he turned and looked at Sam, smiled again, and closed his eyes. The room was quiet. A few minutes later, the young man, Sundance, asked Joey some questions about his studies, to which Joey replied with the utmost compassion and interest. Carlos, meanwhile, was sitting upright as a statue staring fixedly into Joey's eyes, in a state of rapture.

When all questions and comments had been exhausted, Joey asked June if she would play for us. She disappeared for a moment and came back with a small harp. We sat together, listening to the melody. Joey's eyes closed, and not a single muscle moved anywhere. There was no time remaining.

When all was said and done, Joey once again pushed down hard on the arms of his chair, brought himself to an upright position, muttered "KYSH. KYSH," and left the room.

This time I made a beeline for Sam, determined not to let her get away. I felt light again. "Thank you so much for tipping me off about all this," I began.

She looked at me with those same penetrating blue eyes I remembered from the café that first night. "You're welcome. I'm glad you came," she said.

I was struggling for something more to say when Alan poked his head back through the door. He had obviously followed Joey out of the room without my noticing.

"Matt," he said, "Joey would like to see you."

I rose to my feet, disappointed to be separated from Sam so quickly. My disappointment didn't last for long.

"And Sam," continued Alan, "you too."

CHAPTER 7

JOEY'S STORY

When Sam and I entered the same little room where I had spoken with Joey the night before, he was nowhere to be seen. We heard some sounds from another doorway, and after a few minutes he emerged with a silver tray bearing three cups and a small plate of Turkish delight.

"Do you like chai?" he asked. "Indian spiced tea, you know."

"Great!" I replied. "Thank you."

Joey asked me about my job at the radio station, which guests I'd had on the show, where my house had been. He seemed to know plenty about everything. When I told him that the bank had foreclosed on my loan, he even knew a surprising amount about real estate, down to the minute details of the legalities involved.

"And where are you staying now?" he asked. "Where is this garret with the mysterious Paul?"

I explained that it was on the other side of town.

"That's quite a ways from here," said Joey. "How do you get home?"

"I take the bus," I replied, my face flushing. Until recently, I'd never been without my own car.

"What time does the last bus leave?"

"Twelve-ten," I replied. Joey looked at his watch.

"Ah," he said. "That's plenty of time." He settled himself into his armchair. Throughout this interchange, Sam was quiet, making slow and studious work of her Turkish delight. A silence fell over the room.

"You're a very good boy," said Joey finally, looking at me affectionately. "I've waited a long time to find someone like you." He paused. "And especially I like it that you have a family. Being a parent keeps your feet on the earth, you know." He glanced over at some framed photographs on a little table. Sure enough, one of them showed a previous version of Joey embracing one teenage boy under each arm. "They're grown now," he said. "But they sure kept me busy for a while."

"Yes," I said. "But that seems to be my challenge. If I hadn't created such a complicated life, I think it would be easier just to stay in what you're pointing me to."

Joey shook his head slowly. "No, that's not the way," he said. "That's not the way. You're here in a body to lead a human life. You don't graduate from college by dropping out."

I wanted to know more about this mysterious man who seemed to have mastered the art of being human. I looked back over to the table at the photographs. There again was the autographed photo of JFK, grinning next to a younger Joey. A larger frame held multiple photographs, peering out through little ovals in the mat mountings. Some were faces I recognized, many I did not. In the middle of the table, crowning this hall of fame, was the most benign face of all.

An ageless face, probably Indian, was radiating unspeakable peace. Wearing only a piece of cloth covering his pelvis, the man sat cross-legged on a rock. I was lost, gazing into those eyes. He looked very familiar.

"I was twenty-five when I met him," said Joey, following my gaze. "It was after the War, 1948. I was an engineer in the Merchant Marines, working on a ship running between America and Asia. We used to load up in Philadelphia or New York with machine parts, Ford motor cars, you name it. We'd unload in Bombay or Mangalore and then load up with stuff to bring home."

"How did you end up on a ship?" I asked him.

Joey chuckled at my curiosity. "I guess you want the whole story. I was born in Chicago, 1923. My parents were both first-generation Irish Catholic immigrants. I was the second to the youngest of seven children. My father was a good man." Joey stopped and looked at the floor, then sipped his tea. "Probably the best man you'd ever meet. When the Depression came in '32, he lost his job at the car factory. We were dirt poor; there wasn't any such thing as welfare and all that then. We had no family in the States; they were all back in Ireland," he chuckled, "probably more dirt poor than we were. My dad tried to get all kinds of different jobs. Finally in '33 he landed a job in another factory. He was so desperate trying to get the family back on track that he was working all the overtime he could get, fourteen, sixteen-hour days. Nobody minded about that back in those days. He was running a big sheet metal press when he fell asleep on the job. That was the end of him.

"That left the seven of us kids alone with our mother, and we certainly didn't have the money to go back to Ireland. Everybody pitched in and started working. When I was sixteen they sent me to school to study technical engineering. I think the family had me pegged as the best hope to be a breadwinner. After I finished, I went straight into the Navy, 1941, and worked on an aircraft carrier. Two of my brothers were already fighting. Only one of them made it home. When the war ended, I just hopped straight from the Navy to the Merchant Marines. It was the best I could do for the family, because all my expenses were paid, and I could send every cent that I made back home to my mother, my sisters, and my little brother.

"Anyway," Joey continued, "in 1948 we docked in Mangalore, that's on the west coast of India. We unloaded all the heavy machinery we had on board: cars, two printing presses, lots of stuff. We were scheduled to load up the hold with manganese ore they mined in Karnataka. But India was very disorganized in those days. The poor buggers were trying to recover from more than a hundred years of British tyranny, and they didn't have the cargo ready for us. We had ten days to wait.

"One thing I didn't mention to you was that when I was a boy in Chicago, I used to have a lot of strange visions. They thought I was a little cracked, I think. I always excelled at math because this little fella with a white beard and kind eyes would pop up in my mind and tell me all the answers. He used to come to me at night in dreams and tell me that he'd been waiting for me forever. I liked that line; I use it myself. More tea, Sam?"

She looked startled, then smiled and shook her head.

"So there I was in Mangalore in 1948 with nothing to do for ten days. The first afternoon, I walked into a bookstore and saw this guy's photograph." Joey nodded at the picture on his table. "It was the same face I'd been dreaming of all those years. I asked the clerk in the bookstore who it was. And he told me, 'Well that's the Guruji,' and as he said it, his eyes sort of glassed over in reverence."

"Guruji?" I asked.

"They're all called Guruji there, just means teacher. More accurately, very much loved, First-Class, Grade-A teacher. That's 'cause of the *ji* bit, see. It's an upgrade. I asked where he lived, and the shopkeeper gave me elaborate directions to some mountain, a good day's train ride away, over near the other coast. I knew I had to meet the guy, so I went straight to the train station, booked myself a ticket, and was on my way. I stopped off in a hotel a few miles from the place that night, and the next day I hired a taxi to take me to the mountain."

Joey turned to Sam. "It wasn't what you'd call a taxi here. Just a cart and driver pulled by a bullock. Took all day to get there. Finally, the driver dropped me off in front of a group of buildings at the base of a mountain. I had no idea where I was or what I was doing there. Very colorful, it was, the women all wrapped up in those sari outfits. Bullock carts and donkeys everywhere. It was a beautiful town, too. The biggest temples you've ever seen in your life, with towers reaching right up into the sky. Dogs and pigs and cows everywhere you cared to look. Not like Chicago," he chuckled.

"I walked into the compound and asked if I could meet a Mister Guruji there. Luckily, the guy who greeted me spoke English, gave me a room, very plain and simple. Concrete floor, brick walls, plain wooden bed with a thin coconut mattress on top of it. But I was happy. For some reason this felt like home. After I got washed up and all, he led me into a little hall where a bunch of people were sitting, mostly Indians, with one or two Westerners, too. Then I saw my man. Turns out his real name was Ramana. He was half-reclining on a couch. A couple of other guys, very scantily dressed, were fanning him with big leaves. I sat on the floor along with the others."

Joey paused, as if listening to something deep inside, his face softening.

"He turned and looked at me with the quietest, kindest eyes I'd ever seen, or that I've ever seen since. Didn't say a damn word, just went on looking and looking, and the longer he looked, the quieter I got. I hadn't the faintest idea why I was there or what was happening. I just knew that each minute that passed, I was falling into a deeper peace. Finally he spoke to me, in English, and said just the same words that I'd heard in my vision. He said, 'I've been waiting for you forever.' I didn't know what he meant, but I knew it was true. And I knew I'd been waiting for him, too.

"I stayed there for eight days," Joey said softly. "I never really knew what to say to him, so I'd just show up every minute I was allowed in that hall and sit quietly on the floor. He used to look in my eyes a good deal, and I'd look back into his, and neither of us said a word. Then came the last day before I had to take the bullock cart and the train back to the ship. This whole time the others were talking to him in a language I didn't understand. Every now and then a Westerner would chirp in, but even in English, I couldn't understand too much. Finally, I plucked up the courage to say something. I said to him, 'I don't want to leave. I don't want to leave you.' He just looked at me for the longest time, and by the time he did speak, he didn't need to, because what he said, I already knew. He said, 'You cannot leave me and I cannot leave you.' Then he asked me, 'Can you find the one who leaves?' And I looked. I tried to find Joey Murphy, but there was nothing there. All I could find was that same quietness that was looking at me."

Joey turned to me. "Just like you did last night, Matt." I nodded.

"When it was finally time to leave, I didn't mind at all. I said goodbye, but even that seemed like a lie. He just smiled at me, like he knew and I knew no one was going anywhere. All the way back in the bullock cart, all I could feel was the stillness and the kindness in his eyes.

When I got back on the train, all the noise and dust and commotion of India was resting in the kindness that I felt in his eyes. And when I got back to the ship, the body of Joey Murphy went through all its normal functions and duties, but I didn't feel involved in any of it. I just stayed embraced in that kindness and that stillness.

"We set off from Mangalore, I kept up with my duties, but it all felt like a silent movie, like nothing was happening. On the way back across the ocean, a wire came for me. Mama had died. Pneumonia, poor dear. I felt the grief in my chest, but even that grief, to lose the sweetest, gentlest mother anyone's ever known, was welling up within that kindness and that peace, and I felt his eyes still caressing me. They gave me some leave when I got back to New York so I could go to my family and help put things in order. Everyone was all churned up, and I was too, but that kindness and peace just kept on growing and multiplying, and it overflowed onto my sisters and my brother, Pat. With mother gone and my siblings older, I didn't have to come up with so much money. I asked the trading company if they'd give me three months' leave the following spring in India. They thought I was crazy. I had to do several more trips back and forth to Asia, biding time to be back with my Beloved, with those deep eyes."

"Why did they think you were crazy?" I asked.

"Why d'ya think? Everyone wanted leave in Italy or Greece. It was the first request they'd had for India. Anyway, finally February of '49 came around and I made that same trip by train and then on to the holy mountain. When I walked back into the hall it was like no time had passed. Ramana looked at me like I'd just stepped out for five minutes and everything was just like it had been the year before. I spent three months working in the kitchen. I learned to make idli, and curry and chai," Joey chuckled. "Yessir, I grew to love my chai. The old man was getting sick, he had some problem with his arm and he was in a lot of pain. He kept refusing painkillers, but it didn't seem to make any difference to the kindness and peace in those eyes.

"I never talked much, I was too shy, but I noticed one thing. Whoever came and sat before him, he would melt and merge and blend into that person. Even though he was sick, if somebody came asking a lot of intellectual questions, he would just give intellectual answers like that's what he always did. One day, a woman came with some baked stuff she'd made for him. She was tearful and loving, and he was crying, too, and loving her back. Another time, a guy came who was real churned up and angry about something, and then the old man got really stern and angry, too. Although his eyes never changed, his means of expression just shifted to match the person he was with. Watching in those months I learned that's how you get along with people. You just put yourself aside and meet them in who they are.

"One night, when the kitchen chief went back to Madras to see his family, they let me take the hot milk in to the old man before he went to sleep. He motioned for me to sit quiet by his side. There was only his attendant in the room with us. The old man looked at me, again for the longest time, and then he said a few words, which wound up shaping the rest of my life. He said, 'That which you love is That which you are. You will share it wherever you go, you have no choice. But you are an American boy; you are not Indian. It will share itself in an American way.' Then he closed his eyes. He must have been in a lot of pain at that time, and the attendant motioned for me to leave."

Joey picked up his empty cup, looked in it for a few seconds, and put it down.

"Soon after that exchange I had to head back again to Madras and back to the ship. After that three months, nothing ever changed again. It's like I've spent the rest of my life without ever moving from that spot beside his couch where he said those words. We sailed to America, and I made it back just in time for my brother Patrick's graduation from college. I had one more year of my contract with the trading company, and then I didn't know what to do after that."

"Was that the last time you saw him?" I asked.

"I got one more chance," Joey said. "We were doing more trade with the Far East: Hong Kong, Australia, Indonesia; but early in 1950 there was a ship sailing for Madras. I managed to swap with another engineer so I could be on it. When we arrived, the Indians had tightened up their act a bit and all the goods were ready for an immediate turnaround. I heard that Ramana was really in bad shape. So I went to the captain and told him that I needed three weeks off. He was outraged, and told me if I didn't go back on the ship I'd lose my job and my severance pay. Now that was quite a dilemma because it meant I'd be stuck in India without a cent in my pocket and no way to get home. But I felt a command from inside, and I had to follow it. So I got on a train and the ship sailed without me.

"When I made it to the holy mountain, he was bad. They'd built a little shack for him where he was staying, no bigger than ten foot square, and it was obvious he was in his last days. He had cancer. There was a lot of spare time in that period, because he needed a lot of rest. There were visitors coming and going, wealthy Indians, even Indian politicians, and a fair share of Westerners, too.

"I filed by with the rest of them to see him. His body was really weak, but the look in those eyes never changed. Finally, he sent a message to me through one of his attendants, that I should go back to America, there was no need for me to be there anymore."

Joey stretched out his legs, leaning back. He closed his eyes for a moment.

"When I got to Bombay, I picked up a newspaper and found that he had died. Strangely enough, it didn't seem to bother me one bit. Even people who didn't know him too well were all churned up and crying. But those kind and peaceful eyes seemed just as alive with his body dead as they were when he was alive. That night I looked up in the sky and I saw the biggest comet I'd ever seen. It lit up the street like it was daylight. People saw it all over India."

Joey suddenly noticed the empty plate, sprung to his feet with it, and left the room. Sam and I sat there, without a word. I tried to catch her eye, but she became fascinated by the weave of the blanket covering the chair and studied it with concentration.

Joey returned after a few minutes with a full plate and fresh tea. His story continued. "When I got back to Madras, of course I was on the black list. No one would give me a berth home or a job. There was a very well-dressed-looking fella wandering around supervising the unloading of refrigerators, name of Klein. When I was done with getting rejected for the fifth time, he asked me if I wanted to go for lunch. It was his first time in India; he was lost like a fish out of water. I showed him around the town. By the time the day was done, he offered me a job as a technical engineer back home. Of course, having no backup plan, I had no choice but to accept.

"We got to talking on the voyage home, turned out the guy was filthy rich and filthy unhappy. Had a drinking problem, a marriage problem, and a personality problem to boot. Almost every night he would drink too much, then yell at the crew about something or another. I was mighty embarrassed, I must tell you. But I just found myself listening and blending in with him just the way that the old man had blended in with me. And as the days went by, he seemed to soften and get happier. Once we got back to New York, he got me set me up, and latched onto me more as some kind of support and friend than as an engineer. Within a few months I became like his personal assistant with his real estate deals. I learned a thing or two, and I figured out that you didn't need money to buy real estate, you just needed credit."

Joey stretched again, obviously enjoying this bit of the story. With Klein's help, Joey started to buy property himself, and within a couple of years had the titles to four buildings. He met Katie, a secretary in Klein's office, married her, and had two sons. Seems Joey had the golden touch: every real estate deal was a triumph. By the mid-'50s he went into building new homes in the suburbs of New York. Then he started to buy lumber in Canada, had it milled, and had enough for his own projects as well as plenty to sell at a markup.

"By 1958 I had enough for five men to retire. We had a nice brownstone on Madison Avenue in New York. I was selling houses to all of New York's rich and famous. When the Indian guru fad hit, a client who knew I'd been over there invited me to his house to give a talk. Soon we were having informal meetings around New York. That was really how I began a sort of teaching thing, and the seeds Ramana had planted started to bear fruit. It was almost ten years later, although it was very informal, just a meeting of friends."

Joey got tired of business, put it all in the hands of managers, and took his family to Europe in 1960. They lived there for several years, he got involved with rock bands, with theater people; whatever was hot,

Joey seemed to have had a finger in it. In '62 they came back to the States, moved to L.A. He became involved in the Actor's Workshop and met Marilyn Monroe.

"She was trying to climb out of the rut of being a sex symbol and become a serious actress," Joey went on. "One night Milos Forman told me Marilyn was in a bad way and sent me over to try to calm her down. I had become some sort of guru-cum-therapist to that crowd. She was a beauty, that woman, not just to look at. She had deep passion to find out who she really was. We soon struck up a friendship, she would call me or Katie any time of the day or night. We lived nearby, off La Cienega in Hollywood.

"That was how I met Jack Kennedy. One night I was at home late, and the phone rang. It was Marilyn, she was over at Frank Lurie's house, the fashion photographer. She was real upset and disoriented. So I went over there, and we talked a while. I took her home and made her ginger tea. She liked that. Suddenly, after midnight, there were three rings on the doorbell downstairs. Next thing I know, I'm sitting in the kitchen with Marilyn and the President of the United States and a bunch of Secret Service agents patrolling in the garden. He was all caught up in a fight with Fidel Castro and right on the edge of going to war with Cuba. We wound up having quite a conversation there. I think he was surprised that I didn't bow and scrape to him. I think I helped him see that warfare and intolerance were only going to lead to more of the same, but I was surprised when he came out a few days later and reversed his policy on Cuba. That would have been the spring of '63. We met up a few times after that, too, before he got himself killed. Jack was a good man, but in talking to him I realized that if the head of the whole shebang was that stressed out, man we had to do something different.

"So we bought up a bunch of land out in Virginia and looked for people who were interested in living for something more abiding than money and fame. We started our first community with thirty people. It was a great time; everything was up for grabs. Every value we had held sacred was being questioned. I got to know Fritz Perls and Ginsberg and Ram Dass. Seemed like there was nothing we couldn't change."

Joey's story continued to weave among actors, musicians, and writers, some of whom I'd heard of, all of whom had been formative. In the mid-'70s he was in the middle of anti-Vietnam activism, and had to go to Canada for a while to avoid arrest. In this way, he later became involved with the United Nations as an informal advisor. He traveled to India, and befriended the Tibetan community in Dharamsala, helping to establish several Tibetan compounds in Southern India. In the late '70s he saw the great potential of computers, and learned how to program them, as a hobby. He helped out a couple of students start their own company out of a garage, who went on to spearhead the computer revolution.

You name it, he'd been there.

"So that's what I mean," said Joey. "You've got to live a full human life. There ain't no way to avoid it. Life's going to send things your way, and there's not much you can do about it. I figure I've done everything I ever wanted to in this life." He paused. "There's only two experiences I missed out on."

My curiosity was certainly piqued. "What are they?" I asked.

"I've never been arrested, and I've never jumped out of an airplane." He paused, seeing if there was anything to add to the list. "Nope, that's it. I've done everything else." With that he glanced over his shoulder at the clock. "Now what time did you say your bus was?"

"Twelve-ten is the last bus."

"Well my, look at the time. It's seven after right now." He laughed. I was shocked. I couldn't believe we'd been sitting there for two hours.

"Even sprinting, you'll never make it," he told me. He turned to Sam. "You'll have to put him up for the night, Sam."

Sam was visibly shaken. She looked almost angry. "But Joey, I just have a one-room studio."

"Don't matter. You brought him here, you'd better look after him."

"But—," stuttered Sam. "But can't he stay here with you?"

"No one ever stays here, Sam, you know that. Can't an old man have a bit of peace?"

And with that, he pushed down on the arms of his chair in characteristic fashion, bade us goodnight, and disappeared into his bedroom. Sam looked like a cornered animal.

"Look, it's okay," I said. "I can walk home. I don't mind."

"No," she said. "I've got to do what he says. You can sleep on the couch."

CHAPTER 8

THE SOFA BED

We stepped out into a much heavier rain than the night before. This wasn't drizzle; this was a downpour, and neither of us had an umbrella.

"It's several blocks," Sam muttered, still looking very bitter.

We hurried through the rain in awkward silence. By the time we reached her building, we were both drenched. At first sight, it seemed the converted warehouse couldn't possibly be home to anyone. She led me through the sliding heavy gate to an industrial elevator and pressed a button for the top floor. The elevator had no door, just a metal folding grill from floor to ceiling. On our ascent we could see the corporate offices of an outdoor equipment firm, then an aerobics and fitness center, then some more offices, until finally we were delivered to the studio apartments on the top floor. A rough Hessian carpet ran the entire length of the long corridor. Outside the many doors were parked strollers, bicycles, even skis. Her apartment was one of the last. She opened the door, still in moody silence, and let us in. She wasn't lying about its modest size. It was truly one room. A sofa, chair, TV, stereo, and coffee table filled the main area and just an open arch led to a space that held a bed and a dresser. There was a kitchen sink and hot plate in a corner of the living room. The only doorway led into a tiny bathroom.

"You're very wet," she said, avoiding my eyes. "I'll give you something to change into." She stepped into the bedroom alcove and reappeared moments later with some sweatpants, a T-shirt, and a towel. "You can sleep there," she said, pointing to the couch. "Do you want a cup of tea?"

"Sure," I said, "and thanks. I know this is a little awkward for you."

"It's okay. I'm going to take a shower now," she muttered. "Do you want one after I'm done?" I declined. She put the teakettle on the hot plate and flipped a switch on the very impressive stereo that dominated her apartment like a large lion in a small den. It would have better suited a downtown disco. The song was something I knew, but could not quite name. She disappeared into the bathroom.

I dried off my hair with the towel, took off my wet clothes, and put on the ones she'd given me. A few minutes later, she came back from the bathroom in a white bathrobe, modestly pulled tight around her body with a belt. Pink pajama legs poked out at floor level. Her blonde hair was much longer when wet, her eyes an even more penetrating blue. She made the tea and sat down in a chair. The stereo mysteriously whirred for a moment and then began to play something quite different. Random shuffle mode. Clever.

"That was very unusual tonight," she said, obviously feeling a little more relaxed. "I've never heard him tell his story before to anyone."

"I was riveted," I admitted. "Someone should write all that down."

"Maybe that's why he told it to you," she smiled.

We fell into a silence that was part embarrassment and part fatigue. The track on the CD changed to Sarah McLachlan singing "Sweet Surrender." After several minutes, our eyes met.

"I'm sorry," she said. "I'm not very good with new people. I don't mean to make you unwelcome."

I saw the same unassuming compassion in her eyes as that first night. I wanted to say something, to acknowledge her beauty, her generosity, the enormous gift she'd given me, but nothing seemed appropriate.

"Thank you for reaching out to me the other night," was all I could finally come up with. "It's probably the biggest gift anyone has ever given me."

"You're welcome," she smiled, and paused for a long time.

Our eyes met again; thoughts were dropping away. I was transported back into the same feeling of the night before at Joey's, of looking into myself. The room became very still. I sensed the faintest smells of vanilla and of sandalwood.

"I know what you've been going through," she spoke softly. "I've been there myself. I've been in that same despair. He helped me then, just like he's helping you now."

I could feel, from the way she spoke, she had no intention of filling in the details, so I just stayed quiet as we sat there, looking not at each other, but into one another. This was an involuntary looking, the kind where the volition to look away is melted by the looking itself. The corners of her mouth curled up just the tiniest bit into the hint of a smile. Vaguely I recognized that our bodies were breathing in absolute unison, although I wasn't trying to breathe with her, and I'm sure she wasn't with me. I could feel her chest rising and falling, as though I was fully within her body, feeling from the inside. By the time the CD player stopped, it must have been close to two in the morning, but that now seemed irrelevant. She stood up, smiled, and stretched. As she rose, her terrycloth robe loosened a little; I glimpsed the hint of her full breasts, the freckles on her upper chest. Her facial muscles winced as she tightened the belt of the bathrobe.

"The sofa folds out into a bed," she said. I helped her move the coffee table a few feet, and sure enough, the sofa offered up a metal-framed mattress from out of its belly. She produced sheets and a pillow for me.

"Good night," she said. "Sleep well."

She stepped toward me tentatively; I held her against my chest. She turned her head to the side to face away from me, and I placed a hand on her damp wavy hair. I could feel the softness of her breasts now against my chest, the soft beating of her heart, the rising and falling of her breath, and the pulse in her belly against mine. Her hair smelled of vanilla. She turned her head back a little, just at the same moment I turned mine, and, without intention on either of our parts, our cheeks gently brushed. Driven more by impulse than permission, I lowered my head just a little more, and touched her lips lightly with my own. I was starting to feel aroused. She pulled away.

Without another word, she turned away to her bedroom alcove, and I climbed into the sofa's offering. As lights were extinguished, I realized that my whole body was alive with desire for this woman. In that desire, I fell asleep.

When I awoke it was still dark, but the room was infused with a bluish glow. I was too groggy to bother finding out where this bluish light might be coming from. The sofa bed had become considerably more comfortable after a few hours of use; the mattress was feeling thicker and softer.

"Are you awake?" I heard a voice whisper from out of the darkness. Sam was standing in the archway that separated her alcove from the main room, just a few feet from my sofa. Her voice was very soft, stroking the darkness with its gentle intimacy. The white terry robe hung looser on her body now. Her hair had dried and was hanging in little ringlets on her shoulders. I mumbled an assent, and she moved toward me in the nocturnal blueness and sat on the edge of the bed. She had abandoned her heavy mantle of defense—now she showed her undefended tenderness plainly for me to see. Everything that words had not said, her body was now telling me. It wore its longing for touch, its flickering demand to be held, like a heavy musk perfume. She hung her head slightly, waiting, shy, driven by the simplicity of human need. I took her hand in mine.

My heart beat with greater vigor in my own chest. I felt the same quickening in the pulse in her wrist as I caressed it. Her breath drew in ever so slightly as she lightly sucked her lower lip into her mouth.

There was music playing again, very faintly, so softly that it was more felt through the skin than heard. Still drugged by recent sleep, I did not question if she had left the stereo on from the night before, or switched it on again. Sarah McLachlan had made up her mind on the other side of the room, "I won't fear love . . . " We were fumbling our own way behind her.

"I have feared love," Sam murmured, still looking down into her lap. "I always turn away from letting myself be touched like this." There was an explosion in my chest close to crying. I wanted to offer reassurance and did not know how. It was spoken with my hand, as it stroked the back of hers, as it touched the skin on her forearm, as it felt the soft hair on the top of her arm, as it traced the bones in her slightly arched spine, through her robe.

"From the moment I first met you that night, I have been feeling with you. I can feel your courage and your strength. I am sorry to push you away from me; it is just my habit, such an old habit . . ."

"It's okay," I murmured. "It's all right."

As I put my arm around her shoulders, she leaned silently toward me. Her body was trembling. I again smelled the faintest hint of vanilla. I inhaled the warmth of her breath, in an endless savoring that knew no goal, no direction, only this endless, overflowing gentleness. Our lips united like long-lost friends who rush toward each other in mutual recognition. She moaned on an in-breath, as her body relaxed even more into mine. My heart was pounding. I could feel hers beat back from the other side of the robe. My left hand held hers, offering the gentle reassurance that words could never touch, while my right hand continued down her back, around the small of her waist, up and down each arm. When it finally made its journey from her hip down the outside of her left leg, it reached the nakedness of her skin. She was freezing cold.

"Come here," I whispered, and raised the comforter. She giggled softly. Our bodies met. I looked up for a moment and saw a painting hanging on the wall, in the corner by the door. It was Klimt's *The Kiss*. *Perfect,* I thought. Like a perfect movie.

Then we were swimming together in an ocean of liquid love, drowned so completely in it that only the liquidity itself remained, moving in huge waves. The line melted between where she ended and I began. The dance of passion in search of meeting itself flowed on and on. Our naked bodies became increasingly still, till only the slightest movement was enough to open another cavern of infinite and explosive yielding to the mystery.

When I woke up, the sofa bed had restored itself to its original functional rigidity. Strangely, I was again wearing the T-shirt and sweatpants she had given me the night before. I sat up and looked around. Her bed was made and she was nowhere to be found, but I noticed the note on the coffee table: "I've gone to teach yoga. Please help yourself to breakfast. It was very nice to spend time with you, sorry for being a bit guarded. Just close the door, it locks on its own. Seeya. S."

I sat there for a moment, still rapt in lovemaking. I had no idea which impressions were factual and which were dreamed, they all seemed to blend into one another. The note seemed a little formal, relative to remembered passion, I had to admit to myself.

I got up from the bed and then noticed the clock. It was a quarter to ten. I showered and retrieved the clothes that she had hung to dry above the heating vent in the bathroom. She'd left some cereal and rice milk on the tiny kitchen table. I ate a small bowl, folded the bed back into the sofa, then noticed the painting near the door. It was a Van Gogh. Not the Klimt. Sure enough, the door locked itself as I closed it behind me.

CHAPTER 9

Which Is the Most Beautiful?

It was a miraculously sunny day for December. Not only did my body feel like I had just come from a night of exquisite lovemaking, but it seemed to me that everyone I saw on the street had as well. The entire city looked deeply, sexually satisfied. Instead of walking to the bus stop, I was filled with a boyish confidence and wandered back toward Joey's apartment. As I retraced our steps of the night before, it didn't feel like my feet were actually touching the ground. I was floating about two inches above the sidewalk in a state of utter satiation. I climbed the now familiar faded staircase and knocked on Joey's door. It took a few minutes for him to answer, but he finally appeared, wrapped in an ancient-looking Eastern cloth, the kind that bicycle rickshaw drivers wear in Indian movies. He had a toothbrush in his mouth and massive amounts of white foam spilling out onto his goatee.

"You're just in time for your own arrival," he mumbled, and went back into the bathroom, leaving me to face my adultery, even if only imagined, along with J.F.K. The place was full of the smell of brewing Turkish coffee.

"D'ya drink coffee?" he asked, popping his head through the door.

"Um, yeah, sure." Joey disappeared again and produced some kitcheny noises from another room.

"Come on in here, don't be shy," he called out. I stepped into the kitchen, which was a work of art in itself. All kinds of glass jars were arranged on shelves, displaying rice, other grains, various kinds of beans, and a wide assortment of spices. "This is Alan's place, you know. They let me use it."

"Yes, they told me that."

"They're very good cooks, you know. They have a café downstairs."

"Yes, I had a sandwich there last night."

"And . . . " Joey added, with a twinkle in his eye. "How did you sleep?"

"Oh," I looked at the floor, still unsure where reality had ended and my erotic dream had begun. "I slept great, thanks." I watched Joey pour the coffee. "On the sofa bed," I added.

Joey said nothing, but placed the coffee before me and sat down in front of his own. "It's day two."

His reminder sent a wave of anxiety through my body. I was supposed to be learning something, passing some kind of test, but I had no idea what the rules were or what was expected of me. Like one of those dreams where you show up for an exam at school and realize you haven't read the required textbooks. We drank our coffee in silence. I had the feeling Joey was constantly testing me, scrutinizing me, reading me like a book. He disappeared again and came back after ten minutes or so showered, fresh, and sparkling.

"Well, watcha sittin' around for? It's a beautiful day, let's go have ourselves some fun!"

He opened the door of the apartment and bounded down the stairs like a teenager. I followed in hot pursuit. He was whistling a sea shanty to himself, saying good morning to every other person who passed him on the street. Everyone smiled back, even those who had looked quite sullen on approach, as though he were some aged Disney character, sprinkling happiness dust and waking all he met from a trance of melancholy. He gazed with fascination at every shop window, even lingered wistfully for a long time in front of a display of an infinite assortment of vacuum cleaners. He led me down past the bike shop, past the food co-op, past the public utility office. We made a sharp left turn on Clarendon Street and entered the public park.

The sun had not quite melted all the frost from the ground. School must have been out, because kids were Rollerblading. Young mothers and nannies pushed strollers, and old people were meandering along. A few were accompanied by dogs, some leading, and others being led by their owners.

"It all looks so beautiful," I ventured. "I feel so overwhelmed with love. You know last night I—" Joey took no interest in my attempted confession, but grabbed me by the arm and led me into the park's magnificent greenhouse, kept at tropical temperatures throughout the year. The air was full of the warm, wet smell of soil and luscious tropical plants. It's one of the most famous in the country, boasting a unique collection of roses from all over the world that seemed to be in bloom at any time of year one chose to visit. He showed me one of the hybrid roses, red on one side and orange on the other.

"There's a lot of roses here," he said, stating the obvious. "Now tell me, which rose is the most beautiful?"

I took his question in earnest and began inspecting one after the other, but it was difficult because there were so many and each was so different.

"Which one is the most beautiful?" Joey asked again, studying me intently.

"Well, this one here is very pretty," I said, choosing a soft orange-pink specimen.

"How does it smell?" he went on.

I bent over the rose and inhaled its delicate perfume. "Apricot."

Joey bent over to smell it, too, and closed his eyes in a moment of intense savoring. He swooned, with his eyes closed in rapture. Was it parody or real?

"You like that rose, do you, Matt?"

"Um, yes, it's a very . . . ," I paused, "intriguing little rose." I was much more interested in talking to him about Sam, finding out more about her, telling him about the brewing intimacy, both real and imagined, that had reawakened my heart.

"When was the last time you smelled a rose as good as that?"

"I can't remember smelling a rose that good," I answered, not fully engaged by the conversation.

"But are you sure it's the most beautiful one here?" he asked, with great concern.

I had no idea what he was playing at, but offered a few other specimens as backup. Just at that moment, Joey appeared to completely lose interest in the roses and gazed off toward another part of the greenhouse.

The middle of the greenhouse hosted a lotus pond. Green leaves sat flat on the surface of the water with the lotus flowers rising up above them. He stood there and looked at the lotus flowers, eyes filled with adoration.

"Look," he said. "The lotus is growing out of the water." His botanical commentary didn't seem to offer any very useful information. "But the lotus itself is completely dry. It grows out of the water, it gets its life from the water, it makes the pond beautiful, but can you see one single drop of water on the lotus?"

I had to admit the lotus was totally dry. It bored me completely, relative to thoughts of my beloved Sam.

With that he turned and led me back out of the greenhouse. I tried to continue my confession. "I feel really touched by Sam," I said. "She's very beautiful."

Joey looked up into the sky, which was almost completely cloudless. He appeared to be lost for a moment. Finally, I followed his gaze and saw a pair of swallows circling overhead.

"See the way they dance?" he asked.

I saw them flying in interweaving patterns, sometimes very close, sometimes apart.

"Tell me something now. I just can't tell who is chasing whom. Which one is following, and which is being followed?"

I watched for a while, the dance, the in and out of the patterns, the separation, the coming back together, always in harmony. And for the life of me I couldn't distinguish who was the leader and who was the follower. They seemed to be free in flight yet connected.

Joey led me on.

"I slept at her house, Joey, on the sofa." He was making faces at a baby in a stroller now. "This morning I felt such fullness in my heart. We looked into each other's eyes last night and I've never ever in my life experienced such love, such ecstasy. I feel we have a destiny together."

Joey remained silent.

The edge of the park was bordered by a low concrete wall. Students from the local high school had undertaken an enormous project one summer to paint a mural the entire length of the wall. It featured endangered animals from all over the world and had won awards for its high quality and intricacy. It was truly a splendid sight.

"'Ain't that something?" Joey asked.

"It's beautiful," I replied, flatly.

"Just look over there at those eagles, don't they look like they're flying right out of the wall at you?"

"Yes, very realistic."

"Oh, and look at those panda bears there," he went on, "they don't look like paint and concrete at all, do they? They look quite . . . " he hesitated, and smiled mischievously, "cuddly."

"Very cute pandas."

"Which of these animals do you like the best?" Joey asked.

It took me a while to take in the whole array. Finally my eyes rested on a pair of tigers, leaping out of the wall with fierce energy.

"The tigers," I said.

"You really like them tigers," Joey said.

"They're beautiful."

"I wonder if we could get them off the wall and keep 'em?" Joey mused. "We'll have to ask."

We walked deeper into the park, and all around the lake, with its swans and weeping willows. Again, I felt compelled to broach the subject of my newfound love. "I think I'm falling in love with Sam," I finally blurted out.

"You and many others," he laughed. "But she's married, you know."

This came as a complete surprise. I knew I was still married, but she showed every sign of being as single as can be. "She's married?" I asked. "Who to?"

"She's married to that which you will marry, too, if you have any sense."

Joey was obviously talking about some kind of impersonal, spiritual marriage.

"But Joey, I love her personally. Don't you ever feel a love for a person?"

"Yeah, I feel a very personal love, Matt. I'm on fire with love."

"OK, well for whom? I didn't know there was someone like that for you. You just seemed so . . . alone."

He turned to me, his blue eyes sparkling with amusement. "There's only one person right now, Matt, who's special to me. And that person has my heart completely."

"So spill the beans, Joey. Who is it?"

"It's you."

A shock ran through my body. All was clear. Joey liked young men, and I was his prey. At that moment he turned to an old lady standing just next to us and addressed her directly, looking into her eyes.

"I'm in love. I'm completely in love with whoever stands before me in this moment."

The old lady smiled nervously, giggled, and sidled away toward the greenhouse. As she increased her distance from us, she broke into a trot.

"I mean that I love what's before me, and when it ain't before me no more, it's no longer here. That kind of love won't get you in trouble. You watch what happens when you start clingin' to this and that. You're gonna end up with a bunch of dead flowers and broken concrete from the kids' mural. Every rose has its beauty, Matt. Feel it all. Be like the lotus, a part of this world, but untouched by it. Be like a swallow, endlessly dancing in the open sky, but without any clinging."

With that he spotted some children flying kites. Within minutes he was part of the gang, taking turns with this one and that, offering a wealth of information about the aerodynamics of wind-borne flight.

We walked down Florida Street, and back onto West Broad Street. It was time for lunch. Joey led me into Alan's café. We sat down, and pretty soon both Alan and June came to sit with us, and produced soup and enormous sandwiches. "How's it going, mate?" Alan asked me, with an invigorating pat on the back. Before I could open my mouth, Joey answered for me.

"The boy's smitten," he chuckled.

"Sam?" asked Alan, with a grin.

"Acute Samitis," nodded Joey.

I began to study the sprouts in my sandwich with great intensity. This man is absolutely heartless. He has the sensitivity of a sleepwalking bull. My shame marinated slowly into anger. I had just decided to get up and leave, when first Alan and then June moved back behind the counter to do their work, and I was left alone again with Joey, my humiliator.

He looked at me. His eyes smiled as his mouth stayed somber. "It's only day two, you know. If you're serious, everything has to go."

His words were sobering. I had completely forgotten both his promise and the commitment it had inspired in me. I had assumed our work was restricted to the evening meetings, but now a deeper truth dawned on me. Absolutely nothing would be held sacred.

We finished our food in silence. I relaxed into the presence of the man, deeper than his actions or words. I remembered back to long ago when my father would take me to the beach on a Saturday afternoon. He was a quiet man, serious and shy. He lived his life behind thick glasses and a measured manner of speech. He would roll up his gray polyester pants, take off his shirt and sit on a rock in the shade, while I played in the waves, sometimes alone, sometimes with other children. His presence was always a reassurance, a safety net; nothing could go wrong with my father's eyes gently resting on me. Decades of insecurity separated that memory from this lunch with a man I hardly knew, but the feeling of protection remained the same.

When we finished eating, Joey stood up and made his way to the bathroom in the back. His presence seemed to linger at the table, that safety, that same feeling of being watched by a protection that would allow no ill to befall me.

As we left the café, Joey turned to me, just for a moment, and looked directly into my eyes. Without words, his look transfixed. I almost collapsed onto the pavement with its authority. His eyes seemed to ask, "Are you really ready? Are you serious? When I take you to the cliff's edge, will you really jump with me?"

"All is well," he spoke. "You are doing very well. It is unfolding as it should. Come tonight." With that he turned and walked the few steps, opened the door off the street, and was gone, up the faded staircase and into his sanctuary.

CHAPTER 10

UNKNOWN WATERS

I wandered the university district, filling time before the meeting. The feeling of protection and safety continued to envelop me. I was sobered now, no longer elated from notions of spiritual attainment. I was entering an unknown world where every familiar map and habitual strategy could no longer help me. I walked the streets in a daze. I was now faced with a world neither populated by hungry demons nor celestial beings, things just as they are. No meaning.

I came to the colorfully decorated shop window of Mysterium, which proudly announced itself to be the city's largest spiritual bookstore. The window offered me ten steps to financial freedom, the final truth on what makes men and women really get along, and ancient secrets of longevity. None of it had much of a hook. I was wandering in the hinterland, surrounded by a people whose ways were unfamiliar. With nothing else to do, I pushed open the bookstore's glass door. Here was a virtually infinite supply of tools for better living, many of them by authors I had hosted on my show not long before. I browsed the shelves. There was a longing in my heart, but for none of this. For something else. Something which words could not name, but my heart would not leave alone.

Then I saw the eyes. At first I was shocked, they seemed to be Joey's eyes, but looking out from a different face. An Indian face with a beard. I took the book from the shelf. It was the same face that I had seen on the table in Joey's room. It was his old man. There was a sofa at the back of the bookstore provided for patrons like me with time to kill. I opened the book at random.

"There is no greater mystery than this, that we keep seeking reality, though in fact we are reality." A wave of relief swept over me, although I was not sure if I even understood what I was reading.

A woman was perusing the occult section with a man who worked there, looking for a book on Scottish Kabbalism. My vision became wide, it took in everything at once.

"The mind, turned outwards, results in thoughts and objects. Turned inward it becomes itself the Self . . . " I closed my eyes. What would happen if I turned my mind inward on itself? The first few times my mind just did a somersault and arrived at a conceptual conclusion: I am consciousness. I am the witness. Cute. Empty. This was like trying to hold on to a slippery eel. Then after about five minutes, there was just a moment of pure looking, pure seeking for itself. Everything became still.

I opened my eyes. A middle-aged man was speaking earnestly with a girl in her 20s about the comparative merits of different translations of Rumi. He was doing everything he could to hide his obvious deeper carnal intentions.

"Surrender is to give oneself up to the original cause of one's being." I got ensnared in that for a while.

I watched a boy of no more than five picking out a statue with his mother. He loved every one, and with each new choice, his mother would agree completely. It was a gift for Daddy. I felt a wincing below my ribs, and closed my eyes.

As I lingered with the pain a while, I could feel how much I did not want it to be like this. A whisper from nowhere said surrender. As I relaxed into welcoming pain, just like this, it melted like ice, and there was just the resting.

"Only if one knows the truth of love will the strongly entangled knot of life be untied . . . "

A good two hours passed in this way. I must have read virtually every word, but not in sequential order. I would dip in and then stop, intoxicated by the power of what I was reading. When I looked at my watch, I was astounded by how much time had passed. I had just enough money in my pocket to buy the book, still leaving a dollar for the bus. I walked out with it in my pocket, back into the city's twilight. Joey's words and his teacher's words seemed to melt together into one calm certainty that brought me back, always, to my Saturday afternoons on the beach. I wandered some more, my hand in my jacket pocket, clasping the book like a raft in choppy waters.

As I turned the corner, onto Pine Street, a familiar face greeted me. Sam was walking in my direction with a grocery bag cradled against each breast, two French loaves poking out of one bag like rabbit ears. She looked startled.

"Where are you going?" she asked me softly, studying the sidewalk, as though she had dropped a speck of gold dust there.

"Um, nowhere, I'm just waiting till it's time to go to Joey's." My belly tensed. It seemed I could feel Sam's body underneath her clothes. Did we make love, or did I dream it?

She tightened her lip, and withdrew just for a moment, like a cat still uncertain if I was friend or foe. "Well, do you want to eat something before the meeting starts?" she asked a lamppost.

The tightness in my solar plexus suddenly exploded in my chest, as if she had asked me if I'd like to move to Hawaii with her, have babies, and start a new life.

"Oh God, I'd love to," I blurted. I took a breath. "That would be nice."

She laughed. "So let's go."

I took one of her grocery bags and followed her across the street. Only then did I notice we were having this conversation across from the entrance to her building. Back in the industrial elevator she studied the bare wooden floorboards during the five flights of its ascent. I was learning now not to take this personally; it was her default setting. As we stepped back into her apartment, the memory of the dream swept over me again. I wanted to tell her all about it, but I knew that any hope of a relaxed dinner would be abandoned in the process.

She disappeared into the shower, leaving me with Van Morrison forcefully asking me, "Have I told you lately that I love you?" Would that I had his courage and directness with my dinner host. I realized now that Sam's entire life took place to a soundtrack; even when she visited me in my dreams, she managed to activate the hi-fi in my sleep world. As she moved from bathroom to alcove in her white bathrobe, I had to look away. I was overwhelmed with the memory of the previous night.

She reappeared in a turquoise sweat suit. Her feet were pink and naked; I was consumed with the thought of sucking her toes. I looked out the window in embarrassment.

"Hungry?" she asked.

"Um," I replied. "Sure." I crossed my arms over my chest and huddled a little. I felt transparent.

And so, to the accompaniment of a CD player on endless auto-shuffle, we chopped carrots and potatoes together into tiny cubes, as she prepared minestrone soup. Rebecca had cooked this dish many times; it seems to be to Italians what clam chowder is to Bostonians. But this was beyond cooking; this was more of an art form I was observing. Sam treated each vegetable with the care of a lover; her sauté style was as though she was massaging the naked tomatoes and their friends in warm oil.

We sat down with our bowls of minestrone, French bread, Parmesan cheese, and a spinach salad. She was relaxed now, laughing, as though we had been dining together for eternity. She started to ask me more about my life, filling in the pieces from the clues I had delivered at Joey's meeting on the first night. When we got to the children, her eyes lit up.

"Do you have pictures?" she asked. I delivered tattered offerings from the wallet in my back pocket.

"Oh, they're beautiful," she cooed. "They're so beautiful. You must miss them."

"I do. It's true," I replied.

"Will you be with them for Christmas?" she asked. It was only a few days away.

"No, I can't this year," I muttered. "They're with my wife in Chicago, and I'm not really welcome there."

"I'm so sorry," she replied. "I'm really sorry."

In the moments of silence that followed, I could sense her feeling with me.

"It will be okay," she said softly. "Everything will be okay. Once Joey takes you on, everything works out."

That was the knowledge I had rested in all afternoon.

She told me a little about herself, but it was in fragments. She taught yoga in a local studio on Monday, Wednesday, and Saturday mornings and worked in the late-night café where I had met her, to fill out her income. If I tried to turn the subject to her past or anything more personal, she became quiet and changed the subject immediately.

By the time we'd finished eating and were washing the dishes, Enya was celebrating with us in song that on her way home she was committed to remember only good things. It was time to go. As we walked the few blocks to Joey's, Sam put her hand through the crook of my arm. My chest tightened as we ascended the faded stairs. I hid my pride behind a nonchalant exterior. We were together now.

The same regulars were there as on the first night, with the addition of a stocky-looking woman who must have been in her mid-50s. She sat erect, looking mildly discontented with everything. She reminded me of someone I didn't like at all, but I couldn't remember who it was. It became increasingly difficult to sit in the room without noticing her. She was like an itchy substance on my skin. Then Joey came and sat. I felt defiant. I was sitting next to Sam now. What was he going to make of that?

After sitting in silence together for a while, Roy, the owner of the artsy cinema, asked Joey a question about creativity. A long discussion ensued. Then the Austrian psychotherapist, Maryanne, asked him about being of service. In the midst of his long answer I remember him saying, "Real love only gives; it seeks for nothing in return. Real love can only arise from knowing who you are. When you recognize your own self to be limitless, then there is no sense of lack, no sense of limitation, there is only giving. If you perceive yourself to be small, limited, only a name and a form, there must always be lack, always need, always a feeling of something missing. When the heart is awake, it overflows. When it sleeps, it lives in acquisition." As he finished, he looked at me, making his big blue eyes even bigger than usual.

When the meeting ended and Joey had left, Alan stood up, cleared his throat theatrically, and announced that there would be no meetings for several days, due to the Christmas season. Sam had put her shoes on and slipped away before I had time to notice. I followed down the stairs in hot pursuit, but resigned myself to walking to the bus stop alone. There was a longing in my heart, and that now familiar tightening below my rib cage, but just as in the afternoon, everything was contained in an ocean of protection, a feeling that defied understanding.

I walked the few blocks to the bus stop. Soon the bus came, with the same driver as two nights before. We exchanged a grin and I took my seat. Sitting opposite me was a black woman, her little boy asleep on her lap. I could feel from the look on her face, and the way she held her body, that she was exhausted, bewildered by her fate; that her feet hurt. She would probably never know the feeling of a couple of weeks off in Hawaii; her sense of struggle would probably only lift once the confusion of her life was done. Her exhaustion was my own. There was only the drudgery of it all. When she looked back at me, her eyes told me she wanted to be left alone.

My gaze shifted to a teenage boy slumped back in his seat, long gangly legs cumulating in large worn sneakers, hair completely shaved off on one side and left unkempt on the other. He was chewing gum, immersing himself in the luxury of not needing to care about anything. I sank into my own seat and stared out the window.

This was neither the universe of doom I'd walked through the night before I met Joey, nor was it the universe of rapture the night I met him. Reality was shifting constantly; nothing had any solidity.

I was home by 11 P.M. Paul's light was on. I went straight to his door.

"Well, well, well," he greeted me, a twinkle in his eye. "Someone didn't come home last night." He switched off the footage of Detroit traffic in rush hour.

We sat on his tattered brown couch. This was going to be difficult. "Okay, so?" he asked. "The suspense is killing me."

"I can't explain, Paul," I said. Then I remembered the book in my pocket. "I bought a book today." Long pause, he was waiting. "You know, nothing is the way it seems."

"Never mind books," he said. "What about the girl?"

"Well," I replied. "Yes, I ended up staying at her place last night."

"Ho ho ho. That's my boy. No wonder you're feeling better."

"But that's not it, Paul," I interrupted. "It's not about the girl. And yet it is about the girl. Everything's different than it seems to be."

Paul was looking impatient. "Cut the crap, Matt. What happened? Did you . . . ," he paused dramatically, and changed his voice, "have a good time?"

"I slept on her couch, Paul. But it's not that. There's something this guy is showing me that makes everything different."

Paul was looking even more impatient. "For God's sake, Matt. You've had a terrible time lately. You've met a beautiful girl, and you're talking to me about an old man. What's wrong with you?"

"It's not the girl, Paul," was all I could say. "Yes, I like her, but that's what I've always done. Chased after a girl or a job or something. There's something else happening that I can't explain. It's when I let go of the girl that the peace comes. And when I let go, the girl appears. It's when I chase the girl that things get difficult." Our eyes met, I felt a roar arising from my belly. "It's the same for all of us, Paul. It's the chasing that pushes everything away." Whatever was speaking, it was talking to me as much as to Paul. I saw that his heart understood even as he was simultaneously oblivious. In the briefest window, out of time, we both knew. Then he looked away.

"You're crazy, man. You've always been crazy," he laughed. "Just get the girl. You'll feel better, you'll get your job back, and all will be fine."

A thought machine was talking, based in habit, based in what it had been taught to think. It wasn't his thought machine, it wasn't mine, it was everyone's. It was the thought machine, which keeps telling us to chase after dead ends. I could say nothing to that machine to convince it. Yet I could see that Paul's heart already knew what I knew, just had no way to trust itself. I recognized the futility of convincing him, and abandoned the effort.

"You're right. She's beautiful, I'm smitten, and I know it's going to work out great," I grinned.

"That's my boy," the machine responded.

"Want to meet her?" I asked. The words came out of nowhere, surprising even me.

"Of course," he replied, automatically.

"Great. Well the next time I go over to Joey's, she's bound to be there, so come along, too."

He hesitated, the machine sensing it might meet its demise. "Okay. I'll come," he laughed. "But believe me, my eyes are going to be on the girl, not on your old man."

CHAPTER 11

THE YOGA CLASS

When I finally fell asleep that night, Sam and Rebecca and every other woman I had ever known were merging in and out of each other. I was on the threshold, equally pulled by desire and transcendence.

By the time morning came, I had fallen asleep and woken up again many times. The fire in my chest and the tension in my solar plexus were becoming unbearable, but I no longer knew what I was longing for. It wasn't exactly for Sam, and yet it was her, too. It wasn't exactly returning to the bliss of the first night with Joey, and yet it was that, too. It wasn't exactly having things back the way that they had been, and it was that, too. I lay in bed for a long time, caught in the inevitability of just not knowing. An aerial view of Machu Pichu, courtesy of National Geographic, seemed to advocate transcendence, while the market scene from a town in Northern Thailand next to it reminded me there was no escape from the reality of the world. I couldn't go back, yet I had no idea what going forward meant; it was out of my hands.

Sometime after nine, I went back down to Paul's apartment to beg the use of his shower. I opened the door, and he just called out to go ahead. While I was getting dressed again and shaving, I heard Paul's phone ring; as I came back into the living room he was sitting in his bathrobe sipping coffee.

"Your old man called," he said. "He wants you to go over to his place about four o'clock."

"Oh, I gave him your number. I'm sorry." Paul said nothing, just scratched himself and messed with something on a shelf.

Wednesday, no evening meeting. Paul and I drank instant coffee and ate Twinkies together. It had come to this. Then things began to get very clear. I was wasting precious time in distraction. All that mattered, and urgently, was that I be with Sam. That was our destiny. I knew. She was teaching yoga in less than an hour. No problem. I would go surprise her, and that would be that. Happily ever after. I pictured us proudly announcing our engagement to the assembled students later that day. How could I have missed such a simple solution? My already married status did not even rear its head as an impediment. I jumped up from the breakfast table, excused myself, and got on a bus headed toward the rest of my life.

The class was in a ground floor studio: soft music playing, a statue of the Buddha in the corner, some flowers in a vase at his feet. The floor was covered with coconut matting. There were 10 or 12 people already in the room with very professional-looking mats rolled out. Most of them were graying women, in an all-out war with the aging process. Sam looked surprised to see me, suspicious even, but pointed to a corner and gave me a mat of my own. She wore tight yoga pants and a tight shirt, her hair tied back in a ponytail. She taught yoga with the same grace with which she had served coffee and cheesecake on that first night, the same grace she had brought to the minestrone soup. Each movement seemed like ballet.

Yoga has never been a primary strength for me. I prefer gentler approaches to caring for the body, like taking long baths, lying in bed, or receiving massage. Sam soon had us doing things I would not have thought possible or advisable. We had to stretch our legs straight out in front of us, and bend forward from the waist. Some of the ladies were kissing their kneecaps in smug flexibility; as hard as I tried, my knees were still a long way from my head. Next we lay on our backs and raised our legs and feet up toward the ceiling, then raised up the whole torso, so only head and neck remained on the ground. That was bad enough, way beyond my pain threshold. Every tiny space between every vertebra was announcing revolt. But it did not stop there. It went on and on. We lowered our legs even further behind the head, until the feet were touching the ground. That was the idea, anyway, and it seemed to work out fine for the ladies with rubber spines. My feet dangled in midair, like disoriented insects. Sam cruised among the urban yogis, murmuring words of encouragement. As she came close, I lowered my feet even further to the floor, in a kamikaze bid for her approval.

"Don't strain, Matt," was all she could offer my heroic self-torture.

"Would Hawaii suit you for the honeymoon?" I tried to reply. Too late, she had moved on. "And what about children, I'm really okay to have more." We could discuss it later. We had the rest of our lives.

We finished with a balancing posture, for which I was truly unprepared. First we stood on our mats, in two long lines, one behind the other.

"Place your feet together, feel your head pulled to the sky as though by a golden thread," Sam said.

I relished every word, made mental notes to encourage her to write poetry.

"Now, reach back with the left hand and catch your left ankle. Pull your foot up to the buttocks."

I felt a shiver of excitement as she said that word. *I love your buttocks, darling,* I rehearsed for Hawaii.

"Stretch your right arm out in front, and lean the head and torso forward."

Every tiny part of me was now relying on my right ankle to stay upright, and my right ankle was feeling quite unsure of its credentials for the job.

"Now, stretch your left foot and leg out behind you."

A very trained foot, proudly adorned in a pristine white sock, appeared perfectly still in mid-air before me, offered as a challenge from the lady on the next mat up. I was already wobbly before Sam did her tour of the room, but the more desperate I felt to excel at this feat, the more elusive it became. I held out as long as I could, but when it was truly time to abandon hope, raw instinct kicked in. I reached out for the nearest stable object I could find, in hopes of staying upright. I grabbed that still and strong white sock. We went down together.

I was disappointed in that lady. With all her yogic practice, the perfect outfit and all, I would have expected greater control of her emotions. Her assumption that I had done it on purpose, and her quite needless aggression to me betrayed her yogic training to be very immature. I made a mental note to have a word with Sam about this, when we were alone later.

"So sorry," I offered as I helped the lady back up to her feet. "I trained in partner yoga in India, you know. More interaction in those schools." She was unimpressed, and looked at me as though I were both mad and dangerous. Sam giggled. I winked at her. We would have a good laugh about this later, maybe in bed gazing out at the sunset, sipping white wine. Organic.

Finally Sam had us lie flat on the floor and close our eyes, spreading our arms wide. This, I could do really well. I am sure that no one else in the room could do that posture as well as I could. I was dropping, falling back like a dewdrop meeting the ocean. At some point, Sam came over and touched my belly. I opened my eyes right away. Was she ready to discuss where we would settle now, health insurance, one car or two? But she closed her eyes in an invitation for me to rest, and was gone as quickly as she came. Then it all fell away. It must have been some form of sleep, although it didn't seem like it. I felt I was just falling back and back into ever deepening relaxation. Everything disappeared. The next thing I knew, the urban yogis were all sitting in a circle. I sat up and joined them. They were bowing to each other, and offering knowing smiles. I did my best to offer a suitably holy greeting, especially to the victim of my inexperience, but it was too late. I was branded as a terrorist.

I hung around for a while waiting for Sam, feeling sheepish. A little slimy even. Like I was about to try to sell her life insurance or a used car with bad transmission. I walked out of the studio in retreat, made it to the street, and then went back in again. She had disappeared somewhere into a back room to change into city clothes, and I lingered, rehearsing my big line. When she reemerged, she was booted, jacketed, and scarfed for the December weather. Her eyes were an even more vibrant blue. She was wearing a knitted hat with a pom-pom on the top, tied underneath her chin. It framed her rosy cheeks, and very red lips. Her face looked plump, childlike. I wanted to kiss her and take her for hot cocoa. When she saw me, she couldn't hide her crestfallen look. I wished I had left with the rest, but it was too late now.

"You want to have lunch?" I asked her.

She looked trapped again, as she had when Joey sent me home with her.

"I can't today, Matt," she replied. "I have things to do."

"Okay," I replied, and felt the yearning in my chest intensify. "You know, I feel really touched by you." I felt like an idiot. My heart was racing, pounding. My legs felt very weak, as though her yoga class had lasted 43 hours and this was our first break. Every muscle and joint in my body was aching. I wanted to run away. I wanted to grab her to me. "I'd really love to spend more time with you, to get to know you better." I cringed. The words sounded impossibly corny. I was truly out of control.

She frowned at the ground, as always. "Matt," she said quietly, "it's not about me. It's not about anybody else. You've got to trust him, Matt. You've got to trust him completely. When I came by you in class, I could feel the longing in you. But it's not for me, Matt. You've got to understand, it's not for me. It's nothing that any person or experience can satisfy for you. Remember that night when he told us his life story?"

I nodded.

"I've never heard him tell anyone else that story before. In some way he's chosen you, Matt. He's working with you. And if you let him, he'll lead you beyond everything you ever thought you wanted, beyond all the pain you've passed through while not getting it."

"Yes," I said. "I feel like something is watching out for me. And . . . and . . . " It was a strange moment. The words that wanted to speak had a force of their own, but they were accompanied by an equally strong knowing that they were not true, just mechanical speaking from habit. They spoke anyway. "And I feel like meeting you is part of all this. I feel like I've waited an eternity to meet you." Now the machine was in full swing, unstoppable. "You know that night I stayed at your house? I had a really strong dream about us."

Sam was looking increasingly uncomfortable, but the machine was oblivious. Like a steamroller, it was determined to smash aside anything that did not conform to its agenda.

"I need to know, do you feel the same for me, too?"

"I can't explain now, Matt," she replied. "It's not what you think. You have to let go and trust him before you can see things clearly. I have to go now."

"Well, can I see you later on, or tomorrow?" It was out of control; it would stop at nothing now.

"I'm going out of town this afternoon, for a few days. I'll see you when I get back." She tried to force a smile.

"Are you involved with someone?" I implored, leaning toward her. As much as the compulsion kept pushing forward with its agenda, the clear knowledge of its insanity resounded more clearly.

"No, Matt, I am going to spend Christmas with a few friends, that's all." She swallowed hard. "If that is all right with you." She swung her backpack over her shoulder and walked toward the parking lot. I watched her get into an older Mazda. The rear left taillight was smashed and was held together with tape. As she pulled out of the parking space, I could see that the front left side of the car was severely dented and the damage had accumulated rust. As she drove away, I was left holding the whining child of my discontent.

CHAPTER 12

THE VOICE OF DIVINE GRACE

Sam was going to spend Christmas with friends; I would be alone. For the first time I could remember, alone. Paul had taken all the shifts at the studio no one else wanted. He didn't care. My children would be unwrapping presents, probably toy guns with their Mafia-funded grandfather. My wife of 11 years refused to even speak to me on the phone. And I couldn't even try to start an illicit affair, without acting like a complete idiot. Despair descended again like a black cloud.

I walked from the yoga studio over to the little square nearby, where a bookstore-cum-coffee-shop sat in the middle surrounded by outdoor tables and chairs. It was warm enough, even in December, for patrons to sit outside.

As I waited to order my bagel and coffee, I could not force myself to look at the other people in line. I was sure that not a single one of them would be alone for Christmas. I was a beggar for love, wandering in a land of kind hearts and warm welcomes. Plenty for everyone, but not for me.

I noticed the fliers that had been left near the counter. Crystal healing workshops, aromatherapy, multilevel telephone companies. One caught my eye. "The End of Suffering." Sounded familiar. There was a picture of a charismatic-looking woman in her mid-50s. She was smiling so thoroughly from ear to ear that every glistening white tooth in her mouth was exposed. A little blurb announced her to be a fully realized being, surrendered completely to the will of the Divine. "If you're tired of dead end streets," the flier said, "come listen to Diana Milton Jones. The voice of Divine Grace will set you free." A few dates were listed at the bottom of the flier with the address of a church hall near Joey's house. I picked one up, folded it, and popped it in my pocket.

I was floating in and out of a self-invented hell. Whenever thoughts turned to my unrequited love, to my precious children far away, to my uncountable mistakes, the contractions increased, I was back in a pre-Joey universe. The seduction of guilt and worthlessness was very strong— it would catch me unaware, like a wave on the ocean, and drown me in itself. Then, as I brought my attention to the smells, the people, to the blue winter sky overhead, it all fell away, and I felt absolutely protected. My father was once again on his rock on the beach, and no wave was big enough to frighten me.

The book was still in my pocket; I spent the afternoon wandering and reading. The more I read, the more I faced the fact that nothing I thought I knew about anything was going to help me now.

"Peace is your natural state," my little book told me. "It is only your mind that covers over what is natural in you. Look for the mind and it will disappear." Each time it wandered, back I came. It was becoming another habit stream, ripping holes in the continuum of thinking. Just here, through the rip, all is just like it is, without a problem needing solving.

I arrived at Joey's upstairs apartment at four o'clock. He was waiting for me, sitting in the same little room where he had delivered his life story to us a couple of nights before. A cup of tea was waiting for me on the table, next to his own. He looked at me for a long time. "It's day three," he said, finally.

"I know," I replied.

"What else do you know?" His look was piercing.

"That's what I've been wondering all day. Nothing seems to be very reliable just now. I think a lot about Sam, but at the same time I'm realizing now that she can't really give me what I want." This wasn't entirely honest. The lines were more hers than my own, and I think he knew it.

"What do you want?" asked Joey accusingly. "That's the question you have to get clear about before we can go any further. What is it you really want? Once you find the genuine answer to that question, you can have it, but there's no point in driving with your foot on the accelerator and the brake at the same time."

I had to experiment with several answers before I spoke. "Actually, I have no idea. Every answer I try to come up with doesn't quite fit. I could say I want my old life back, but that's not quite true. I could say I want my wife and kids, and I do, but there's something more. I could say I want to get close to Sam, and that is also true. I don't know what I want, Joey."

"That's a good beginning," he reflected. "You don't know what you want."

"I want to live the way that I felt after the first night with you. I can remember everything was perfect, shimmering, my mind stopped working. I was full of optimism and hope. I want that." I breathed a sigh of relief.

"Very good," he said. "Not everyone wants that, you know. You get whatever you put on your altar. If you worship money with unwavering totality, that will fill your days and nights. If you worship sex and relationship, you can have that movie, too. If you worship fame and power, you can dedicate your life to them, and that obsession will fill your life. It just takes a little more time, but desire brings things to you, like a dog when you whistle." He paused, chuckled, and added, "And then they leave again. If you want what you say you want, you can have that, too. But how much do you want it?"

"I don't know. I don't feel there's any alternative left."

"Very good," he replied. "That is indeed true. But so far you are just dicking around with it. How are you going to get what you say you want?"

"I need help," I replied. "I'm hoping you can give it to me."

He burst out laughing. "Ah ha!" he said. "So you want someone to give it to you. What price are you willing to pay?" He had teased Carlos in the same way. "What are you willing to give?"

"I don't have anything," I replied.

"Not true, not true," he muttered. "Oh, if only that were true. You've got a lot that you're still holding onto. And the price you'll have to pay is all of it. There's nothing I can do about that." He dabbed his mustache with an ornate handkerchief.

"There's no meeting tonight," he announced. "So we'll go out, you and me."

I remembered the flier. "I found this today." I passed it to Joey. "Do you know who she is?"

Joey read every word on the flier with diligence. His face was expressionless. "This sounds very important," he announced. I had no way to know if he was joking or serious. "We'd better go tonight and listen to the voice of Divine Grace. Now let's have some dinner."

I followed him into the kitchen; he motioned for me to sit at his kitchen table. He took a jar of yellow goo from the shelf. It looked like glue. He doled out a couple of large tablespoons into a pot and lit the gas. He pulled four or five little jars of powder from the shelf and sprinkled some of the contents of each, one by one, into the melting yellow goo. Within 30 seconds, the kitchen was filled with the smell of an Indian restaurant.

"Curry," I said.

"You don't need no curry," he laughed. "You're what they call a *vata* type. Curry powder's too stimulating for you. What you need is a bit of calming." He went on to tip some rice into his aromatic concoction, and then some small yellow beans. After a couple minutes of stirring, he added water and put a lid on it. He went to the refrigerator and pulled out carrots, cabbage, potatoes, and a turnip. He was chopping now, but not quite with the ballet-like strokes I had observed in Sam the night before. This was more of a martial art. He declined all offers of help. He didn't talk during his culinary preparations, just hummed gently to himself while I sat at his table and watched. After a while, he opened the pot again, tossed in the vegetables, and stirred.

"My Guru taught me to cook, you know," he said. "There's a science to it. Here in America we just eat for pleasure. But food is important. The right tastes, even the right consistency, it all affects the way you live." Finally he produced a couple of plates and served some of his concoction onto each one. He put a plate before me, put one on the other side of the table for himself, and then between us he put a plastic tub of yogurt, a glass jar that looked like some kind of preserve, and another jar of white powder. "Help yourself. Yogurt, mango chutney, and coconut."

I did as he instructed. The food was delicious. Within minutes I did indeed feel my body calming. We ate in silence. I savored the rich blend of tastes and textures he had miraculously woven into one tapestry. When we were done, we washed the dishes together and put everything away. I noticed how meticulously clean he kept everything. Although the apartment was not fancy, nothing was out of place.

"Time to go," he announced, glancing at the clock on the kitchen wall. As he was getting his shoes and coat from the closet, there was a knock on the front door.

"See who it is."

I opened the door and found the stocky-looking woman who had appeared at the previous night's meeting.

"Where's Joey?" she barked at me.

I stepped back, my chest tightening. "Um, he's just getting his coat."

"I'm Cheryl," she announced and pushed past me into the apartment.

Joey came back into the room and grinned at her. "Well, well, well," he said. "How are you, dear?"

Her manner completely changed. It became subservient, almost devotional. "I need to talk to you, Joey. It's very important." She modified her brisk voice with a tone of pleading. "I must see you alone," she went on, motioning to me with her eyes.

I was ready to go to battle. There was no question now that this woman was electing herself as a foe.

"We're just going out, Cheryl. We're going to see a teacher Matt's found. We're going to hear the voice of Divine Grace." Joey looked triumphant.

The woman turned on me. "You're going to take Joey to see a teacher? Joey doesn't need any teachers. Do you have any idea who you're dealing with here?"

I was staggered. This was a visitation from hell. "I, umm . . . "

"Joey," she continued, turning back to her mentor, "please don't let people waste your time like this. I must talk to you about something very important."

Joey just grinned. "No, no," he said. "I'm all excited now to go hear the voice of Divine Grace. You'll just have to come with us."

And so we set off, the three of us, back down the faded staircase and into the street. It was only a few short blocks to the meeting hall. Cheryl walked on the other side of Joey from me, ignoring me completely. She fed him reports of people I didn't know, obviously students of his from some other city. Joey hardly responded, just grinned and nodded. Every now and then he asked about someone whom she hadn't mentioned. I couldn't help but notice that almost everything she said was critical. "John's got totally identified again. He opened his heart for a few days after your last visit, but he just can't seem to stay out of that ridiculous mind of his."

I wanted to jump in with a comment like "Well I'm sure that's a predicament you can relate to," but I kept quiet, and Joey just went on nodding and smiling.

"And Miriam and David, they're having a second baby."

"Hmm," said Joey, in appreciation.

"They just don't seem to be able to recognize what's real and important and what's just distraction."

"Ahh," said Joey.

This woman was driving me completely crazy.

We made it to the church hall. There were a hundred people already present. We found three seats together three-quarters of the way toward the back. Some people were sitting silently with their eyes closed. Others had bought books from the overflowing tables at the back of the hall and were now studying them. I looked around. Most of the gathered audience looked well-to-do. There was an atmosphere of heightened anticipation. The people sitting toward the front of the hall looked smug, betraying their pride in being the chosen few. Joey sat quite expression-less, without looking around the room. Cheryl was fuming on the other side. Without breathing a word, she left no question that she considered the entire expedition to be a complete waste of time and held me en-tirely responsible.

A good 20 minutes after the event was scheduled to begin, there was a flurry of excitement from the doors at the back. A woman strode in with the confidence of a celebrity. She was relatively plump, wearing a flowing red outfit and very expensive-looking shoes, the kind that would make even Imelda Marcos want to go shopping. Her curly brown hair was streaked with gray. She was followed by two other women carrying clipboards and a man bringing up the rear. She walked straight up the middle of the hall, occasionally glancing with a smile at a few people. She ascended the podium, and sat down on a thronelike chair surround-ed by flowers. One of the women stepped up onto the podium and, kneeling before her, fastened a lapel mike to her gown. A few people in the room were crying now, some were stretching their hands toward her in supplication. Joey continued to sit motionless, while Cheryl's body movements suggested that she was close to violence. The room became quiet for 15 or 20 minutes, broken only by the occasional sounds of sob-bing. A man behind me was chanting, "Dianama, Dianama, Dianama." I was tempted to warn him that Cheryl was dangerous; he was putting his life in danger by continuing. But she managed to contain herself.

"You think you want truth." The Voice of Divine Grace had started to speak. "But you are fooling yourself. You come here to my feet saying that you want to surrender, but who is really ready to surrender? You have been wandering for lifetimes, chasing after this and that, saying you want God, saying you want love, saying you want freedom. Now I have come to free you, but who is willing to surrender to the will of God? Who is willing to give up your petty life?"

She had an intense presence to her. At least half the room was sob-bing. Some were sitting bolt upright, perhaps hoping if they kept still enough she would not see them. Among those sitting on cushions in the first few rows, many had bowed their heads to the floor in supplica-tion. Her talk continued in the same vein for what to me seemed like a very long time. Joey was in his waxwork mode, with which I was now familiar. Cheryl just kept breathing deeply and flexing her muscles. She would have thrown rotten fruit, I'm sure, if we'd had any. After 20 or 30 minutes a handheld microphone was produced, and questions were invited from the floor.

"Diana," began an earnest-looking man, balding, with glasses and well dressed. "I want to surrender to you so much. I want to give you my life, but I feel so weak."

The Voice of Divine Grace glared back at him. "The path of liberation is not for the faint-hearted," she replied. "I'm interested in warriors, not weaklings."

The man looked crestfallen.

"The path to God is the most rigorous of all," she continued. "Stay with me and you will be splattered like an egg dropped from the roof, until nothing is left of you. Are you ready for that, or are you just a wimp?"

"Oh, Ma, I want so much to be ready," pleaded the man.

"Then get serious," she barked back at him. "And drop all this pathetic nonsense. I want men around me who are strong. I have no time for cowards."

The poor fellow sunk dejectedly back into his seat. I didn't know what to make of all of this. She certainly had something. She had the self-assurance of a television evangelist, and I was just as repelled.

The next question came from a woman who announced herself as Martha and held the mike with evangelical fervor.

"We've been doing the home study course at Stephanie's house, Ma," she gushed. "It's been so beautiful. And every week I've felt my surrender to you deepening. I gladly give you my life. Do what you will with me."

This little speech seemed to please Diana much more than the last.

"Yes, sweet one," she cooed. "The lamb must lay down with the shepherd and be comforted. You are home. Trust in the protection of divine grace and you live a blessed life. Come here, come here!"

The lamb cavorted urgently to the podium, as though afraid someone might take the opportunity before her. She threw herself at Diana's expensive shoes and began kissing them fervently. The Italian shoe manufacturer was missing the photo op of a lifetime. Finally she knelt at Diana's feet. Now that they were close to each other, I noticed their similar hairdo. They were also wearing the same style of outfit, although something subtle betrayed the fact that Diana's came from a shop on Fifth Avenue and her devotee's from a retail chain. Tears streamed down the woman's face. "I love you so much. I love you so much."

"Yes," Diana said. "This is an open heart." She glared disapprovingly at the man who hadn't made the grade. "This is divine surrender. I gladly welcome you into my heart. Welcome home."

A good third of the audience was crying by now. This was obviously an evangelical moment for many of them. I glanced again to my left. Joey hadn't moved a muscle. He was barely breathing, as if dead. Cheryl, on the other hand, left no doubt that she was alive and kicking. The jugular vein in her neck pulsed with life force. Each minute she was spending doing something other than she had intended seemed to add to her torture.

The evening went on for at least another hour. Doubts and questions were treated with disdain. Expressions of surrender and devotion were welcomed. Toward the end of the evening, Diana closed her eyes and opened her fingers wide, exposing her palms to her devotees. Strange gyrating music struck up from speakers all around the room and before too long she had turned into a wrathful deity, or at least an impersonation of one. Her eyes rolled up behind their slightly opened lids, exposing only the whites. She moaned and cried. Her upper body was writhing and gyrating. Most of the room was going nuts. People screamed, laughed hysterically. As the tempo and volume of the music increased, some were standing up, raising their hands to the ceiling. I think I even heard someone on the other side of the hall vomiting.

As suddenly as it had started, it was all over. She stood up and raised her hands to the ceiling, obviously a cue for the faithful to follow suit, with a two-armed version of Hitler's famous greeting. And with that, she swept back down the aisle, followed by her band of trusty servants. The whole room was left in wild chaos. Many people were crying hysterically, a few were screaming, others were just laughing.

Joey turned to me, eyes twinkling. We joined the rest of the hall in shuffling back out again.

The deluge at the tables at the back made it difficult to leave. Eager hands grabbed up books entitled *You Are Divine,* the cover sporting a gloating picture of Diana. Photos were available in every pose imaginable, sitting, standing, lying down. Even pictures of her feet were available, now de-robed of those expensive shoes. Audio tapes, video tapes, little bottles of perfume—purported to be the same one she wore—were all being seized like there was no tomorrow. As we left the hall, I could feel that Cheryl had warmed to me a little bit. The evening had offered her a new enemy to focus on.

At the exit a number of very determined-looking characters held out baskets. From each handheld basket hung a sign requesting a donation. To my amazement, Joey was the first of the three of us to comply. I followed suit, but Cheryl just glared menacingly at her basket carrier and marched right passed him. Mercifully, he offered her no resistance.

We left the hall and descended the stairs back toward the exit onto the street. There was a flurry of activity outside a door in the corridor. As we got closer we could see that the Voice of Divine Grace herself was the cause of the commotion. She was talking to another look-alike, her clipboard-clutching band of assistants waiting at a respectful distance. It was not until we were almost level with her that her eyes met Joey's. I have never seen someone's composure and expression change so quickly. The blazing self-assurance evaporated in an instant, and she looked visibly shaken.

"Um, Joey," she exclaimed. "I didn't know you were in town."

Joey just grinned at her.

"Um, why don't you, um, why don't you step in here with me, Joey," continued a clearly disoriented Diana. The two of them disappeared into a little room off the corridor. Glancing through the open door, I could see this was the minister's office, obviously given over for her use that evening. She glared at her band of assistants, who responded like sheep barked at by the dog. They huddled together and looked down at their clipboards. For the first time in the evening, Cheryl initiated conversation with me. We had to stand right over to the side of the corridor so as to make way for the faithful to leave.

"So what did you make of the whole thing?" she asked me.

The question felt like a trick.

"Quite a show."

"Do you go to a lot of things like this?" asked Cheryl.

"No," I replied. "Actually, no. I just found this flier in a café today. It was Joey who suggested we come."

Cheryl jutted her chin toward me a little; her eyes bulged slightly. They betrayed a seething distrust.

Finally Joey emerged from his meeting with the great Voice. Her little herd of assistants scampered in through the door as he came over to join us. He motioned to us with his head, and soon we were all out of the building.

"You didn't tell me you knew her," I exclaimed.

"You didn't ask," he replied. "Diana spent time with me about ten years ago. She and her husband were on some kind of disability at the time; I think he'd just come out of a nut farm. Anyway, they were both down on their luck, but they took to me like ducks to water. They were very serious, you know, very sincere. The husband had a very good experience with me. He was a good boy. His mind got really quieted. Still as a mountain pool. And then she told me one day she'd had a dream. She said that in the dream she'd become the queen of the whole universe and everyone was sitting at her feet." Joey chuckled; even Cheryl seemed tickled. "That's what happens, see?" said Joey. "Everyone gets to live out their dream."

"So do you support what she's doing now?" I asked Joey.

"It doesn't bother me," he said. "Don't suppose it hurts anybody too much."

"Yes, but something felt very wrong about it all."

"Ah," he said. "Just leave it alone. You see, that's what people have done with the truth for centuries now. It's nothing new. Everyone would rather worship an idol or a semi-god or some fancy lady wearing expensive shoes. That's the old way," he said. "And if people want that, let them have it. They can get all worked up and all, nothing wrong with it. Just a little old fashioned, that's all."

A random thought crossed my mind. Joey is a man, his teacher was a man, maybe he thinks women are not cut out for this.

"Man or woman, makes no difference," he said, seamlessly following my thought with his words. Every time he did that, it was unnerving. "In fact, over the years I've come to find that most gals are a whole lot more open." He winked at Cheryl.

"You come tomorrow," Joey added, as we got to the corner, "and I'll show you the true teacher. Either you worship name and form, or you discover that which was never born. Name and form, name and form. Diana's a name and it goes along with a very dolled-up form. Come tomorrow, I'll show you the real teacher. Come tomorrow at ten." Then he muttered, "I think she might have had a face lift, too."

He grabbed Cheryl's arm, and started walking away, back in the direction of West Broad Street.

He stopped, turned and added, "And bring a car."

CHAPTER 13

The Arrest

I woke with a start the next day. I didn't have the faintest idea where I was going to get a car. Mine had been repossessed by the loan company, and I hadn't paid my credit card bills for so long, I seriously doubted that I could rent one.

I'd almost completely made up my mind to abandon the whole thing. Maybe I should call Rebecca and try one last attempt at reconciliation. Maybe the bridge was the best thing after all. I made my way down to Paul's door, ready to admit my foolishness. I would start taking the psychiatrist's pills on that very day.

I let myself in to Paul's with the key and called out to him. He was already up, watching video footage of Samurai mud wrestlers.

"How's it going?" he asked. His patience was definitely running out, I could tell from the way that his eyes didn't move from his TV screen.

"Listen, I'm sorry I've been a bit stupid. You're right. I need to pull myself together. I've started taking the pills," I lied. It was almost true. I was definitely going to have started taking the little pills by the time I saw him next, and the difference seemed to be a technicality.

"You were out late last night," I said.

"Yeah, took my parents to the airport," he replied. He warmed to me, yet again, and patted the sofa for me to sit down. Old friends can't be cool for too long. "They've gone to Hawaii for Christmas. Not bad, huh? Left me their car, too."

Now a second pair of Samurai mud wrestlers leaped into violent combat—inside my skull. They made the wrestlers on his screen look benign in comparison. A mean and ruthless character, called Ask to Borrow the Car, was now in furious mortal combat with his gentler opponent, Don't Be a Fool. Paul went on sipping his coffee, oblivious to the splattering of mud, blood, and vengeance between my ears.

"So you've got two cars, now? Way to go . . . coming up in the world." I tried to make casual conversation, hoping that neither of my wrestlers would poke a fist or knee out through one of my eardrums and betray the furious battle going on inside.

"Yup, my old Honda gets a rest for a few days. I'm now the proud driver of a Cadillac Seville. So what did you do?"

"Oh," I said, scrambling for something acceptable. "I just went out and, um, heard someone giving a talk."

"Any good?" asked Paul.

"Nah," I said. "Just boring stuff." It was probably the first time that Diana, the Voice of Divine Grace, had ever been referred to as boring.

"So Matt, it's Christmas. The geese are getting fat. What are you going to do?" He looked awkward as soon as he had asked the question. He knew it was a painful topic for me, with my loved ones out of reach.

"Could I borrow your Honda?" I blurted. I was shocked; my evil mud wrestler had somehow managed to bury his reasonable opponent, face in the mud, and had taken the opportunity to assume temporary control of my brain.

"Where do you want to go?"

"Oh," I said, realizing I had no idea where I would be going. "Just a job thing," I lied again. "No big deal, it can wait anyway." At least the weaker but more reasonable of my assailants had managed to revive himself from the mud and restore temporary sanity.

Paul looked back at his own mud wrestlers for a while. "I don't have insurance on that car, Matt, you know," he went on. "What sort of a job thing is it, anyway?"

Once again, the wilder of my two opponents kicked his brother in the dirt and took the microphone. "Don't worry about the insurance, bro, you know how careful a driver I am. It's a good opportunity, I think." And before any restorative action could be taken, Paul had handed me the keys, told me where the car was parked, and I was bounding up the stairs to get ready.

Five minutes later I was behind the wheel of Paul's Honda, heading back over to the man who was proving to be either my savior or my destroyer. I felt completely out of control, driven by a manic force to be free of the mess I had created in my life. I had lied to my best friend. I was making no real attempt to rebuild my life and take care of my family. Instead, I was following the whims of an old man I hardly knew. I parked right outside the café. It was one minute before 10. I climbed the stairs again and knocked on Joey's door. I could smell the now familiar aroma of chai brewing. Joey opened the door to me. He was wearing a heavy coat that came down to his knees, a scarf, and a cap of the kind that English sportsmen wear when they go hunting. His beard and mustache were combed and washed.

"Drink your tea," he said. "We've got to get going. Did you bring your stuff?"

"What kind of stuff?" I asked him.

"You're going to need some clothes and stuff," he said.

"You didn't tell me where we were going, or for how long, or anything."

"Didn't I?" He looked pensively at the table, knitting his brows. Then he brightened. "Don't worry," he said. "We'll take care of you. You got the car?"

"Yes," I said. "I borrowed it from a friend."

"Good. Drink your tea and we'll go."

I was torn. Who was this man taking over my life, causing me to lie to my friend? Why wouldn't he leave me alone? But where would I be if he did? I would do anything to make sure exactly that didn't happen. Joey had a leather bag packed and ready. We stepped right down the stairs and climbed into the car.

"This car okay for a few days?" asked Joey.

Now I felt furious at his presumption. He'd only told me 12 hours before that we needed a car at all, and now that I'd miraculously found one, he wanted it for several days. I had to admit that yes, the car was available for several days. I hated him for the fact that it was true.

"So let's swing by your place," he said, slapping my thigh. "Pick up your kit, and we'll be off."

So it was that I retraced the streets back to my house. I left him in the car while I climbed up to my garret room. It didn't take more than two or three minutes to throw some things in a bag. When I got back to the street he was nowhere to be found, and the car was locked.

Joey came back around the corner after a few minutes, clutching some snacks: dried fruit, a couple of small plastic bottles of juice, a carton of chocolate milk, packets of nuts, and a bulging plastic bag of chocolate-covered everything. Without a word of explanation, he walked straight to the driver's door and motioned me to climb in on the other side. Thoughts of insurance, the current status of his driver's license, and whether or not Paul was still home, flashed through my mind. None of it seemed to make any difference because here I was sitting on the right side of the car, which was actually the wrong side of the car, and Joey was playing with the gears like an Italian sports car driver about to put a machine through its paces. I felt a sense of foreboding, but it was too late. The tires made a faint screech as Joey lunged the car into gear, and we were off.

It's not too many blocks from Paul's house to the outskirts of the town, and before too long we were on our way to I knew not where. Joey had a strange knack of putting me at ease, even in the midst of his most outrageous behavior. As he laughed, joked, and commented on little tidbits of local history, his childlike excitement to be going on an adventure became infectious. I don't think the cassette player in Paul's car had worked for many years, but Joey switched on the radio. Here was the band Steppenwolf, encouraging us to get out on the highway, to start looking for adventure, in whatever might come our way. I didn't want them putting any ideas in his head. I was wondering if I could retune the dial to Mozart or some Christian channel about family values, but Joey was obviously a '60s fan and was singing along with eyes flashing.

Out past Yarrowville the trouble began. We were on a small, two-lane road, very straight, lined by tall yew trees standing naked to the sky, like anorexic models. As the Eagles declared "I'm already gone," Joey's foot hit the floor. The speedometer rose steadily, 50, 55, 60, on and on it went.

"We have to be careful," I warned him. "My friend doesn't have insurance."

"I'm always careful," laughed Joey, and pushed the Honda to increasingly higher speeds. The naked trees were flying past us so fast, that they changed from black, white, black, white, black, white, to one continuous blur of gray.

Then I heard the sound I had most been dreading. A police siren, following us from quite a distance behind. I still faintly hoped it might be chasing some other sinner. "Slow down, Joey," I begged. "You've got to slow down."

"Yeehaw!" came his response, as the Honda lunged forward. I was definitely, irreversibly in the hands of a complete lunatic. It took a while for the police car to catch up with us—the feats that Joey was putting the Honda through were a challenge even to those equipped for pursuit. How could he be enjoying the whole thing so much? The window was cracked just a little on his side, just enough to blow his hair back onto the headrest behind him. His eyes were aflame with pure thrill. Maybe I should just open the car door and throw myself out onto the road, I thought. At least my final moment would be a statement of disaffiliation from this maniac. Perhaps the police would realize I'd been kidnapped. Rebecca and the kids might land some sort of claim. Before too long we heard the sound of another siren coming from the other direction.

"That's it," chuckled Joey. "They won."

I couldn't believe him. He was playing some sort of cops and robbers game with my best friend's uninsured car. Joey reduced his speed and pulled over. We were hemmed in by the police in front and back, and after a couple of minutes another car appeared and pulled off on the other side of the road. The boys were definitely excited. This was a quiet, rural area. Probably the most action they'd seen in many years.

"Get out of the car," cried one of them, obviously the most senior. "Get out of the car and put your hands on the roof." He was shouting, desperate to seem in control. The others all had their hands quivering near their waists, like children who've seen too many cowboy films.

"Get out of the car," he shouted. Joey stepped out of the car and obligingly offered up his wrists. "Put your hands on top of the car," repeated the older policeman. One of them had drawn a gun. Joey shrugged, grinned, and joined me, resting his hands on the icy metal next to mine. The same older policeman was reading us an official statement that sounded very familiar—about the right to remain silent, attorneys, and so on. All I was interested in was how quickly I would have the right to die. They frisked us roughly from head to toe, in a whirlwind of nervous excitement. We were both handcuffed and pushed into the back of the police car that had been parked across the street.

Finally, Joey got his wish.

Poor Paul. I couldn't believe I'd done this to him. Joey had left the keys of the Honda in the ignition, and one of the remaining policemen was now busy searching the car. I was praying Paul was not still in the habit of leaving foil-wrapped little illegalities around. We were driven a few miles back down the avenue of trees to a small town: "Welcome to Yarrowville: population 1,283" the sign read. They took us to the police station, which was really no more than three rooms in a trailer. Still handcuffed, we were motioned to wait in a couple of vacant chairs.

The older policeman appeared, the one who'd been shouting orders at us. He introduced himself as Sergeant Booker. He was a big, burly man with large, friendly hands, and a thick mustache trimmed very squarely above his lip; the kind of policeman every small town can be proud of, the kind who allows little old ladies to fall asleep in the peaceful knowledge of absolute protection. Booker was trying to look nonchalant, as if this kind of thing happened every day, but nothing could hide the excitement bubbling underneath. This was his big moment. Finally, his teenage dreams of excitement, of car chases, of shootouts were coming to fruition.

"Name," he asked me first, assuming from my younger age that I must be the instigator of whatever crime was to be discovered.

"Thomson, Matt Thomson. No P. T-H-O-M-S-O-N."

"Address?"

The question was salt into my wounds. I gave him the address of Paul's apartment building, fully aware that it was not the address on my driver's license. But I was past hope and past care now. Clearly, with Joey's help the demons had me and I was destined to spend the rest of my life in a cold, dark dungeon.

"That your car . . . sir?" His pause was just long enough to make the *sir* sarcastic.

"Uh, no, it's my friend's car."

"Registration?"

"Must be in the glove box," I said. One of Booker's younger acolytes appeared with great pride with the documents.

"And who, might I ask, is Paul Moula?"

"He's a friend of mine."

"Do you have his permission to drive his car . . . sir?"

"Yes, I do," I explained wearily. I knew what would come next. They would phone Paul, and that would be the last straw. I would be truly and completely homeless. I looked around to see if there was any heavy object I could use to bludgeon Joey to death before they put me in jail, but nothing suitable seemed handy.

"Do you have any proof of insurance?"

I faltered. "Um, no," I said. "Don't have proof of insurance." I left it at that. There seemed no point in tightening the noose that was already firmly around my neck.

Booker asked me a series of other degrading questions. Had I ever been arrested before? Had I ever been involved in prostitution? My humiliation grew stronger. Finally it was Joey's turn. He answered each question with the relish and gusto of a claimant for the Publisher's Clearing House prize.

"Name?"

"Murphy, Joey Murphy," he announced with pride.

"Address?"

To my surprise, Joey didn't give the address on West Broad Street. I remembered then that it was actually Alan and June's place. He gave the name of a farm. At that moment a younger cop whispered something in Booker's ear.

"I understand you were driving the car when the officer began to pursue you?"

"That's right, sir," beamed Joey, with the self-assurance of a hero. "I was driving the car when the officer chased us."

"And I understand that you increased your speed rather than slowing down."

"Yessir, that's what I did," grinned Joey.

"And what exactly was your purpose in doing that, may I ask?"

Joey didn't remove his eyes for a moment from Booker's face. He just went on grinning with complete delight at the situation.

"Seemed like it would be more fun that way," he confessed.

"I beg your pardon, sir?"

"It seemed like everyone would have a more exciting day if we had a little fun," Joey went on, with the innocence of a six-year-old.

Our pursuer stepped into the room now. He was in his early 20s, eager to please tattooed over every square inch of his body.

Joey looked straight at him, and challenged him sternly, "Did you have fun, boy?"

The young policeman was obviously startled by the question and didn't have a chance to reply before Joey continued. "Now remember, you're under oath."

That was just too much for Booker. "Be quiet!" he snapped. "I'll ask the questions here. Now, have you ever been arrested before?"

"No," said Joey, with the delight of a child asked if he'd ever been to Disneyland. "This is my very, very first time." He was in rapture now. "Thank you," he added.

Booker had no idea what to make of the whole thing. For that matter, neither did I. I was seething with anger, self-hatred, self-destruction, and thoughts of homicide. Booker disappeared into the other room to make a phone call, but the walls were so thin he needn't have bothered. The move of location offered him no privacy.

"Yes, sir, Sergeant Booker here. We've just apprehended two Caucasian males driving on Route 53. We're holding them here on driving at unsafe speed and resisting arrest." There was a pause while a voice on the other end must have asked some questions. "Two, sir. Youngest is a Matt Thomson, aged thirty-four, sir. No P, sir." Another pause. "Er no, not a urine test, sir. The letter P, sir. It does not appear in his name. No, sir, no previous record." There was another pause. "One Murphy. Yes, sir, Joseph Murphy. That's right, sir, seventy-seven, sir. An address in Idlewild, sir. Yes. Oasis Farm. In Idlewild. I beg your pardon, sir? Could you say that again, sir?"

Booker reappeared, visibly perturbed. "Um, I've been instructed to ask the two of you to wait for the time being. Would you care for any refreshments?" He said *refreshments* like an older member of the fundamentalist Christian right might say *blow job.* "The chief of police will be here in a few minutes," he added.

Booker then stepped forward and unfastened my handcuffs, but when he tried to do the same for Joey, he was refused. "I'll hang on to these for now, thanks," said Joey, only adding to Booker's confusion. We were served Lipton's tea and Oreo cookies, and after more than half an hour we heard another car arriving in the driveway. Heavy footsteps approached on the gravel, and in walked a round, jovial, bald-headed man. He must have been somewhere in his 50s. He had the ruddy cheeks that one gets from good, clean country living, and a tangible patience and stillness to him. He looked virtually impossible to make angry.

He looked around with an authoritative air. "All right, Booker, you can send your men back to their duties."

"Beg your pardon, sir?" Booker sounded deflated.

"I can handle this now."

Booker reluctantly dismissed his cadre, then defiantly returned to the corner with arms crossed over his chest. He was not to be cheated of what was to follow. The chief of police looked over at him. He let out a breath, and motioned to Booker to sit down. I wondered if this was to be a "good cop, bad cop" interrogation, like I'd seen on TV. The chief pulled up a chair right in front of Joey, and sat down, making himself comfortable.

"What's going on, Joey?" he asked in a quiet voice. "Did they give you tea or coffee?"

"What?" I blurted. "You mean you know him?"

"Oh yes," continued the chief in his soft monotone. He extended his hand to me. "My name is Findley. Chief Inspector Findley."

I didn't know whether to laugh or cry or hit someone first. "What the hell is going on here?" I tried not to shout.

"We had a little fun, and now it's over," replied Joey. His voice made no bones about the fact that I was overreacting.

"Joey, Joey," laughed the chief. "A little fun is one thing. But this is going a bit far. You gave the whole local police force more excitement than they've seen in years."

"I know!" beamed Joey with pride. Booker was leaning forward in his chair, looking intent, like a child trying to see how a magic trick is done. He looked from Joey to Findley to me with a knitted brow.

"I'm sorry," I interjected. "But what is going on? That was my friend's car, and . . . " I felt like crying.

"Don't worry. Nothing will happen to you." Findley looked sternly at Booker, who nodded obediently.

"What is going on here?" I could really find nothing else to say.

"My father was an officer on the U.S.S. *Enterprise* during the Second World War," Findley started.

Joey shifted in his chair. "I don't think this is very relevant, is it?"

"Well, Joey, I think your young friend here has a right to know why I'm going to let you go." Findley went on. "When the torpedo hit, it brought the whole officer's bridge down with it. Everyone was running around getting into lifeboats, but my father was trapped underneath crumpled metal, his leg pinned under part of the I-beam that had been supporting the bridge. His leg was badly broken. The ship was almost completely evacuated as he moaned for someone to come and help him. Only one boy, already in one of the lifeboats, heard his call."

Joey looked awkward. "And that young man jumped out of the lifeboat and ran alone back to the sound of my father's moaning. That boy, red-haired with freckles, hardly old enough to shave, managed to use another beam as a lever to lift the weight off my father's leg, and then carried him to the edge of the ship. Of course, my father couldn't swim, let alone walk, but that brave young man jumped into the water with my father, and, holding onto him with one arm, swam through the icy waters to the lifeboat. They got picked up by another ship a few hours later.

"After the war, my father tried every way he could to find the man who'd rescued him. Years later, as fate would have it, my father was working an office job for the FBI. He recognized Joey's name and face on a list of anti-war activists during Vietnam. When Joey was able to return to this country, my father was able to thank him in person. Forty years later."

"Forty-two," interrupted Joey.

"My father died almost ten years ago," Findley went on. "The last thing he said, and I was there in the room, you know, he said, 'I owe my life to Joey Murphy.'"

This was my first experience of Joey rendered speechless. He stared at the floor, not knowing what to say.

"What else could one do?" said Joey finally. "No one was going to help him. He would have gone down with the boat. I didn't want any fuss. Never liked fuss, you know."

The room had become very quiet. Booker was teary-eyed. With a nod from the chief, he stepped forward and unlocked Joey's handcuffs.

"All charges are to be dropped," said Findley. "Escort these gentlemen back to their car." He turned to Joey. "You'll be at the farm for Christmas?" Joey nodded. "I'll come on Sunday with Angela. Now you still haven't told me, what were you playing at, Joey? If I'd been off duty or out of town, you could have spent the whole of Christmas behind bars."

Joey smiled. "You know me by now. I leap before I look. Thing is I'd never been arrested see, besides, I had to test Matt here to see what he's made of before his training starts."

I gulped.

And so we were escorted back to the police car, treated now like dignitaries rather than criminals, and driven back to Paul's Honda by the side of the road. I managed to make it to the driver's door before Joey. With Booker and Findley waving us off, we continued on our way to our mysterious destination.

As they faded from view, I turned on Joey. "I can't believe you did that! We had no insurance, you had no license, it was completely irresponsible. You almost got us arrested!"

"What do you mean," said Joey indignantly. "We did get arrested!"

"Yes, but I mean we could have gotten into real, serious trouble, and it's not even my car, Joey."

"Ah," said Joey. "We could have. That was the exciting part. We could have. But we didn't."

"Why didn't you tell me you knew the chief of police? You left me thinking we were in deep trouble! And all the time you knew we'd be okay."

"I didn't know for sure. I had a feeling. And besides, I wanted to see if you think your life is real when the shit hits the fan." Joey went back to his chocolate-covered almonds. "You do. You've got so caught up in trying to win the game, or should I say trying not to lose, you've forgotten how to play for fun."

"But you can't do that kind of thing, it's completely irresponsible," I said, realizing I was repeating myself.

"On the contrary," said Joey, "I feel very able to respond quite freely to every impulse which life brings. From outside and from within." He was grinning now. "I've lived perfectly well like this for decades. I don't have a problem.

"To live your whole life in fear and restraint is nuts," he went on, cracking open a pistachio. "Calculation is irresponsible. It completely kills the ability to respond. I tell you, I just do what guides me. Then things always work out."

"But if you just do whatever you want, like that, you're going to end up killing people and getting into no end of trouble. What if you feel like walking off a cliff, or . . . or . . . doing something violent?"

"How often do you feel like walking off a cliff? The only time you ever think of a thing like that is when you're lost in pessimistic thoughts! And violence is all the fruit of holding back; it's like a pressure cooker.

"Things always turn out when you stop thinking. There's something guiding all this, see? What do you think it is that makes the trees grow? What do you think it is that makes the flowers all these colors? What makes the clouds so beautiful? You think it's just random voidness? Feel it! There's a benevolence in all this. It can only take care of you, it can only nourish you when you learn to trust everything perfectly. And that don't only mean the things that happen to you, but every impulse of God's desire that rises inside you, too."

Something inside me wanted him to be right. I could feel the ground slowly eroding under me, which just made the whole thing more and more annoying.

"So you are just suggesting that I should never think, and just act completely impulsively?"

"You'll see, you'll see. It will all drop away. It is all dropping away. Once you let go of all that is not you, things become very simple. You just need training. We will start our real work this afternoon." He paused. "As soon as you start to think, you create doubt. And I tell you, doubt cancels out that benevolence as quick as pissin' will put out a fire."

"It just doesn't make sense," I complained.

"You've spent your life living from logic," said Joey, "haven't you? You've spent your life doing what you thought was reasonable. And how's it worked out?"

I couldn't answer him. He knew perfectly well.

CHAPTER 14

OASIS

We drove in silence. Then Joey gestured to me and I turned right onto a smaller road. The larger houses and manicured lawns gave way to a different habitat now, paint peeling from smaller houses, yards long overgrown, old cars left out to pasture. Through the slightly open window I could smell the damp crispness of rural winter.

Soon he pointed to a narrow driveway suddenly appearing among the overgrown winter bushes. "Oasis Farm," declared a wooden sign nailed to a tree. The driveway was just wide enough for one car. Leaves brushed us on both sides, dropping recent raindrops on the windshield, in a confetti shower of welcome. Finally, the driveway opened out into a graveled area where several other cars were already parked. Joey was first out, clutching chocolate wrappers and pistachio shells in his cupped hands. I followed in pursuit.

He found the trash can, and then strode down a path leading to a modest two-story farmhouse with a covered deck on the first floor. As we got closer, the front door opened and an older woman pushed the screen door out of her way.

"Well, hello there, stranger," she called, in a thick, fruity voice.

Joey, quickening his pace, bounded up the stairs into the woman's arms, lifted her feet from the ground, and swung her in his embrace. They were both laughing and kissing like teenagers.

"How are you?" She looked him up and down and twinkled, brushing some crumbs from his jacket.

"All the better to be home," he beamed back at her. "Katie, meet my new friend, Matt. He'll be with us for Christmas. Matt, this is Katie, the light of my life."

Katie turned to me, welcome evident in every hint of her demeanor. She wore a long maroon corduroy dress, with deep pockets sewn on a little below the waist, and a thick woolen cardigan. Very colorful socks culminated in strong shoes with thick soles. Her voluminous gray hair was clipped in a barrette at the back of her head. The wrinkles around her eyes and mouth reminded me of a crumpled brown paper bag, but her eyes were bright, like a child on an outing.

"Well," she laughed. "Why are we standing around out here like a bunch of penguins? Come inside by the fire."

We stepped into the house. The front door opened immediately into the living room, which was scented with the rich smell of an open fire. Everything in the room seemed to be a shade of some rustic color: a brown sofa with dark wooden armrests, dark maroon curtains, a large Buddha statue, also in a dark color with hints of gold. Rich, deep music was playing. I knew it in my body, but could not place it. As I looked around I saw the room was filled with little treasures from all over the world, small carved boxes, candles, prints and pictures in dark wooden frames. An older golden retriever dozed in front of the splendid fireplace. He stretched and took in the scene. When he saw Joey, he woke up completely and launched himself at him.

"Matt, meet George Gurdjieff, another longtime companion." The dog looked at me suspiciously. It refused my offer of petting.

"Mahler!" I announced triumphantly. "Mahler's First Symphony. First movement."

"Very good!" Katie stopped, and eyed me more closely. "Do you like Mahler?"

"My grandfather was the conductor of the Boston Philharmonic. I grew up on Mahler and Strauss."

"Ah, deep and dark, like the forest at night. I love to be drawn into the shadow lands, that's where the passion lies," she sighed.

We had a moment there, Katie and I, loving our shared darkness. Then she bustled us into the kitchen. The room was dominated by a very large table, made of a thick slab of wood, rough and dented, a good eight feet long. Against one wall was a wood-burning stove, the kind people sometimes use in the country. She put the kettle on, and sat us down at the table. The floor was rough slate slabs, very thick. The room was full of competing smells: dried flowers hanging besides the window, some kind of spicy soup simmering on the stove, and chocolate. Katie produced an uncut chocolate cake and sat it on the table between us. Joey's eyes lit up.

"You know the way to a man's heart, my darling," he teased.

She found plates, made the tea, and we were soon relaxing together. I used to visit my grandparents as a child for my vacations. My grandmother always had three or four kinds of desserts ready, and made me fresh orange juice, secretly delivered to my bedside in the nighttime. Time stopped when we were there, days stretched forever, on a velvet background of sad, slow classical music on scratched vinyl records.

I was back there now.

"So, who's coming?" Joey asked Katie.

"Billy and Dawn got in last night; they're down in the barn," she started. "And Lilly's here, too, with a new friend."

Joey looked up, interested, his mustache now covered in chocolate.

"You'll meet her." Katie went on to list at least a dozen more names. "And Cheryl will be here tonight. Oh, and Sam. She stayed with Tim last night, and they'll be here soon, I think."

Joey and Katie went on joking and flirting with each other like young lovers, but I no longer followed their banter. I felt nauseated. The cake sat heavy in my belly. Sam was coming with Tim. So that was it. Spending the weekend with friends. Lying bitch. Why couldn't she just tell me straight?

Why do women lie? Had she been leading me on, knowing I was falling for her? I felt dizzy, like the life was lifting out of my body, leaving it to die like a wounded animal. I played with my cake, hardly touching it.

"Eat up, Matt," I heard Katie's voice. "Looks like you need a little extra weight on you."

"He chatters like a chipmunk, eats like a bird. Needs Katie's kitchen treatment," added Joey.

I hated them both with a vengeance. There must be a way to drive back to the city. I'd find some excuse. Seeing Sam, after all my protestations of love, was a humiliation I didn't need. Joey glanced at me. His expression gave nothing away, but I knew he knew.

"Well, can't idle away the day," bustled Katie. "Show Matt the room upstairs, my darlin', and I'm going to cook you a meal you'll remember until you're an old man."

Joey led me outside again to get my stuff. I looked at the ground; my skin felt raw. Joey said nothing, just walked by my side back to the car. We got the bag. On our way back to the house, he started in slowly.

"This is it, see. This is what has to be seen. This is where the rubber meets the road. You can have peaks and feelings of freedom, but this is where you find out how deep it goes."

"Why didn't you tell me she was with someone?" I protested. "You could see I liked her. I've had so much loss and disappointment. Why did you leave me in a place where you knew I'd fall?"

Joey looked at me intently as we walked back to the house.

"Keep going," he said. "What else do your thoughts say?"

I hated him for this. I hated his total lack of any reaction.

"I don't know. I feel like everything I touch just goes sour right away. There's no hope."

He led me back into the living room. George Gurdjieff was napping again. Katie must have gone out the back door, for the house was quiet. Joey motioned me to the leather chair by the fire and sat down on the sofa.

"Keep going," he said. "Tell me everything that seems true."

His eyes never left me for a moment. As I softened into the chair, for the first time I felt the sinking sorrow in my chest.

"Love always goes away. I feel like it's all a tease. I loved my parents; they died. I loved my wife, but when I made a big mistake she left me. I love my kids, but I barely know them now when I talk to them on the phone." My throat was tight and dry.

"Keep going," said Joey. "Keep going. What's the core that you feel?"

"I don't know. No one loves me. Everybody leaves me." The room felt cold. My back ached. I wanted home so bad, and had none.

"Good. Just say that. 'Everybody leaves me.' Just keep saying that."

"Say what?" I felt like an idiot.

"Say those words again, 'Everybody leaves me.' Keep saying them, and feel your body."

I was repeating it mechanically, muttering and looking at the floor. "Everybody leaves me . . . everybody leaves me." Was he just trying to make a fool of me?

"Good." said Joey. "Now, where do you feel that in the body as you say it?"

"I don't feel anything," I muttered. But his eyes were piercing. They would not let me off the hook. Reluctantly, I put my hand on my chest. "I guess I feel heavy here."

"Keep your hand there, and go on saying the words."

I kept repeating them.

"Everything you think, everything you feel, has underneath it a vibration, a frequency, like a piece of music. That Mahler thing you liked, it changes your feeling, doesn't it? It has a vibration to it. Can you feel the vibration of 'everybody leaves me'?"

It took me a little while to recognize what he was talking about. I really didn't want to feel anything at all. But there it was anyway, the buzzing in my chest, the nausea, the hatred for anything alive.

"Yes, I can feel it."

"How strong is it?" asked Joey.

"Not really strong. It's there."

"Good, okay. Now you've been fighting this and resisting it all your life. The last thing you've ever wanted to feel is that everybody whom you love leaves you. Instead of pushing it away, try to make the feeling stronger."

It was a strange request, alien to my instinct, but I tried it anyway. Nothing happened. I wanted more than anything to get back in the car. But then it started, a trickle at first. I could feel his eyes on me, like a coach with his rookie. It came in pulses and waves through my body, a thick heavy blanket of pain.

"How strong is it now?"

"Stronger."

"Good. Can you make this more?"

A whirlpool drew me into its center. As it pulled me down into a dark cave of despair, I could hear Joey's voice, as though far away, encouraging me on.

"Keep going. Keep going. Keep intensifying what you've been running away from all your life. How strong is it now?"

"It's very strong," I gasped. I was shocked. My body convulsed, quite beyond my choice or control, making strange noises and jerks. But that was all on the outside. Inside I was being pulled deep into the darkness, to the place that Mahler must have known so well.

"Keep going," said Joey. "Keep going. Don't stop now. Let it take you over so there's nothing left."

I did as he said. Soon my whole body was in spasm. I was hardly breathing. I felt almost ready to burst.

"Can you have any more?" he asked. "Is there any possible way to make this more?"

"No!" I gasped.

"Then relax completely, let go."

I did as he said. I fell back into the chair.

"Good," said Joey. "Relax. Fall back into yourself. Try to find yourself now. Fall back and try to find the one who feels."

I fell into deep relief, as an athlete might on crossing the finish line. Just as on the first night when I had met Joey; it was a falling back into nothing, as though into infinite, empty space. Silence.

"Good," said Joey. "Good. When you look for yourself in this way, what do you find?"

I did not answer. But he must have known.

"Just let yourself be nothing. Allow yourself to be the space that you are.

"Now bring your hand back to your chest where you've been feeling it, and tell me what's here."

I did as he said. To my surprise, it was absolutely still. I reached out, trying to recapture my pain, but it had been stolen, leaving an empty space where it rightly belonged.

"Nothing," I whispered.

"Good," said Joey, and chuckled. "Now say it again; say the words again, *Everybody leaves me.*"

"I don't want to." I was sprawled back in the arms of the chair now.

"Do it anyway." His voice was piercing, firm.

"Everybody leaves me." It was hard to say, it sounded mechanical.

"How does it sound to you now?" asked Joey.

"Just words." I didn't want to speak. "Just empty words, it means nothing."

"Good. Now say the opposite. Say, 'Everybody stays forever.'" I did as he said. "Now how does that sound?"

"More words."

"Good," said Joey, "Good. All a story; very good. Now open your eyes and tell me again about Sam."

It was a shock to hear her name; I had forgotten all about her. And it was a shock, too, to discover that her name, too, was just a word. I tried anyway.

"She knew that I liked her, and now I find out there's this guy Tim. I feel she misled me." I was feeling bored by my own story.

"Good. Is it just Sam who has deceived you?"

"No," I said. "Many women have done that." Did we have to go there?

"Try saying, 'I can't trust women.'"

I went through all the steps with Joey again: repeating it, finding it in my body, building it up till I was writhing, and falling back into deep relaxation. By the end of each cycle, the statement had become meaningless.

Every time we were done with another frequency, he asked me again about Sam, and probed and teased and provoked until I came up with another sentence: "I'm all alone"; "Nobody cares about me"; "It's all too much." Each time we went through, it became easier and quicker to let go. Finally, there was nothing left. I was just in the room. Even Joey seemed different to me. Things were completely still; even in their moving, things were still. Joey spent about half an hour with me in this way.

"Life becomes blessing, when nothing means anything anymore," he then said, so quietly I had to strain to hear him. He took a deep breath. "Everybody runs around their whole lives, on automatic, trying to avoid feeling stuff. I met a man once who'd worked hard his whole life. Gotten up before dawn, got to the office by eight, worked like a dog from dawn to dusk. When I met him he had one of the most successful construction companies in the state. Founded the company private, he did, no shareholders or nothing. He was worth two hundred million. And what frequency do you suppose was running, that man? What was it that got him out of bed before dawn every morning?"

I shrugged.

"There's not enough," he grinned. "That poor bastard wasted his whole life trying to not face a simple feeling. Even with hundreds of millions of dollars in the bank, it didn't free him from what he refused to feel. The week I met him, we did what we've just done here. Took no more than half an hour. A week later he handed the entire company over to his employees, made them all shareholders, and began for the first time to enjoy his life and relax." He looked intently into me. "Every human being is running away from something they don't want to feel. If you're running away from 'I'm weak,' you can go to the gym all you like and build pecs so big you'll need to wear a bra, but none of it makes any difference until you face the dark caves in your own mind. If you avoid your own fears you fill your life with endless distraction."

We sat quietly together. Neither of us had anything more to say. I looked slowly around the room. A Russian icon, dark and still. A statue of a water carrier, baskets hanging from either end of a bar across his shoulders. The ticking of the clock, strangely also frozen out of time, as though hammering into my thoughts, now, now, now. Joey was gazing into the fire.

We were stirred finally by the sound of a car driving on the gravel. Both car doors opened and then closed, and soon we heard slow footsteps making their way up the path toward the house. The screen door opened, the front door handle turned, and the door itself opened inward toward us. In walked an old man, much more frail than Joey. Tall and slender, with a shock of pure white hair and a heavily wrinkled face, he came into the room with the help of a cane. He was extraordinarily shiny and clean, with perfectly pressed khaki pants, a spotless white shirt, a silk cravat tied at the neck, leather shoes immaculately polished. He looked at us and smiled. His eyes were absolutely clear, like a child's. His body was slightly shaking, like a wind-up toy. Behind him, another figure stood in the shadows outside the doorway, holding a bag in each hand. It was Sam.

Joey jumped to his feet and in a second was embracing his new visitor. They held each other at arm's length, grinning into one another's eyes.

"Good to see you, Joseph," the man said in a cultured British accent.

He glanced at me and smiled with one side of his mouth only, as though sharing a private joke at someone else's expense.

"Timothy, what new trouble have you been making?" Joey chuckled, and led his friend through the living room back into the kitchen, leaving me with Sam.

She stood in the doorway. Her feet were turned slightly in toward one another, her lower lip tight. The two bags, one in each hand, pulled her arms down into a posture of defeat. I could feel how she felt as though I'd known her forever. My heart was still. I smiled at her and said hello. She took a tentative step into the room, like a cat that thinks it can faintly smell a dog, but is not quite sure. She looked at me, her head to one side, trying to figure out what was different about me. Her face brightened. She smiled a little. She sat on the edge of the sofa, fumbling with her car keys.

"How long have you been here?" she asked, not looking up.

"Oh, just a few hours."

There was another pause as she blew kisses to George Gurdjieff. "Did you meet Katie already?"

"Yes, we had tea and chocolate cake."

Sam giggled. "You'll have to get used to chocolate around here. Joey says it's what keeps him still on the planet. He's a chocolate 'con-o-sour.'"

I wanted to correct Sam's pronunciation of that word. I knew she knew that she'd said it wrong and was embarrassed. I noticed her left eye muscles were twitching a little. She tried to stop it by blinking, and failed. In the afternoon light streaming in from the window, I could see the little lines on her upper lip and on her neck. "Did you see anything of the farm yet?"

"Not yet," I smiled.

"Would you like me to show you around a little bit?" she offered nervously. "There's just time before dark."

"I'd like that." We left the house and took another gravel path. We walked through a vegetable garden, past endless flowerbeds. She knew the name of every plant and bush, whether it was visible or dormant. We walked down a driveway to another group of buildings, dominated by a large barn on two stories. Sam led me to a woodwork shop, in the basement of the barn, and introduced me to Jesse, a young man dressed in jean overalls, engrossed in making a dresser out of pine. She led me through a pottery studio, and past various bedrooms, some being used, but many simply testimonials to the community's previous, more thriving activities. We met Billy and Dawn, he with a drooping mustache and a belly, she with salt and pepper hair and bright eyes, both lawyers from Philadelphia, working in a legal aid office. We met Lilly and Gretchen, a lesbian couple from Portland.

On the way back we took a longer route, past some other cottages and then through the woods. I must have asked her casually how long she had been coming there, for I still remember her story, almost whispered among the damp trees, her eyes not once looking up from the ground.

She had met Joey more than 20 years before, when she was 17. She had run away from home before finishing high school, seeking shelter in the city. Before long she was experimenting with marijuana, then hallucinogenics, and finally with heroin. Her dreams to live as an artist came to nothing, and before long she was making a hundred a night as a call girl for foreign businessmen, hanging out at the bar at night at the Hyatt. She got pregnant finally, when her delirium from the heroin no longer allowed her to remain clear about birth control. Joey found her one night at the hotel, where he had gone to meet one of his old L.A. buddies from years before. When she tried to proposition Joey, he told her he'd pay a thousand cash for the whole weekend. He never laid a finger on her, but brought her straight to the farm, gave her a room and a home. She stayed for five years, in and out of nervous breakdown, before she had the strength to get her own place in the city again.

We saw the smoke from Katie's chimney getting closer. Sam told me she had never regained her trust of men; she had remained alone ever since.

I turned to her; we faced one another, just in front of the house. I could see the pain and fear written large on her face now. How could I possibly have missed it before? Desire for her seemed almost violent now, a gross insensitivity. I took her in my arms and held her. I touched her head with my hand.

We stood together in mutual understanding.

No one spoke.

CHAPTER 15

NOT TWO

The next morning at dawn, the house was perfectly quiet. I had been dreaming of Rebecca and the kids again, and resisted returning to this strange world in which I had landed without them.

"Come on," said Joey's voice. "We're going for a walk."

I forced myself up from the bed. It was cold. Joey stood there in the doorway, brimming with health. Each breath made steam in the room. I put on my clothes and boots and followed him down the wooden stairs. We went into the kitchen, where he had already made tea. He was wearing a thick fisherman's sweater and what looked like workman's overalls. He exuded an almost tangible feeling of wholeness.

"How'd you sleep?" Joey asked me as we sat at the kitchen table.

"Good," I said. "I dreamed of my kids again. It's Christmas Eve today; the first time I've had a Christmas without them."

"Hmmm. That's hard. So what's to stop you and your wife from fixing things up between you?"

"She's mad at me. She blames me for ruining all our lives."

Joey looked at me, calm and steady, and said not a word. I felt he was reading something inside me, that I couldn't even read myself. I felt uncomfortable.

"Come on," he said again, finishing the last of his tea. "Life's waiting for us."

Out we marched into the cold, damp December morning, thick wet dew on everything, rich smells of rotting leaves all around us. The moss on the forest floor was damp, naked like a sleeping woman. Joey led me on into the forest, singing some sort of repetitive chant just under his breath. Finally, we reached a clearing among the trees. Two trees had been cut down, leaving stumps about two feet above the ground.

"This will do. Sit down; sit down there," he said, pointing to one of the stumps. I assumed he would take the other, but he stayed standing.

"Okay. Now, what have you not said to your wife?"

"Excuse me?"

"What's been left unsaid with your wife? What have you not said to her?"

"Well, I've explained the situation. I've told her how I invested the money, and how it didn't work out, and all those things."

"Yeah, but what else? What's been left unsaid?"

"I think I've said it all, Joey."

"Thing is," he said quietly, as though thinking aloud to himself, "you've only seen half the story."

"Which part did I miss?"

"Hers." He stopped to get chewing tobacco out of a pouch. "Okay. Close your eyes, and just imagine your wife is on that other stump, sitting opposite you. Can you see her there?"

"Yeah, I guess so."

"What's she wearing?"

"I don't know. She's in Chicago."

"Well make it up, for pity's sake. Don't dick around, Matt, we've got work to do." He looked stern for just a moment, just long enough.

"She's wearing her blue dress, a jacket, and black leggings and running shoes." I felt a familiar wave of longing in my body as I remembered how Becca would dress to go for a walk with me in the forest.

"Good," said Joey. "Now just feel her there with you. Feel her with your body and say what you want to say to her."

I kept silent, feeling foolish again, like the day before. But I could sense his unwavering gaze, and I knew, as always, that there was no point in fighting.

"I miss you," I began. "I miss you, Becca. When I see you sitting there, you're so familiar to me. You've been my best friend for so long . . . "

I opened my eyes for a moment, and stared into the distant trees, wondering what more to say. Joey shuffled impatiently. I closed them. "I feel lost, I feel incomplete. I'm so sorry for what I did."

"Okay," Joey prompted. "Now keep your eyes closed and with your inner eye take a look at her. How does she feel?"

I hazarded a guess. "I guess she'd be angry; she has been every time we talk."

"Don't think, feel her. Feel her in front of you."

"Yes, she's angry, but I can also feel that she misses me. She's sad."

"Keep talking to her."

"Becca, I'm so sorry. I had no idea it would work out like it did. I'm so, so sorry. I know I've caused suffering for you and the kids, but truly, my love, I've also caused myself so much pain with my mistakes."

I was surprised to hear myself say "my love." It felt real for a flicker, and then corny. I felt like Joey was a voyeur now, intruding on my privacy.

"Good," said Joey. "Now listen; just close your eyes and listen to what she has to say."

I did as Joey told me. I had to wait a while. I could hear Becca's voice, I could hear the twang in her accent, but I wavered, uncertain if this was real or not.

"Okay. Now repeat out loud what she says."

"I'm sure you're suffering, Matt, but you've got to." This still felt contrived, like the therapy group Becca herself had dragged me to when our marriage was floundering. "That wasn't even your money. It was money from my dad. That was our house, Matt, that you gambled away. That was our house and our kids' future. You've got to make it right, Matt; you've got to make it right if you want me to come back to you and if you ever want to be with your kids again."

There, that should satisfy him.

"Okay," said Joey. "Take it in. Hear what she says, and now say what you want to say."

"I'm trying, Becca. I'm trying. I don't know what I can do. I've got nothing left. I feel like I'm just at the bottom of everything. I haven't even got my confidence left. I'm lost, Becca. If I knew what to do, I'd do it." I was getting into it now, getting lost in the movie I was scripting with his help.

"What else do you want to say? As if this is the only chance that you've got. As if you're never going to see her again." He said the words loud and fast. "What's the deepest thing you want to say to her?"

"I love you, honey. I'm sorry. Even though I know I'm a failure, I love you. You've been my best friend."

"Now," instructed Joey, "don't open your eyes. You're going to stand up . . . "

He came over and helped me to my feet.

" . . . and you're going to let everything about being Matt just drain away. All the habits of being Matt; all the thoughts, all the feelings in the body . . . just let them drain away into the ground. You're going to take a step now, you're going to move across, and you're going to become Becca."

He helped me move my body so that I was ready to sit on the other tree stump.

"And as you sit down, really feel what it's like to be this woman, looking at her husband; feel the feelings in this body. Feel what it's like to have these legs, this chest, these thoughts."

I sat down on the stump. At first I felt stupid, like I was playacting. Then I felt something less familiar welling in my chest; I felt resentment, I felt the hurt. I felt the pride that would not forgive this man unless he made amends. I could feel the swirling eddy of feeling that was too much, out of control, that had to be contained, even though the very containing was a small death.

"Now, Rebecca, what do you have to say?" asked Joey. "Look at your husband. Look at this man who lost all your money, who has turned out to be a failure. What do you want to say to him?"

"I hate you," spoke something in the body. It was in shock, it felt like a kind of ventriloquism. "I just hate you, Matt. You lied to me. You betrayed me. We had such a great life together; we were so happy. We were raising the kids in such a beautiful way. You had a decent job. Why, Matt?" I, she, whoever, was screaming now. I could feel the swirling of emotion out of control in my body. "Why did you have to do that? Why did you have to take our security?" Now it really was a scream. Tears, her tears, were flowing down my face now through the anger. "Why did you have to take our security and throw it away? What kind of a fool are you? You're just stupid. I hate you!"

"What else do you want to say to him?" prompted Joey.

"And I miss you, too." Inconsistent as this might have seemed to the remains of my controlling mind, it seemed quite harmonious within the swirling feelings. "I don't even want to tell you. I don't want you to know how much I miss you. I miss our life; I miss everything! It's been awful here with my parents. The kids . . . I can see them messing up the kids, but I just can't come back to you until you turn yourself around."

"Okay," said Joey. "Take a deep breath." Again he helped me stand up.

"Now let it all go and let Rebecca drain completely out of the body. Let it go."

He helped me move my body across to the first stump again. I was shaking from head to toe with raw emotion.

We went on like this a few more times. I became Matt again, I told her I was sorry, that I wanted to work things out. I asked her to give me a chance. I moved across and became Becca, I could feel my husband's sorrow for what he had done, I was touched, melted. I knew I missed him. But I still wanted some real action from him before I would relent. And I became Matt, and told her I loved her, that no matter what I would be her man.

"Now stand up."

I started to move toward Becca's stump again, but he stopped me.

"No, no. Stand in the middle. Stand between the stumps, so that you can have Matt on one side of you and Becca on the other, and feel who you are now. Who are you when you are aware of these two people speaking?"

A falling back. I could feel them both, like hand puppets suspended in space. I was watching them both. I was the space. All limits dropped away.

"I am just here."

"Tell me more."

"I see a man who's caught in guilt. He's stuck; he can't take action. He's in fear. And I see a woman. She's proud. She really wants to forgive him, but she wants something from him first."

"That's right," said Joey. "Let it be like it is. Experience it like it is. This is what is true between these people now. Open your eyes."

The forest smelled crisp, fresh. It was a new morning.

"What's true now?" asked Joey.

"I can see you. I can smell the forest. I feel hungry."

"What about your marriage?"

It was a strange question, like there was no marriage; there were just these two tree stumps, quite content together in the forest. I said nothing. Joey nodded and laughed. My silence was the answer he understood. He beckoned to me and we continued our walk.

"So what problem remains?"

I shrugged. "In a way, I had to do what I did. So did she. There was no choice."

"Right. All beings follow their nature. It's not the situation that hurts, see. It's the separation. It's the feeling of 'me' and 'her' as separate, as two. Whenever you take away the separation, the suffering stops."

"But she's still in Chicago, and I'm still here."

"At the core of everything between people," said Joey, "is your level of separation. When the feeling of separation is high, the way you speak, the way you feel, the way you act, your body language, and ultimately where you physically find yourself will all reflect that separation. When you dissolve the separation in yourself, everything else follows suit. Wait and see."

We walked on through the forest together. I could feel it all through my skin.

"When you feel a conflict with another, don't bother trying to fix it by doing stuff and saying stuff. Just take the place of the other person, giving them your own, and you will heal the split within your own heart. Everything else works out just fine and dandy on its own."

He led me back along the way through the forest. He returned to singing his chant under his breath, sometimes stopping to point out to me the moss on a tree or a rabbit hole in the ground.

When we got back to the house, Katie was bustling in the kitchen, making us scrambled eggs, toast, and more tea. I felt extraordinarily light. Small things, like the black and white photograph of a cat in a swing, made me laugh out loud. I devoured Katie's food like an animal and eagerly pushed my plate forward when offered more.

As Katie cleared the dishes, I offered my help. She refused.

"It's two hours ahead in Chicago," said Joey. "Go call your wife."

"What?"

"Go call your wife. It's Christmas Eve. Go call your wife and kids."

He pointed out an old rotary phone sitting in the kitchen. I dialed the number, heard the first few words of my father-in-law's answering machine, and hung up right away.

"What's wrong?" asked Joey.

"They're not there."

"Well, don't they have an answering machine?"

"Yes." I stared at the wall, in a state of catatonia. "But it's my father-in-law's."

"Call them back. Leave a message and leave this number."

I wanted to argue. He gave me that look again. A fixed expressionless gaze, like the face of a lion. I did as I was told. My father-in-law's message was just as abrupt and in-your-face as his attitude about everything.

"We're not here. If you want your call returned, leave a message."

I swallowed, hard. I knew Becca's dad would not be happy to hear my voice on his machine.

"Uhhh, this is a message for Becca. I wanted to call and say, 'Merry Christmas' to you and the kids. It's Christmas Eve; here's my number." I read the number off Joey's phone. I had to force the words out of my throat and chest, like glue out of a tube after forgetting to replace the cap.

"Good. Now, ready for some work?" asked Joey.

Without waiting for an answer, he led me outside to a pile of cut wood.

"Ever split logs before?"

"A couple of times," I exaggerated.

"Good! Then this will keep you busy."

CHAPTER 16

JUST LIKE ME

By midmorning, the pile of logs awaiting execution was half the size it had been. Despite the crisp cold of the day, my body was sticky with sweat, and there was a roar in my belly that would take flak from no one. Fragments of wood lay spread all over the small cobbled area outside the back door. My father-in-law had been brutally and mercilessly massacred dozens of times, surrendering his position only briefly to make way for Bruce Pushar from the station, Dave Harmer with his infamous SolarBike, every telemarketer who ever called during dinner, and various representatives of banks and other creditors who had contributed to my demise. The sun was shining, it was midmorning on day five, and I was dangerous.

Water finally led me back into the kitchen, both the taking in of it and the letting out. Were it not for these biological urges, I could have cut the entire forest into neat burnable chunks. The door banged loudly against the washing machine as I threw it open. And there, sitting at the kitchen table, spine straight and disapproval perched on her nose, was Cheryl. My first impulse was to go back and get the axe.

"Matt, dear, this is Cheryl, an old friend of ours," Katie said hurriedly, before there was time for violence. I grunted. My feet made loud noises as I crossed the kitchen to get water. Cheryl fidgeted, like a librarian faced with a customer whose very demeanor threatens to throw books around and to hell with the consequences.

"Will you be here for Christmas?" asked Cheryl, pursing her lips.

"What the fuck has that to do with you, you sex-starved, mean-spirited, wart-infested witch?" I might well have replied to her, had Katie not stepped in between us. She could feel the force her axe had unleashed in me, and was now intent on assuaging bloodshed.

"Yes, Cheryl, Joey brought Matt up yesterday. We are so happy to have him here."

"Lovely," said Cheryl, forcing a smile, as if a deranged rapist had a stiletto blade pressed against her ribs, and was whispering, 'Act nice, and you won't get hurt too bad.' "And have you been enjoying the farm, Matt? What have you been doing here?"

"I've been chopping wood." I looked her right in the eye, sinking my axe right into the heart of her disapproval, and with it every judgment I had ever suffered from anyone.

Joey's whistle saved the day. He stepped into the kitchen, took a look at us gathered there, and grinned. "Aha," he said. "Looks like those logs did you a world of good, Matt. Now come with me, we've work to do. Ladies, excuse us."

With that he turned his back and was out the front door. I followed, my sigh of relief mixed with disappointment. I felt like a dog yanked forcibly by the leash from a cat I was about to dismember. My chest was exploding with a need for revenge against all the mean people I had ever known.

"Where are we going?" I asked Joey, slamming the screen door behind me. "Whoops." For the first time I noticed how much smaller Joey was than me. An old man, frail even. I could carry him under one arm while fending off a couple of dragons with the other hand.

"Don't matter to me, I had to get you outta there before you killed somebody. Let's go take a look at the horses, not seen 'em yet." We walked back out on the driveway, the silence only interrupted by the sound of our feet on the gravel. I kicked stones off the pathway, and spat from time to time. Joey hardly seemed to notice. I felt awkward with so much energy in my body, like I was wearing pants with large red checks, and had to explain or change my clothes or both.

"I love you, Joey," I tried on for size. "You are the wisest and most innocent person I've ever known. You are beautiful."

Joey looked at me from the corner of his eye, and scowled a little. "Tobacco?" he offered, as he stuffed a wad into his mouth.

"No, thanks."

"You seem a little feisty." Joey raised one eyebrow.

"Well," I grinned broadly, "give a man an axe and some wood and there's no telling what will happen."

"Ah," said Joey. "Yes, that must be it."

I took a long steamy piss against a tree, and had to run to catch up with him. "And," I went on, "that woman drives me crazy."

"Katie bothering you?" asked Joey quizzically, knowing perfectly well that was not what I meant.

"No!" I said, not meaning to shout. "That . . . " I wanted to not remember her name, just as a statement of disgust, but it came anyway. "That Cheryl."

"Cheryl?" asked Joey, acting surprised. "Innocent as a lamb. What's bothering you about Cheryl?"

We were getting near the horses now. I was distracted for a moment by their beauty. They were perfect creatures, poised like statues. Joey followed my eyes.

"They were a gift," he said, ruefully. "Many years ago. I helped a man out starting a computer company, and when it got big, he bought me four Arabian stallions."

"I only see three."

"No one had computers back then," he said, "except the government and enormous companies. Just the word *computer* to the average person would conjure up images of rows and rows of huge machines with tapes flying backward and forward. You needed all that just to do simple arithmetic. But this guy was into something small, zany, with pictures to represent things." Joey paused. "Well, I guess that was my touch. And then he had this little gizmo you could hold in your hand to choose things on the screen. He called it a floating icon selector," Joey went on. "I took one look at the thing first day I walked in the garage, and I said to him, 'Looks like your computer's being nibbled on by a mouse.' He laughed like crazy and the word stuck. He figured later on that calling it a mouse was a big part of what made the thing catch on. So that's how I got the horses." By now we were close to the picket fence surrounding Joey's three stallions. I plucked a blade of grass and chewed on it.

"So," said Joey. "I'm sorry. I interrupted you. What's the problem with Cheryl then?"

"Well, she's cold. She's . . . " I was at a loss for words. "She's kind of bitter, you know? Like the world's done her wrong and she bears everyone a grudge. Yeah, that's it. She's got a chip on her shoulder. She's got an attitude."

"Ah, yes," said Joey. "And what else?"

"She just takes. You know, nothing to give."

"Yes," said Joey, thoughtfully. "I see." It sounded as if these revelations about Cheryl were completely new and he'd never considered them before.

"Well, what else?"

"Well, she's unfriendly. And pushy," I said.

"Ah," said Joey. "Yes, that will never do."

"And she needs to relax; she needs to let people be. She only finds fault."

We stood there leaning against the picket fence, Joey gazing into the distance. I was restless; in trying to get some mud off my boot I kicked the fence post just a little too hard and stubbed my toe. I pulled another blade of grass from the ground by the post and chewed on it.

"So what do you see here?" asked Joey after a moment.

I looked. The horses had turned toward us now. They were absolutely still. The eyes of one burned into me. Slowly it began to walk toward us. Joey reached into the deep pocket of his duffle coat, and produced an apple, with a flourish, like a magician. Behind the horses was a red barn with white trim. The paint was peeling. A huge bush, an ivy of some sort, cascaded over the roof and down toward us.

"Tell me what you see," said Joey, so softly it was almost intimate.

"I see the horses walking." They were almost up to us now. "I can smell the horses. I can see the barn and the ivy."

"Wisteria," said Joey. "But, never mind. Go on."

"I see the color of the sky, the orange behind the trees as the sun is setting."

"Keep going."

"I can see the way the grass is overgrown toward the back of the pasture, but chewed down the middle."

"Good," said Joey. "But what's wrong with this scene? What makes it less than perfect?"

My mind was blank; I struggled for something to say. "Well, maybe the grass needs cutting."

"Are you sure?" asked Joey.

"No, I guess not."

"Certainly not," said Joey. "The horses will eat it as the winter wears on. What else is wrong with this picture?"

"The barn needs painting."

"Aaaah," said Joey. "Are you sure that's true?"

"No, I guess not."

"What else is wrong? Tell me what makes this scene less than perfect."

This time there was a longer silence. I had run out of things to say.

"I'll tell you what I see when I look here," said Joey. "I see only three horses. My favorite, Morning Star, died two years ago. Every time I come here to this pasture that's what I see . . . no Morning Star. I love the other horses, too, mind you." He was feeding one an apple now from the flat of his palm and gave me an apple to feed to another.

"When I look at this pasture I see a lack, a lack of my favorite horse. But you don't see that, do you?" he asked, his blue eyes piercing into mine.

"No," I said. "I never knew your horse."

"Right. So the lack of perfection I feel here is not real, is it?"

"What do you mean?"

"I mean the only way to create something less than perfect is to compare it in your mind with something else. It only exists as my mental process."

I was lost.

"You see, if I let go of the idea of Morning Star, there's nothing wrong with this picture. If you let go of the idea of a freshly painted barn, there's nothing wrong with this picture. If you let go of the idea that the grass should be even, there's nothing wrong with this picture. If you abandon the idea of how someone should be, there's nothing wrong with them. The difference between heaven and hell is comparing." He turned back toward the horses. He seemed to enter into a silent dialogue with each one.

"Now, that's just the beginning. That's just the very first step, to see, to know that anything less than heaven is just a creation of your own mind."

I wanted to ask him about starving babies, mass genocide, and the globalization of the economy, but he interrupted me before I had a chance.

"Now," he said. "What about Cheryl? You say she's not giving; she's got a chip on her shoulder; she's mean-spirited; she needs to relax and let people be as they are, but do you know for sure those things are objectively true?"

"Sure!" I said. "It's obvious."

"Well, she doesn't bother everyone the same, does she?"

"You mean you actually like that woman?"

"Sure," said Joey. "I've known Cheryl for years, love her to pieces. The important thing to see is why do you feel the need to change her? What is it about how she is that disturbs you? Try saying it again. Try saying, 'She's a victim.'"

"She's a victim," I said.

"Say it again. Really say it with venom."

This wasn't hard. "She's a victim!" I said, grabbing hold of the fence post. "She's a victim! She's a victim."

I was almost retching on the word now.

"Good," said Joey. "Now just let go of the idea of Cheryl and say that word a few more times. Victim! Victim!"

I did as he said. I was attacking the fence post now with such ferocity that I was surprised it survived. "Victim! Victim!" I screamed at the innocent piece of wood, eyes glaring.

"Good," said Joey. "Now you see, you've still got the charge on the word, even with Cheryl gone. So where's the victim now?"

Everything did a flip again. I looked into his eyes. It all stopped. When the word came, it was involuntary. I heard it more than said it.

"Me?" I felt totally busted.

Joey's eyes laughed while his mouth stayed perfectly still. "Right," he said. "Right. Now try saying the whole thing. 'Cheryl's a victim, just like me.'"

I repeated his words. "Cheryl's a victim, just like me."

I burst out laughing; a mad, deranged laugh. My body was rippling with energy. It felt loose.

"Just like me, just like me," Joey sang under his breath, to a melody from Verdi's Rigaletto. "Now try the other ones."

"What do you mean, what other ones?"

Try saying "She's a taker, not a giver, just like me."

I did as he said, and laughed again. A tight knot was unraveling somewhere in my body.

"She's mean-spirited. She's mean-spirited, just like me. She's cold, just like me."

Joey prompted me under his breath, without expression. "Needs to relax."

"She needs to relax, just like me." He prompted again. "She needs to let people be, just like me." The absurd and obvious truth of the last two statements sank in. The horse near me became frisky suddenly, and did a small dance, from back feet to front.

"Simple, eh?" said Joey.

I had no idea what he was even talking about anymore. The air smelled good, the horses were enjoying the end of their apples as they did their polka, and it really felt like Christmas Eve.

Joey turned away from the fence, and I walked alongside him. I was a little weak in the knees. I wanted to sit down, muddy as it was, and play in the dirt for a while.

"That's pretty much the ticket for whatever you have to say about anybody," said Joey. "Whether it's praise or blame. Add the words *just like me* and you'll find out what your work is."

"Work?" I asked, quickening my step to keep up with him.

"All that keeps you from the sweetness of this moment are the ghosts you will not own," said Joey. "The victim, the mean-spiritedness, the taking, is all good, it's all God, except when you say 'no' to it. When you deny that in yourself, you'll find a way to make someone else wrong, too. It's just the same with your beauty. So what was that you were saying to me when we were walking over here, what was that smoochy stuff?"

"That I love you."

"Then what did you say?"

"I said you were sweet and wise," I guessed.

"Good," said Joey. "Can you own that, too, that I'm sweet and wise just like you?" He grinned at me like a shy teenage girl. I obeyed. I laughed and put my arm around him. This time he laughed too and put his arm around my waist.

"Just like me . . . just like me . . . ," he sang, this time to his own tune, as he danced in a circle around me. "Can you feel this has taken residence in your body now?" he whispered conspiratorially, wrapping his tongue around the word *body* as he poked me painfully in the ribs.

"Yes," I winced. I was at that moment entranced by a rabbit hopping between the trees.

Turning a corner, we saw two people walking toward us from the house. One waved an arm in the air. It was Katie, with Cheryl. They were both wrapped up in scarves and hats and holding each other's gloved hand. They looked like schoolgirls.

"Been to see the horses, darlin'?" asked Katie as we got closer.

"Hmmmm," he said. "Come here." He pulled her toward him, as if they were married just yesterday. I looked into Cheryl's eyes. I waited for the reaction to come in my belly. I waited again, our eyes still engaged.

Someone had stolen my feeling of repulsion, and I was quite lost without it, like a warrior suddenly stripped of all his weapons. Undefended, unprepared. Cheryl cocked her head to one side, frowned, then burst out laughing.

"It's Christmas tomorrow," said Katie. Unable to contain her pleasure, she wriggled her body. I felt a sudden wave of panic. Gifts! I didn't have any gifts. They were being so kind and generous, but I hadn't even known I was coming here. Christmas means gifts, and I didn't have any.

"Now, Matt," said Katie, taking me by the arm as we walked back to the house. "Sam told me you were interested in the pottery. Well, you're in luck. We fired up the kiln a few hours ago, since our master potter is back in town."

"Oh?" I said.

"Yes. It means you can go have some fun and maybe even make a few Christmas presents." My mind had been read like the cover of a magazine. Again. "And Matt, I was wondering if I could use your car. We're out of nutmeg, and the store will close in half an hour. My battery's dead."

I hesitated, wondering if Katie had taken driving lessons from her husband.

"Sure," Joey interjected, before I had time to speak. "The keys are in the glove box." That took care of it. Out of my hands. I was past caring.

"So, who's the master potter?" I asked.

"Cheryl," Katie beamed back.

CHAPTER 17

THE REAL TEACHER

There we were, dressed in aprons that looked like they'd seen better days, cutting up a big piece of clay. Cheryl had changed. She'd softened. I was wondering if Joey had tipped her off. She showed me how to cut the clay into the right kind of chunks, how to moisten it with water. Then she put it on the wheel and we spent a couple of hours learning how to make a flower vase, a milk jug, and a bowl. She was thorough in her instruction, and when I was a little too eager with shaping my creation, she touched me gently on the arm.

"Easy," she said. "Easy, boy."

I tried to remember what the problem had been. Whenever my creation collapsed completely into a wobbly mess, we both burst out laughing. We were actually having fun. She showed me how to apply glaze, and we put our creations in the kiln and washed up. The afternoon passed without ado.

When we got back to the house, Joey was fast asleep with George Gurdjieff on the floor at his feet. There was no one else around. I crept up to my room and lay on the bed, an indescribable feeling of goodness in my body somewhere in the unclaimed zone between sex, good food, laughter, and sleep.

They called me down at six for dinner. By now, there must have been more than a dozen gathered for Christmas Eve. Joey, Katie, me, Cheryl, Sam, the old man Tim, the lawyer couple, even the police chief and his wife.

We ate meat loaf, brussels sprouts, and brown rice pilaf, and drank red wine. The tiniest things seemed funny. Joey regaled us with stories that brought tears of laughter to our eyes. Finally, after chocolate pudding (Joey had three helpings) and some kind of spicy tea, a man called David stood up.

"Time for the meeting, folks. We'll see you all in the yurt at nine o'clock."

There was a scurry of activity as people rose with plates and bowls and started cleaning. Cheryl disappeared. They all seemed to know what to do. I felt helpless; Joey rescued me. He gave me a wink, and nodded his head toward the living room.

"Come on," he said. "You've done your share of the work today with that firewood. Sit yourself down here."

We sat by the fire together.

"How are you?" he asked, as though he were quoting someone else, like he did not believe his own question.

"Wonderful," I said. But it was also as though someone else said it. It was very odd. We were having a conversation in which we were both caricaturing ourselves. The joke of it all. Something else eclipsed the small talk.

"You don't miss your kids?" said Joey.

"Yes, I do," I said, and thought for a while. "It's the same missing, but now it feels . . . well good, I guess. It's not painful. Does that sound really weird?"

"Ah," said Joey. "Everything can be like that. Your wife called," he added after some silence.

"My wife?"

"Yes, don't you remember you left a message for her?"

"When did she call?"

"While you were doing your pottery. I talked to her for a while. Nice woman. I had a word with your kids, too."

"You talked to my kids?"

"Yep. Dominic and . . . "

"Sarah."

"That's right. Anyway, they said they were going to some sort of family thing tonight."

Probably Mafia, I thought to myself.

"She asked you to call her in the morning."

"She did?" I tried to appear matter-of-fact, but my heart was pounding. "Yep," said Joey. We lapsed into silence again. The room was spinning. The wine had suddenly taken hold. I felt tired and dizzy and sick. Joey had talked to my wife and kids.

"What about the real teacher?" I asked. "You said when I came here I would meet the real teacher. Is that you?"

Joey laughed. "It's not me." He paused. "And it's not not me. You'll meet the real teacher tonight."

Soon the others were walking back through the living room on their way out of the house. Joey gave me a nod; we rose and followed. We walked over to a round canvas building on a platform. This must be the yurt. From the outside it seemed as though it would be freezing sitting in a canvas building, but inside it was quite cozy, with a wood-burning stove even. The temperature was quite comfortable enough for a T-shirt. About 20 people sat in a circle. The chief of police grinned at me and winked.

David hit a metal bowl with a wooden mallet, and the room fell silent. We all closed our eyes. I found a well of physical pleasure in my belly so intense I was tempted to scream. My body began making small, jerky movements that originated in my belly and hinged my body at the solar plexus. Inside I was smiling, a total smile. I wasn't only smiling with the lips; I was smiling in my lungs and liver and through the whole length of yards of intestines. My genitals and asshole were smiling.

After some time the bell rang again. There was silence. I waited for Joey to conduct the meeting. But it was obvious, not only from the seating arrangement, but also from the disposition of the people, that this was not going to be his show. No one was looking at him any more than at anyone else. Finally, Tim cleared his throat.

"Well," he began. His cultured British accent reminded me of an Oscar Wilde play. "Someone has to begin. It might as well be me, before I drop dead."

Someone laughed nervously.

"Yes," Tim said. "Sam was kind enough to drive me here yesterday. My eyesight is so bad, I can't even tell how many we are tonight." His voice was so thin and frail it felt like he was speaking to us from another room. A room I sensed I had never been to.

"I got my tests back last week," he said. "They confirmed that it is malignant." A perfect stillness in the room. "As we already knew, or at least suspected. And I have to tell you that it's a wonderful and interesting experience to finally arrive at the place we all avoid. The tumor is too deeply buried in the spine to make it worth considering the possibility of surgery. And it is too far gone for chemotherapy or radiation."

His eyes were as clear as a June sky.

"All my life, just like everyone, I wondered how this day would be. And I was surprised," Tim said. "I felt no pushing away of any of it. I've lived fully. I've done all I need to do, and probably quite a bit more than was actually necessary." He chuckled quietly. "I'm ready for the next great adventure. I guess I'd like to add . . . " Now his voice quivered just a little; his already shaking hand shook a little more visibly, " . . . how deeply I feel blessed by this circle of friends. I've known some of you for decades." He glanced at Joey. "I've seen us all go through hell and high water. It's almost certainly my last Christmas here. I know that I can die and say that I've loved for real."

When he finished speaking, the only sound was the wood crackling in the stove.

One by one, people offered a few words. Never more than a handful at a time. Appreciation, even humor.

"You're the wickedest old pervert I've ever known," said Joey, deadpan. "I'll miss you when you're gone."

The room settled once again into the same stillness from which Tim had spoken. The silence was like music. I could feel it pulling me into its depth, caressing me from within my skin.

This time the silence was broken by Jesse. "Yeah, I've been kind of torn up since Lizzie left." Early 20s, greasy shoulder-length mousy hair, old sneakers, sweater with a hole. He sat quite still. His body indicated one could say anything to him, anything at all, and he would not flinch. His openness was not just a lack of defense; it was extraordinary, worn out loud.

Jesse looked at me and explained, "She was my girlfriend. She went to New York to go to dance school. I've thought a lot about following her there to be together, but I don't know anybody. Besides, I wonder sometimes if she still wants to be with me. It's been a few months now, I think about dating other people, but I just can't replace her. I feel stuck." Even in his stuckness, his vulnerability contained raw power.

Again, a silence in the room, a waiting. Katie spoke.

"Lizzie is a beautiful girl, Jesse. And I absolutely know that even though she's pulled to her studying, she still loves you very deeply." No one spoke, but I could feel the assent like a wave.

A couple of other people offered comments. Suddenly my heart was beating faster, my spine straightened, and I realized that quite beyond my control, I was also about to speak. It was a body sensation, like being about to sneeze, and knowing there is no longer any choice.

"I don't know you." The words began, all on their own. It was a relief of pressure. "But I can feel you. And it feels to me really good to just stay where you are, feeling what you're feeling. It may be painful to be separated from the one you love, but if you just sit with all this, it will take you deeper into yourself. It will allow you to love more deeply in the future because you'll have passed through this pain of being left."

I could feel the attention with me. I had the room. "I am where you are, and I'm learning this, too."

I was surprised. My mouth was dry; my heart was beating so wildly, I was afraid I would croak. Who just made me say that? I looked at Joey; he raised one eyebrow again at me. His eyes twinkled.

The gathering continued like this for perhaps an hour. Someone would speak, describe what was happening for them, and there would follow a silence. Then different voices in the room would respond. I spoke two or three more times, each like the first, without premeditation, as though being used. A couple times we agreed on little tasks people had to do that the group agreed on. Jesse's assignment, for example, was to write a poem every day, turning his longing for his girlfriend into art. Charlie, who'd brought his heart problem to the group, was given an assignment of 20 minutes of exercise every day.

Eventually our words ran out, as the fire died down to glowing embers. The gong rang again, and we closed our eyes. My body was very alive, absolutely sober and awake.

We stepped out of the yurt. The moon was shining brightly. The air was cold and damp, but refreshing. It felt good to deeply breathe in huge gulps, as though it was washing my lungs clean. I sauntered a bit, waiting for Joey. We walked back together.

"Good," he said. "It's starting to flow in you."

"Is it?" I asked.

"You'll see," he chuckled.

"So, who's the real teacher?" I asked him.

He stopped, looked me directly in the eyes, and paused.

"You are," he said with an absolutely calm voice. "You are, and it's more than you. As soon as you put yourself in the position of listening, feeling into others, feeling what's best for others, you discover the real teacher, invisible, never seen, behind your own eyes. It's you and it's not you.

"The real teacher is not a person, it's a meeting."

CHAPTER 18

ETERNAL NOW

Christmas morning. The air in the room was cool, the warmth under the comforter in my bed made it seem like the best place to stay all day. I lay still, marveling at how relaxed and full my body felt. The ocean in my belly sent ripples as I moved in the bed, out into my arms and legs, satiated as though I'd just feasted. I reached out drunkenly to find a logical cause for feeling so good: I'm going to talk to the kids today; Joey and Katie's kindness toward me; Cheryl with the pottery.

My attention turned to noises coming from downstairs. As if awakening from a dream, I realized I had been tuning them out for quite some time now. I had no watch. I pulled on my clothes. Opening my door, I stumbled over a neat pile of folded laundry. I almost fell down the stairs into the living room and found everyone gathered from the night before. The clock above the fireplace said a quarter to 11.

"We'd given you up for dead," said Joey. "You're too late for breakfast, you know."

"Oh, nonsense," Katie said. "There's plenty. Don't tease the boy; it's Christmas."

"Your wife called," Joey went on, shifting the chewing tobacco to his cheek.

"What?" Now I tripped on the dog, conveniently lying across the bottom of the stairs. I had to grab hold of the kitchen door to avoid throwing myself full force into the Christmas tree.

"Yep, about nine o'clock. Nice woman," he said as an aside to Tim. Tim raised his eyebrows and looked interested, ready for a good story.

"You talked to her?" I tried to calm the tone of my voice.

"We had quite a chat," Joey told Tim, ignoring me. "Into photography, you know."

"Really?" said Tim with an exaggerated rise in the music of the word, as though Joey had just told him my wife was this month's centerfold in Playboy, and loves to offer oral sex to strangers.

"Well, I, uh . . . ," I tried to get control of the conversation. This was my wife they were carving up for Christmas here. But I was still off balance.

"She's mighty keen on Cartier-Bresson," Joey went on. "I knew him, you know. I have a few of his original prints."

"Aha!" exclaimed Tim, full of hidden meaning.

"Well that was big news to her!" Joey laughed. "She wants to get together and see them as soon as possible."

"You're going to get together with Becca?" I blurted, now more or less free of the Christmas tree. I noticed my zipper was down. I pulled it up, which completely deflected everyone's attention from what I was saying.

"And the children . . . very sweet," Joey continued, offering Tim tobacco. "I had a long talk with the young boy about Legos." Tim waved aside the tobacco, but seemed very excited about the mention of a young boy.

"You talked about Legos with my son?" I interrupted.

"Oh, yeah," said Joey, looking at me for the first time. "I helped design some of the early models back in Denmark in '63."

I might have guessed.

"I had a chat with your father-in-law, too. Now there's a deep man, that Paulo. Sicilian. That's a mighty lush part of the world. Remember, Katie? Those weeks we spent in Palermo?" Katie smiled. "Best olives in the whole world. But hurry up, boy. They're waiting for you to call, almost a couple of hours now."

I stumbled into the kitchen; my heart was racing. Fuck them all, these dirty old men. I got the numbers mixed up on the rotary phone, and had to redial three times.

"Hello!" Becca's sing-song voice always played my heart like a lute.

I grunted.

"Good morning, darling! Happy Christmas!" she went on.

"It's me, Matt." I don't know who I imagined she thought it was, and was calling "darling," but it couldn't be me.

"Yes, I know! Happy Christmas!" she laughed.

"I'm staying with some friends." I felt she needed some sort of explanation.

"Yes. Such a nice man. We had quite a talk, Matt."

"Oh, Joey. That's good. That's good, Becca." I found a piece of bread someone had left on the kitchen counter. I crumbled it between my fingers.

"He says you're going to do really well, Matt."

"He did?" I mushed the crumbs together into a tight ball.

"Yeah!" Her voice reached an almost operatic pitch with enthusiasm. "He said everything's going to be really fine. Honey, I was just waiting for you to pull it together. I knew you would." I pushed a hole into the mushed bread ball with my thumb.

"Oh! Um . . . right. Well, it just took a little time, that's all." My throat felt dry. I stuffed the mushy bread ball into my mouth, realized what I had done, and spat it out again.

"Do you want to speak to the kids? I can't wait to see you, darling!"

I wiped the mess from the counter with my shirt. A storm brewing in my chest. What lies had Joey told her? I didn't have much time to think about it.

"Hey, Dad! Happy Christmas!" Dominic on the phone.

"Happy Christmas, Dom. How are you?" A bird sang outside the window. What kind of bird sings in December?

"Great! Hey, thanks for the gift, Dad. I miss you." It might be in a cage.

"You're welcome, sweetheart. I miss you, too." My voice was mechanical, flat. Here they are, all my loved ones opening the doors to peace again, and I'm screwing it up. "Have you been having a good time?"

Dominic lowered his voice to a whisper. I could hardly hear him. "It's boring, Dad. Grandpa's kinda weird. He's got guns. I want to come home." The birdsong became louder, as if inside the room.

My throat tightened. "Yes, darling. Soon. I want you to come home, too." I hated this, this enactment of what I had most desired. I was getting my postponed dreams, but not on my terms. Set up like this I felt like a cheat.

"Daddee!" Here was Sarah. "Happy Christmas, Daddy."

"Happy Christmas, poppet. Are you having a good time?" Christ, give me something better to say. I was spoiling it all. My head hurt, I was thirsty.

"Yes, Daddy. I miss you."

"We'll see each other soon, honey." The bird stopped. I could only hear laughter from the other room.

Becca back on the line. "Heey . . . " Her voice raised in the middle and dropped at the end. Sexy, almost. I could taste her lower lip between mine. She spoke in that guttural voice that always ended us up between the sheets, her pretending it was me who was horny. "Well, I can't wait to hear what you've been up to."

"Neither can I," I said. My voice was still flat, as much as I tried to squish some innuendo into the bread ball of this new intimacy.

"What do you mean, Matt?"

"I mean, I can't wait to hear what you've been up to."

"Oh, yes." She giggled.

"Looks like things are going to work out now. I'm really . . . I'm really . . . hmmmm . . ." I cleared my throat. "Confident." Silence. She had to have known I was bluffing. I didn't even fool myself. I found a sticky spot on my shirt and tried to wipe it off with my spare hand.

"Call me soon?" A question, a tentative one at that, more than a demand.

My breath tightened. I felt like I had won a prize by accident, and it was only time till I had to give it back. A pause. Sadness. "Bye."

I turned around. Joey was standing in the kitchen doorway, grinning at me.

"What did you tell them?" My voice was cold, accusing.

"Just the truth." I hated his innocent, deerlike eyes in these moments. "Which is?"

"That you're doing very well. She asked me how you were doing."

"And you said?" There was a kitchen knife a few inches from my hand. I pulled away from it.

"I said you were doing very well. I said that you were an intelligent and capable young man, who would have no problem turning his life around."

"That's it? That's all you said?" I was staring. I knew him a little by now.

"Let me see . . . " Joey looked pensive. I knew there was more, and I knew he'd do everything to wriggle out of confessing. "Well, hurry up and make your coffee. We're going to open our gifts now."

I did as I was told and joined the others in the living room. Cheryl patted the sofa next to her where there was an empty space. "I wrapped the things you made," she whispered, theatrically. "Something for Joey, something for Katie, and plenty left over for your family."

"Thank you," I whispered back and squeezed her hand, trying to conjure up Christmasy feelings. I noticed the mess on my shirt from my misadventure with the bread ball.

And so began the strangest game I ever played at Christmas. It didn't need much guesswork to figure out who made it up. Somebody would get a gift from the tree, and open it. The next person could either get another gift or take away the gift that the first person got. If your gift got taken, you would take another. Then the third person could choose, either from under the tree or from one of the previous two. The person having a gift taken from them got to choose another gift, either from under the tree or one already in possession, but couldn't take back one of the gifts they previously had taken away from them. This went on in the same vein until all the presents had been opened. Much later I found out that this was another of Joey's little ideas that had spread virally from one party to another all over the world.

I was the third to receive a gift, which was a bottle of red wine from Napa Valley. Not bad stuff at all. I lost it in round five. I spent two rounds wondering what I would do with an ugly, fuzzy red steering-wheel cover, when Charlie greedily exchanged it for a CD of *NSYNC. Jessie took that from me in round 11, and I wound up with a nice woolen hat, clearly one which Katie had made, which suited me just fine.

Around noon everyone dispersed to do various tasks. I went in the kitchen to see how I could help, but Katie insisted I sit down to eat the eggs and toast that I had missed for breakfast. Then, with a quick jerk of his head, Joey motioned me outside. I found my jacket, put on my new hat, and we were off again into the forest.

"It's day six," said Joey. He paused for a long time. "How did you sleep?"

"Great. Thanks."

We were walking thick into the woods now, deeply off the path through the underbrush. The damp moss greeted us, as though this was our own home. The forest washed us with its dew, as if to remind us that the world of people had dirtied us unnaturally. A squirrel ran up a tree into a hole. I breathed the smells in deep. I wanted to take my clothes off and rub in the mud and moisture and texture of it all.

"Did you dream?" asked Joey.

I had to think. "Yeah, I dreamed of my parents again."

"Ah, tell me about them."

"They died in a plane crash."

"When?"

"I was still in college."

"Do you miss them?"

"Yes and no. We were kind of distant when they died."

"Where were you when you heard the news of their death?"

I thought about it. "I was working at a late night café. It was after two in the morning; we were just closing when a phone call came."

I could feel a burning sensation on the left side of my face now, as though remembering something violent in my body, as well as my mind. "They had called the shared house that I lived in, and someone there gave them the number of the café."

"Who was calling?"

"Some government agency. They were very diplomatic, I remember. It took them ages to get to the point."

"What did you feel?"

I tried to remember. "Nothing. That was the strange thing. I didn't feel anything; it was more an absence of feeling. After I hung up the phone I just went back to washing the dishes."

"What did you feel later?"

"Numb. Like I said, we'd grown apart."

"Okay," said Joey. He motioned toward a tree stump. "Close your eyes." I sat and did as he said. "Now go back to your memory of a few minutes before you got the call."

"I was doing the dishes."

"Okay, now play it slowly forward till the phone rings."

"I just remembered one thing."

"What's that?"

"I'd smoked a joint about one hour before. I was stoned."

"Aha. Good to know." He was playing Sherlock. "So listen now to the voice on the phone."

"Yeah, he's asking me for my name and various irrelevant details to prove that it's me. Now he's talking about flight numbers, giving various disclaimers about the liability of the government."

"And?"

"Well, he hasn't said that they're dead yet, but I sort of know it. I can feel it."

"Where do you feel it?"

"There's a tightening here." I put my hand to my gut.

"Okay," said Joey. "Put your hand there and forget all about the memory now, and just like we did yesterday, make it stronger. How strong is it now, if one is almost nothing, and ten is as strong as it could be?"

"Maybe four."

"Make it stronger."

A fire was beginning to burn in the middle of my body. It started as a smolder, but it was soon raging. With every breath, it took over more and more until my head ached and my mouth was dry.

"How strong is it?" I heard Joey's voice, from far away.

"Nine," I said through gritted teeth.

"Keep building it; keep making it more. Let this overwhelm you."

Soon I was convulsing completely, imploding into a tight knot of not wanting to feel. I heard Joey's voice again.

"Relax; let go. Relax back into yourself."

I breathed deeply and sighed out. It was like taking off a tight shoe.

"Now. Could you forget all about what has happened before? Could you start fresh?"

"Yes," I whispered.

"Bring your hand back. What's there now?"

I was surprised. "Nothing, it's, it's . . . there's nothing there at all."

"Good," said Joey. "Go back again to the phone call. The man is asking your name, for proof of your identity, and now feel."

As I returned to the memory, it was quite different. Instead of numbness there was grief. "Mummy," I whispered involuntarily.

"Yes," said Joey. "Let yourself feel."

Suddenly I was soft. I had lost my mother and my father all at the same time.

"Let go of the images and feel your body."

It was all in my lower belly, a vacuum. A pain too strong to feel.

"Give it a number," Joey whispered.

"Four," I said. I was falling into it, falling out of control; consumed by a fire that burned so strong it destroyed. It took much longer to work our way up through the numbers this time. I would contract completely, and then he would encourage me to breathe until I could feel again. Finally, after what was maybe a few minutes, but seemed like hours, I was feeling it fully. There was nothing but an overwhelming agony; nothing left but a universe devoid of all the support I'd ever known. It was searing, like an operation on the nervous system without anesthetic. It was pure scream without any sound. Finally, I heard his voice again.

"Relax, let go; fall back into yourself."

My body was trembling. I could hear the sounds of the forest, very fresh and vivid. My body felt tremendously soft, as though this were my first moment, newborn, innocent, absolutely innocent, just pure hearing. I could feel the wetness of the moss against my skin as a caress.

"Put your hand to your belly," said Joey softly. "What's there?"

"It's warm," I said. "It's sweet; it's soft."

"Good," he said. He waited a few moments and then asked me to return again to the phone call. He had me replay it a couple of times, but there was no charge. It was as if I was listening to someone else's memory.

Joey came over and put his arm around me. He looked into my eyes like a parent or a lover.

"You've been resisting that one for a long time."

I laid my head in his lap. He placed his hand on my head. Together, we listened to the forest; neither of us spoke. He hummed to himself softly, under his breath; I could feel the rise and fall of his belly with my head. Finally, without speaking, we slowly stood up together and continued our walk through the moss and the ferns and the dew and the hint of animals, for whom this was home. It was quite some time and some walking before we spoke again.

He squeezed my elbow. "You jumped in at the deep end. Most everything we do and say is the product of memory. We almost never respond innocently or spontaneously to what's before us. It's all filtered through what's gone before, and not even the clear memory of that—a distorted, filtered view of what's gone before. Instead of responding, we react." He turned from me, stretched his back, and opened his arms wide toward a tree.

"We react inappropriately, based upon the distorted perceptions we carry in our bodies," he went on as he turned back to me. "Memory can have a charge when it's carried in the body, or it can be factual, you remember the facts of a situation with no feelings attached to it. To live freely you need to be able to know how to transform charged, emotional memory into factual memory. Feel now in your body whatever you couldn't or wouldn't feel then."

"But Joey," I said. "There must be millions of events that happened in my life. The number of charged memories must be virtually infinite."

"It's not a process of time," he went on. "It's not a goal you have to work toward, to become finally complete. It's a dance, an endless exploration. I didn't say you have to liberate every charged memory to be free, only that you have to know how to. You have the God-given ability to feel each impulse as it arises and return again and again to your natural state."

We walked back into Katie's cottage. George Gurdjieff was sleeping by the fire. It felt warm after the walk. Katie had been baking bread, the whole cottage smelled sweet and reassuring. Some knitting had been left in the chair next to the fire. Joey motioned for me to take a seat at the dining table, and he put on the kettle for tea.

"You know, Joey," I began. "None of these lessons are exactly easy. It could take me years of practice to master even one of them."

Joey opened the cupboard above the kitchen counter. Dozens of kinds of herbal teas. He opened his eyes wide, and whistled. "What kind of tea do you want?"

"Whatever. Whatever you are having."

"Lipton."

"I mean we have habits that have lasted all our lives, habits like judgment and fear."

Joey wasn't listening. He had found a little bottle among the tea, and was eyeing it with rapt curiosity.

"Vitamin C. One thousand milligrams."

"It's all very well to go out into a field, with a teacher there to remind you, and to have an insight of how things could be, but what about daily life? What about the marketplace?"

"Made from organically grown rosehips," Joey went on.

"Joey, I just don't feel it is enough. Are you expecting me to master all this stuff you're showing me overnight? Just because I get it once?"

"Patented time-release formula. What's that mean anyway?"

I was feeling impatient. "It means that you take a big dose in one shot, and they've figured out some clever way so that it slowly absorbs into your system."

"Ah," said Joey. "Yes. That's the idea."

He twinkled, and put a large handful in his mouth.

CHAPTER 19

BLIND MAN'S BASEBALL

I don't remember too much about the rest of the day. At five o'clock we all gathered for a magnificent dinner. There was turkey and gravy, mashed potatoes, salad, and an infinite variety of vegetables. Tim brought some very special wine he'd had for many decades. Enough to lubricate every one of us. We stayed up late playing Pictionary and Charades and a number of very bizarre games that Joey appeared to make up on the spot.

Sam looked so beautiful that evening. She wore a black velvet choker with a stone set in it and a dark blue dress. Her blue eyes were shining. We could look into each other, my heart was free like an animal released from years of living in a cage. I knew she knew it. She had become closer to me than a sister.

The next day we all woke late. There was a befuddled morning-after feeling to the whole house. I sat for a long time in the kitchen, drinking Katie's coffee, eating her bread, and listening to stories about her life with Joey. All the details he had dwelt on, that evening in the city, she either glossed over or forgot completely. Her version was filled with colorful, simple people. A single mother in Barcelona who had traveled with them through Europe. Stories of Tim when he was auditioning for his first parts on the stage. Katie would stop what she was doing as she recalled different friends. She would look hazily into the distance, remembering them as "a sweetheart" or "such a honey."

Joey walked in around 11 A.M. He nodded briefly to each of us, but looked serious and determined, like a doctor on call who just got beeped and must hurry to the hospital. He drank his coffee standing up and looked frequently at his watch. Then he strode to the back door, nodded at me, and we were off again.

Near the pile of logs, which I had not yet stacked, was a shed, three walls closed in, but open at the front. He disappeared into the back for a few minutes, then returned with a baseball and a bat. He said not a word to me, nor did our eyes meet. He seemed angry about something, and I couldn't imagine what.

He led me up a dirt road. It quickly rose to a much higher elevation above the farm; as we walked in silence, the trees got thinner, the ground more gravelly. The wind was cold, and made noises in the trees. The combination of remoteness and his silent, determined attitude made me nervous. I looked back over my shoulder now and then at the farm, the warm fire, the warm bread, his warm wife.

We continued up beyond where the dirt road ended, walking on a small path, and finally came to a cleared area overlooking the most incredible view of the valley below. From where we stood there must have been an almost sheer drop of perhaps 2,000 feet to the bottom of the valley. Right on the edge, jutting out a little over the drop, was a large boulder, flat on the top, perhaps three feet square.

Joey motioned me to stand away from the drop, so it was off to our side. He handed me the baseball bat. He looked solemnly into my eyes.

"Focus your mind," he said, quietly and with slightly pursed lips. "Focus your mind, very precisely into this moment. Now we're going to find out just how serious you are."

I completely forgot his soft, gentle humor. Jesus, this guy could throw me over the cliff without a moment's hesitation and lie to the others about what had happened. Was I with a raving psychopath? It really didn't seem like any of this made any difference to him. He did seem to care, but without giving a hoot for consequence.

Without a moment's warning, he threw the ball forcefully toward me. For a man in his late 70s, he had the pitching power of a 20-year-old. I missed completely. The ball sailed off behind my head. I went scurrying after it. After a search of a minute or two, I brought it dutifully back. His face was expressionless as he took the ball. "Focus," he said. "This is just the beginning."

The next pitches were easier. I was ready now. As he threw each ball with great force, I managed to hit almost all of them. Some he caught. Others, I had to run and find.

"Okay," he said after a while. "You're ready for the next level."

He pulled a red bandanna out of his hip pocket. He folded it down into a narrow strip and tied it around my eyes. His touch was rough. He caught my hair in his knot; when I made a sound he ignored it, breathing hard.

"We're going to do the same thing now, but blindfolded."

There was clearly no opportunity for discussion here. I stood holding the bat. I could feel the rings on its handle, designed for fingers to grip. I could feel the slightly wet earth beneath my feet, the heightened tension in my chest. The rush came suddenly. I felt my arms move quickly; a split second later came the thought to do something, after it was over. There was a crack as the bat hit the ball. I heard Joey's voice.

"Stay there," he said. "I'll get it."

I could hear the crunching of his feet. My whole body was electric. Thought completely suspended. I had just hit a ball square on without using my eyes. I heard the sounds of Joey's return. Then another ball. The whole thing happened so quickly. If I break it down, it sounds like a sequence of events. But it was all happening at the same time. The sound of the ball in flight. A thought, perhaps a clenching of fear, the ball might hit me. Instead of swinging the bat, I raised my arm to defend myself. The ball struck my elbow. Excruciating pain. My body crumpled. I dropped the bat. I lay on the ground, gripping the pain in my arm. Joey walked toward me. His voice was cold, crisp, militaristic.

"You have to focus. You have to focus. Stand up."

I did. "Joey, that really hurt."

"We can call this off right now," said Joey. "You can beat it out of here this afternoon. But if you're serious, you need to go all the way."

"I'll go on," I said, my arm throbbing. It would be severely bruised.

"You can't think," he said, cutting his words crisp and short. "You can't think. There's no room here for thought. You must focus. You must focus so clearly on this moment that nothing else exists. If you let yourself follow thought for even a second, the ball could be in your face."

My body convulsed. I felt sick and shocked and very cold.

"Focus," he said. "Focus so that the past and future die. Focus so that only this moment remains."

He placed the bat back in my hands. He walked away. My body was gripped with fear and excitement. I didn't know which was which. Then, somehow, the magic began. Ball after ball: whiz, the crack of bat meeting a hard ball. With every ball, I relaxed even more. I was pure thrill. Something, not me, would hit the ball. My chest was on fire. I was laughing, yelling sounds that echoed off the walls of the valley. I felt huge, filled with light, bursting. Finally, it stopped. He walked over, untied the bandanna and looked into my eyes.

"This is pure response," said Joey, "with no thought. This is how you will learn to live your life. No past, no future, no understanding. Action without thought. Learn to act before you think."

I grinned at him. "Thank God it's over," I said. "I was afraid I would be killed."

"It's not over," he said, "and you may be killed. That was just rehearsal."

He led me to the rock jutting out over the sheer drop of the cliff. I wanted to protest, but I knew it was no good. He stood me there, my back to the drop, my feet inches from the edge. It was either my life on the line or the bus home. He tied the bandanna over my eyes and walked back several paces. I tested the rock with my foot. It was not dry. I could easily slip, lose my balance, and fall. I remembered there were a few trees growing out of the steep drop. Would they catch me? I was blindfolded. Even if I missed with my swing, the ball would go sailing past my head into the valley, thousands of feet below. If I lost focus, as I had before, if the ball hit me, it would almost surely send me over the edge.

"Focus," I heard him say crisply. "Focus. It's no longer a game, Matt. Now it's your life. Take your time. You know the knack now. Find the current; find the place which knows what to do. Breathe deeply."

I breathed through the knot in my solar plexus. I breathed through my thoughts. Time stopped.

Then it happened.

The ball whistled, the response came, the crack, all in the same moment.

I don't know what to call it. Laughter, orgasm, joy, knowing the pure and original face of God? It's virtually impossible to describe that moment. I could try, but it would miss the essence of the thing. I knew. I absolutely knew that life was happening totally independently of my efforts and decisions and thoughts.

That was the last ball. He picked it up and removed the blindfold. He looked into my eyes and we embraced. He knew that I knew. We said nothing.

We walked back down the dirt path and then the dirt road, virtually in silence. Now and then Joey would stop to point out a bird or a tree. My whole body had changed. It was light, strong, determined. It moved from the belly on its own. I was not moving it; it knew. It was not re-sponding to the environment around it; it was absolutely a part of its environment, moved by its environment. It had returned to something more natural than I knew anything about.

Back to the house. Katie had made soup and bread. I said nothing; there was nothing to be said. I tasted the food, felt the people, felt my own body. Every movement was like the hands holding the bat with-out seeing the ball. Everything was moved and guided by a force which knew, unquestioningly, the next move.

CHAPTER 20

How About Now

I went outside after lunch and stacked wood. I gave myself to pure action, this human body a simple animal, engaged in simple tasks.

"Ready?" Joey asked quietly. I looked up. He must have come from around the corner of the shed and been standing there watching me.

"What now?" I asked. I was ready for anything.

"Let's head on back to the city."

There was a great to-do of good-byes on the front porch. Katie and Joey embraced again like newlyweds. Sam and Cheryl and Tim and all the others came one by one to send us off. Finally, we were back in Paul's Honda, plentifully equipped with cake wrapped in tin foil and other little snacks. Joey got started on them before we were even out of the driveway.

He said nothing for a while. I was driving the car just as I had held the bat, with a precision that left no room for thought.

"It's not over yet," he said finally.

I took a breath. "Okay, I'm ready."

"Keep digging for what is between you and perfection." He went back to his bag of nuts, seemingly uninterested in whether I accepted his challenge or not.

"Money," I began. "Money. It's all very well teaching me to hit a baseball with my eyes closed . . . "

" . . . while perched over a fourteen-hundred and eighty-three foot sheer drop," Joey added with relish.

"And it's great that you have somehow persuaded my wife that I am worthy of reconsideration, but I still have no money. And no prospect of any. That is my real problem, more than learning blind man's baseball. Until I can reenter the job stream, none of this really helps me too much. I've lost my house. I've lost my job. Unless I find a way to turn that around, in my books I have a problem."

"How about now?" asked Joey.

"What do you mean?"

"This moment, how is this moment?"

"This moment is fine. I'm driving home. In my friend's car. With a chocolate addict. But what about tomorrow, what about my family cooped up in Chicago? I'm really no closer to solving any of that."

"Now," said Joey, putting aside his food and straightening his spine. "Tell me about now," he said with military precision.

"Okay. We are driving the car."

"We?"

"Okay, I'm driving the car. You're holding a bag of nuts."

"And fruit," added Joey. "And Katie's chocolate cake. Want some?"

"No." "Not hungry?"

"No."

"Thirsty?"

"No, I'm fine."

"What else? Tell me about your body."

I radioed in to the poor creature. It had been pushed out of the scene for a while. "I can feel my belly. I can feel my breath."

"Got any life-threatening diseases?" Joey asked, chewing something.

"No, I feel good."

"Is there gas in the car?" To my surprise there was. The gauge was full. Must have been Katie.

"Are you too hot?" He looked at me with concern, reaching for the heater controls.

"No. I'm fine."

"Too cold?"

"No. I said I'm fine." I was getting irritated.

"Do you need to stop to pee?"

"No, I'm fine. Thank you, I'm fine."

"What about number two?" He grinned like a five-year-old.

"I told you I'm fine. If I need something I'll tell you. I'm fine. Fine. Great."

"Good," he said. He went back to chocolate-covered raisins for a minute or so.

"Are you tired? Do you need to rest?"

"No, I'm cool."

"We're in no hurry; you can have a nap if you need to."

"Listen, Joey, no nap, no food or drink or heat or cold or pee or . . . ," I paused, "number two needed. I am fine like this. Don't need anything. Okay?"

Joey went quiet. Looked hurt, reprimanded.

"Do you need some money?" he asked, pulling out his wallet.

"No, Joey, we have gas and you have food and I'm not hungry, I don't need any money."

"You sure?" he pressed, leaning toward me, offering a bunch of bills.

"Look," I was almost shouting. "What am I going to do with money in the middle of nowhere? There are no shops. And if there were, I don't need anything. What's gotten into you? I don't need anything."

Joey shrugged and put away his wallet. "I thought you said you had a problem with money," he mumbled.

"Yes, I do, but not now."

"Ah," said Joey, sounding confused. "When?"

"Well, later. Before. Generally. But not this moment. I don't need money right now."

He scrutinized my face, bewildered.

"So why were you thinking about it?"

"Well, it is something I have to take care of. It's a problem in my life."

"Hmm." He considered. "Are you sure?"

"Of course I'm sure. I need a job."

"How do you know?"

I was ready to hit him. This was idiotic. "I have a family. I have responsibilities. Of course I need to work. I need to get a job. Soon. Tomorrow."

"What's the evidence?"

"Joey, do you think I don't need to work? Are you suggesting I just drift along like this forever?"

"I suggest you be where you are. Here. Where you have told me with great conviction that you do not need anything. You've told me that a bunch of times. What happens to this drive, to being in the car, to this not needing anything, when you start thinking about money? Do you enjoy the ride more by bringing in your money story?"

I hesitated. Was this another trap? "No . . . " I said slowly, tentatively.

"Do you have more money by thinking these thoughts?"

"Of course not."

"What happens to you here when you think about all this? What happens to your body, to your being with me?"

"I guess I feel tense when I think about money. Everybody does."

"Everybody?"

"Most people."

"What most people do has never seemed to me a very good guide for how to live one's life," he mused. "Just look at how half of them just voted."

"Almost half. Bush did not get the popular vote. He stole the election."

"Try to just be here for a few minutes. Breathe. Feel your body; feel me with you. Crack the window a little and breathe the air." I did as he suggested. "And think about . . . " He hesitated for a moment, then smiled. "Sam."

And so we drove together in silence. I went back over Sam's confession of her life story to me the first day at the farm. I lingered on our embrace near the cabbage patch.

"How does that feel now?" He interrupted my reverie.

I took a breath. I felt alive, rested. The air in my nose and lungs felt refreshing.

"So what makes for a brighter day? Thinking about money, about a lack of something, or thinking about a beautiful woman? Or . . . ," he added as an afterthought, "just breathing and feeling this fine December day?"

I looked at him and did not need to answer. I conceded the round to him. Again. My breath was getting deeper and fuller, as though it were pushing out not only against the walls of the lungs, but the walls of the car, too. It pushed out into the ferns and trees beside the road.

"Feel all this. Feel your full belly. Feel your healthy body. Feel me here with you. Feel the full gas tank. Feel the power of the car, lunging forward as you touch the gas pedal. Feel this, this is life. Your wife and children are safe. They love you. Feel it." There was a pause. "Now tell me about this moment."

"My body feels good. I feel alive. I can feel you." In the saying of it, which was something of an experiment, I found that it was actually true.

"Good," he said. "Tell me about the texture of this moment. What do you bring to meet this?"

"I feel alive." I waited for more words to come. "I feel hungry and horny and ready to sing, all at the same time but with no desire for anything. Gratitude, I feel grateful."

"Yes," he said. "And in this is there any lack of money?"

A small, green, furry demon wanted to argue. But I was getting to know him by now. There was no way to win. Joey had reality on his side, and all my demon could bring to the contest were thoughts of past and future. It was a losing battle; my demon went back to sleep.

"Desire creates lack. Simple. The more you desire anything, money, love, security, anything, you manufacture a universe in that moment where it is missing. Without that thought you are already full, whole.

Desire is a disease. The antidote is the conscious practice of gratitude. Gratitude flips you into now. Into a now that is already full, and lays the foundation for greater and greater fullness. To be free you must learn to recognize the monkey mind. It is always jumping ahead and wanting something more. It skips over this, and so creates a precedent for a life of not enough. Dissolve desire through the practice of gratitude. Start now, and continue till you notice that your heart has stopped beating and your life is over.

"I've made money and given it all away more times than I can remember in my life. Money does not come to you from desire. Or if it does, it's like a whore, all show and no real satisfaction. Learn to sing 'Hallelujah' for what is here before your nose. I swear you will be given more than your desire could ever imagine."

We drove in silence, he nibbling, me feeling. The eternal battle between this, which is real, and the world of thought. A soft decision relaxed, in a moment out of time. What he was pointing me toward was not a hobby or a quick fix technique to accommodate my schemes for success. It was a death of how I had always lived. After some time he spoke again.

"You are doing well. Your training is almost done."

"How much more is there?" I asked.

"You need to finish all the lessons. The hardest are the last."

"How many have we done?"

He was silent. He looked out of the window. "Seven," he said finally. I tried to remember.

"Feel what you most resist, that was number one," he said. "Become the other, number two. Just like me, three. The real teacher, four."

"What about the first night I met you?" I interjected.

"That doesn't count. The remembering is grace. Not to forget takes practice." He paused, and nibbled on something. "Now, where were we? Ah yes, Drop the past, five. Act without thought, six.

"Blind man's baseball?"

"Yep. And practice gratitude, that's seven."

"How many are there altogether?"

He paused for a good time while nibbling on nuts. Like he couldn't remember. When he did answer, it sounded random, like he was picking a number out of the air to satisfy me.

"Ten."

CHAPTER 21

Chocolate Chocolate-Chip Cheesecake

"Pull over here," said Joey. I was surprised at his choice. The Terrace is a fashionable up-market restaurant, about 40 minutes out of town, just off the road. It has magnificent views of the surrounding canyon, thickly covered with trees. The walls on all sides are glass, floor to ceiling, with no interior walls, so wherever you sit you feel you are flying over a forest.

Joey strode into the restaurant, straight past the sign requesting guests to wait to be seated, with the air of a man who has just bought the whole place. He stopped at a table where a couple in their 50s were dining with a young man and woman. The young man looked impatient, brewing a fight for later. Had to be their son, the resemblance was striking. The older woman was obviously disapproving of everything. The young woman looked nervous, fiddling with a diamond ring, ready to do handstands at the drop of a hat, if that would help her chances of being accepted. Must be the prospective daughter-in-law.

"Are you enjoying your lunch?" Joey asked the elder lady. She assented dismissively, but that did not dissuade Joey. "How are the fries?" he went on.

"They're just fine, thank you," the woman replied curtly.

"Yep," said Joey. "I like 'em crispy. Now you look like the kind of woman who's never going to be happy in a restaurant." Everyone at the table tightened. "Because I bet you know you could always do better at home."

The woman's manner changed completely. She looked up into Joey's eyes, as though he were announcing himself as her long-lost brother. On he went. "I can tell a good cook a mile away, because all the men in her life look well fed and well loved. You could put these fries to shame any day of the week, couldn't you?"

She flushed. Joey bent down and took a couple of fries from her plate and put them in his mouth. She looked up at him in wonder, and pushed the plate toward him in case he wanted more.

"She's got a world of good things to teach you, my dear," he said to the younger woman. "She knows the secret to making a man happy." He did that funny thing with his eyebrow. The younger woman leapt into an animated monologue, as though she had been waiting for her cue at a school play. "Oh yes, Maude is a wonderful cook." She flashed a nervous smile at Maude, and giggled. "Dan loves his mother so much, and I feel so lucky to be joining this family. She's also a really wonderful seamstr—"

Joey moved on, leaving the table in electrified confusion. His next stop was a table where an overweight couple was sitting with their five overweight children, all fighting indiscriminately among themselves. Both parents looked exhausted—with each other, with the whole chaos they had landed for themselves. The man was wearing a very loud sweatshirt, Christmas greetings blazing from it in neon letters, in every language known to man.

"Now that, sir, is a magnificent garment," said Joey. The wife beamed, as if to say, "See, I knew it was a good choice." The kids stopped and stared up at Joey in fascination.

"Your Dad is a great man," Joey went on. "I admire him more than . . . ," he made big eyes at the oldest child, only about eight, " . . . Superman." The child took a sudden sharp in-breath. "Make very, very sure," Joey bent toward the child in a conspiratorial whisper, "that you do everything he tells you to do. That's important, if your mission here on Earth is to succeed." The father straightened his back and knitted his brows, trying to remember where he had met Joey before, coming up with nothing.

"And," Joey went on, looking at the wife, "he's easily the best-dressed man in this whole joint." She shuddered a little and looked rapturous.

And so we finally found ourselves an empty table, right in the middle of the restaurant, and sat down. Joey looked back at the five kids and waved. The table near the entrance where Joey had taken the fries was by now bubbling with animated laughter.

"Ah," said Joey. "God, I love humanity."

The waitress arrived with our menus.

"Good afternoon, gentlemen." She greeted us in a thick Australian accent. In her early 20s, she was beautiful and buxom. Her blonde hair was tied back into a little ponytail, she had bright blue eyes, a freckly nose, and a strong athletic body. She had the look of a woman who had grown up with Marlboro men, and had wrestled many a fully-grown kangaroo to the ground, laughing all the while. As she bent down to clear the dishes from the table, Joey looked unabashedly down her white shirt at the top of her full brown breasts.

"Beautiful," he murmured, like an art connoisseur at an exhibition. "Just beautiful."

The waitress stood up again, dishes in hand, and smiled, cocking her head to one side. A healthy clean country smile. "Well, thank you," she grinned, as though she were just done with shearing 200 sheep and taking a break before doing more. "A girl does sure like to be appreciated."

"No, thank you, dear," said Joey. "Your radiant and alive beauty has brightened my whole day. You are like a beautiful painting." His gaze was unashamed, as he took in her whole body with complete relish.

We ordered. A cup of tea each. Joey also wanted dessert, and insisted on hearing in detail about every item. He settled on chocolate

chocolate-chip cheesecake. "And do you suppose you could manage that smothered with hot fudge sauce?" he asked. He tickled her with the word *smothered.* I writhed.

"Oh, I dare say we could do that for you," she joked back. "Anything else now?"

"Marry me!" said Joey.

The waitress left, looking quite perky. I was seething. Joey looked back at me in surprise.

"Got a problem?" he asked, raising an eyebrow.

"How can you talk to women like that?" I blurted. "I mean, you were looking at her like an object."

"Hmmm," said Joey considering. Then he smiled back at me. "But a very beautiful one!"

"Yes, but she's a human being, not just a sex symbol."

"Well, isn't she a beautiful human being?"

"Yes, she's gorgeous, stunning, but that doesn't mean that you can just stare right down her blouse."

"Why not?" said Joey. "That's what everyone is doing, in their minds. And secretly, that's what every woman wants: for her beauty, both inner and outer, to be relished. When her beauty is overlooked, she dies a small death every moment."

I had gotten heavily steeped in feminism at college, and he was committing every politically incorrect chauvinist blunder that had been hammered out of me by various girlfriends. "Well, aren't you making some sweeping generalizations? Don't men want to be appreciated for their beauty, too? Don't women want to be appreciated for their brains and beliefs, and not just their breasts?" I was indignant now.

"Sure, every one of us has masculine and feminine energy. But the trouble with your present generation is you have mixed it all up. Men and women are different. Their bodies are shaped differently, just in case you hadn't noticed. And their psyches are shaped differently, too. A man has about thirty times more testosterone in his body than a woman does. And the woman, she has way more oxytocin. So you see, the average man's life is more bound up with breaking through barriers and accomplishment, whereas most women identify more with being beautiful. If you want to support a man to feel his deepest essence, talk about what he has accomplished. If you want to do the same for a woman, notice her inner beauty."

The waitress returned with our cups of tea. "Here you go, gentlemen!"

"Thank you, my dear," said Joey. He took her hand. "Tell me," he said. "My friend here is very upset that I complimented you on your lustrous beauty. Did it disturb you? How did you feel about it?"

The waitress seemed amused. "Well . . . frankly, I rather liked it. I mean, there are not too many men around who are that honest. You know, direct. I like that. Reminds me of home."

"Ahh," said Joey, reflecting seriously. "Yes, very direct people, the Australians. And how does it feel to be living inside such a young and alive body?"

Now the waitress was more than amused. She flushed. "Mmmm . . . " she made the tiniest sounds with her out-breath. "Well, it feels great, actually! I love to be in my body. I am just doing this job for the money, you know. I am really here in the States for the skiing."

"Yes, skiing," said Joey, "I used to love to ski, too. Too old now, mind you. I am sure that your radiant healthy body gives you a lot of pleasure."

"Well, yes, it does."

"And you give me pleasure, too." He paused. "My friend finds you beautiful, too," he said. "But he'd rather not tell you about it."

"Oh well," said the waitress, "sounds like most men." She smiled at me. "You'd better let your mate here give you some training in girly appreciation, he's a pro." She turned and left.

"I can't believe you, Joey," I blurted.

He was right, I had to admit it; he was only saying and doing what every man feels, but keeps hidden.

"See, the way you are with a woman is just like you are with all of life. One mirrors the other. If you hold back, if you are half-assed, life will turn from you and close to you. If you give everything of yourself," Joey swept his hand to indicate the whole restaurant, and the canyon beyond, too, "she reveals her deeper beauty to you. All of life is just one huge beautiful woman. You have to learn to love her deeply, all the time. Find her ticklish spots, tease her, notice her infinite beauty, and tell her again and again and again."

The waitress came back from the kitchen with Joey's cheesecake. She was standing behind him, waiting for the right moment to interrupt.

"Kiss her, lick her, bite her. Give her everything you have. Whisper sweet nothings in her ear. She is craving for your presence. Give everything to her in every moment, like there has never been any other moment, and there will never be. She is screaming for you to make love to her."

The waitress didn't move a muscle. I was making little eye movements to Joey, a pained expression on my lips. I was dying.

"Huh-hmmm," said the waitress, transfixed. "Here we go." She gave him his cheesecake. "Extra chocolate sauce. Can I get anything else for you?"

Joey looked up, with a twinkle in his eye that would eclipse the northern star. "I'll let you know, my dear."

She laughed. I could feel her opening to Joey like a rose. It annoyed me that he could bring her out like this with his crudities. She tore herself away from him.

"Now it's your turn," said Joey. I groaned, wondering what could possibly be next. "This is the eighth lesson," he went on. "You're almost done."

"Have a look around the restaurant. Tell me what you see."

I glanced around. "I see people. I see the view of the canyon. I see the Christmas tree in the corner."

"No," said Joey, "look at specific people, tune in. Feel the people, feel their fears and pains and hopes and unsung dreams." I looked again. I saw a young couple, sitting next to the window. They were not talking, just looking down at their empty teacups.

"Well, that couple over there, they, ah, they don't know what to say."

"Exactly," said Joey. "They are sitting in withholding. Look deeper; what is he holding back?"

When I looked again, it was as though the scene now offered more information.

"He is angry. He is disappointed. He is jealous. He could cry."

"Exactly, see, it is all there. What else? What about her?"

"Well, she is guilty about something; she wants to say 'sorry' to him."

"What is she guilty about?"

"I don't know."

"Yes, you do. Feel her with your body."

"She is ashamed. She cheated on him."

"Of course. That wasn't very difficult, was it? Now, what do they need? What would bring more love, more space? How could you caress them with your total heart?"

"I guess they need to let go and feel that they love each other."

"Right. Okay. See that vase of flowers over there by the entrance?" I looked. Sure enough, there it was. "Okay, when no one is looking, go take a flower, give it to them, and tell them that you can feel the love between them."

"But I can't feel the love between them."

"Exactly. That is where you can bring your gift. Do you think I actually liked that guy's shirt? Give a little." He paused. "Now." He glared at me.

In agony, I forced myself to get up and sidle over to the flowers. Looking around like a pickpocket, I slipped a flower out of the vase, took a huge breath, and strode over to my prey.

"Excuse me." They looked up, startled. "I'm so sorry to disturb you like this." I grinned stupidly. "And I know this must seem rather unusual. But my friend and I . . . ," I cleared my throat sounding theatrical. "We were just remarking on how much . . . um . . . well, you know . . . um . . . . love we felt between you. And in grateful appreciation, no I mean in . . . um . . . celebration . . . " God, I sound like an idiot. " . . . We would like to present you with this . . . um . . . er . . . rather small rose."

There was a stunned silence. They both stared at me in shock. They looked at each other. The man turned panicky for a moment. He scanned the room, as if looking for law enforcement. Then he spoke.

"Well, thanks. Actually, we really needed someone to say something just like that today." He laughed nervously.

"Yes, how totally sweet of you," she added. She almost sang the word *sweet*. She had a cultured voice. "Such an unusual gesture."

They looked at each other and she reached for his hand.

"Well, good," I said. "Um . . . mission accomplished. I mean, good luck to both of you." They both smiled and I beat a retreat back to Joey, kicking myself.

"Good," said Joey.

"Thank God that's over with." I slumped back into my chair.

"What do you mean? That was just a warm-up. Look around, what else do you see?"

"No, Joey, really, I am not very good at this."

"I know," he replied. "That's why you need practice. What else do you see?"

Reluctantly, I scanned the room again. There were probably 50 tables in all. And then, on the far side of the restaurant, I saw something I could not believe. Bruce Pushar, the man who forced me from my job, and Will Thurston, the owner of KYQD, were engrossed in a fierce argument.

"My God," I said to Joey. "My old boss is there with the man he hired who pushed me out."

"Pushar and Thurston?" Joey had an amazing memory. "Nope," he said, absolutely unimpressed by the coincidence that they were here at all. "That's too advanced for you right now. Pick another table, look for someone else."

All kinds of feelings swirled in my chest. So there they were, the man who had most blessed my life, and the one I held partially responsible for ruining it. But obediently, I moved on.

Two teenage girls sat in the corner. They wore heavy makeup and tight sweaters with plunging neck lines. I could see platform shoes under the table. "Well, those two girls look bored, like they are waiting for life to begin. They are pretending that they are above it all, but actually they are dead scared."

"Pretty good," said Joey. "You forgot to mention they are both virgins and obsessed with getting laid." Now that Joey mentioned it, I saw that he was right. It was written all over them.

"So what do they most need?"

"Sex?" I offered.

"No," said Joey. "They are young tender flowers. That's what they want but not what would most open them." Once he put it that way, I looked beyond the layers of makeup and provocative clothing, and also felt their innocence. "No, they just want to feel wanted," he continued. "Okay, so go and ask them to go out with us."

"Joey, no, absolutely not."

"Do it," Joey said. He looked at his watch and started to read the menu. The unspoken message was clear. This was day seven. I was running out of time. I was failing my eighth lesson.

So I just did it. Like pulling a Band-Aid off a hairy part of one's body, I strode straight over.

"Well, hello there, girls!" They looked up. The one facing me sneered just a little. Her expression said "weirdo," but I braved on anyway. "My friend and I noticed how gorgeous you both are, and we were wondering if you would grace us," I was on a roll now, "with the pleasure of your company." There, done. Still alive. Just.

"You what?" said Sneery.

Her friend was obviously more of a gambler. She had more acne spots on her face than I had ever seen. The makeup did a poor job of hiding them. "Where's your friend?"

"He's the . . ." What was the best adjective here? " . . . mature gentleman sitting over there."

"Him?" said Acne, disappointed.

"You've got to be fucking joking," said Sneery. "Piss off."

"Well, thank you for your time. Have a nice day." I walked back.

"They turned us down," I reported.

"'Course they did. What did you expect?"

"Then why have me do that?"

"Not to spend the evening with them. Have a look now. How are they doing?" I looked over. They glanced at me, but immediately looked away. They were talking to each other and laughing. They looked happy.

"See, you don't give a damn to get something. You give a damn to give. To add color where it is missing. You just made their day. You just allowed them to feel desirable and beautiful. Now look at your other handiwork." He gestured to the first couple with his eyes. She was crying big tears into her empty teacup, and he was caressing her hands, obviously pouring forth forgiveness.

"Now how do you feel?" he asked me.

I checked in. I was surprised. "I feel alive," I admitted. "I feel open."

"Exactly," said Joey. "You become what you give. This is the eighth lesson. Be generous with yourself. Make love to life in all her forms. All the time."

Our waitress brought the bill. "This one's on me," said Joey and pulled out his wallet.

Just at that moment, Pushar and Thurston rose from their table. They were still involved in their dispute. I realized they would have to walk straight past our table to make it to the entrance. I braced myself.

Thurston saw me before Pushar did.

"Matt, is that you?" he said. He looked worried and angry. Pushar stood beside him, sullen.

"Hello, Will," I replied. "Good to see you." I ignored Pushar, just as he was ignoring me.

"I was just hearing," he breathed deeply, "among other things, that you are no longer with the station. And I'm sorry to hear that, Matt. I always thought you were the best we had to offer." Pushar flushed. His lip quivered.

"Yes, I'm sorry, too. I've missed you, Will. How have you been?"

"Hawaii has been good to Carol and me. Gave me a complete break from the station." He paused and added in a lower voice, "which was perhaps not such a great idea after all."

He turned to Joey, apologetically. "Will Thurston, KYQD." He extended his hand to Joey, who grabbed it with enthusiasm. "And this is Bruce Pushar, our station manager," he added reluctantly.

"KYQD?" said Joey. "Ah yes. Joey Murphy." He paused, and added very slowly, with a sparkle, "KYSH. KYSH."

"Really?" replied Will in surprise. "KYSH, eh? So what do you think of our Matt here?"

Joey looked over at me, sizing me up as though we had just met for the first time. "Matt," he said thoughtfully, "is one of the most inspiring people I have ever met. He has a heart to ignite the world." There was a pregnant silence.

Will and Pushar offered a few more pleasantries, and then left. As they made their way out of the restaurant, I could see that Will was even more angry with Pushar, who was cowering at his side.

"KYSH is his main competitor, Joey. It's a radio station. He thought I was being courted by the enemy."

"Really?" he replied, looking bored. "Innocent mistake."

CHAPTER 22

DARK NIGHTS

We got back to the city, still in its post-Christmas repose, that evening. Joey slept most of the way after we left the restaurant. I drove him to West Broad Street and stopped the car. Without opening his eyes, he spoke.

"Go home. Get some grapes and some water. Then go up to your room. And sit still. Don't read, don't write, don't meditate, don't exercise, don't go out, don't talk to anyone. Sleep when you need to, otherwise just sit there and wait. With your eyes open. Eat once tomorrow, in the middle of the day. And come to the meeting in the evening. Don't use a watch. I will arrange for someone to collect you and bring you there." He opened his eyes, looked at me with an empty expression, and casually added, "Good luck." With that he got out of the car, pulled his bag from the back seat, and was off down the alley.

I went to bed that night looking forward to a couple days' rest. This must be a pause in the training. I had done well, passed all the tests, and deserved a break. Three more days, two more lessons, and it's over. Then who knows? Perhaps just better luck. For now, I was happy to be home,

ARJUNA ARDAGH

like Ulysses after his voyage. I sat on my foam pad for a while, quite content with my spartan surroundings. I felt like a monk. Finally I slept.

All would have been well, had it not been for the dream. I was in a hotel somewhere by the sea. An old world building, wooden panels half-way up the walls, flowery wallpaper above. Genteel. I was checking in at the reception desk, when I saw my parents there. My father was fussing with the locks on the luggage, my mother discreetly eyeing herself in a mirror, patting at her cheek with a very clean handkerchief. When they saw me, they tried to look the other way, in confusion. Finally, they reluctantly said, "Hello." I wanted to rush to them, throw my arms around my mother's neck, hug my Dad after so many years. But they were acting so cold to me; I held back, in resonance.

"I thought you were dead," was all I could find to say to them. My father looked at the floor, very seriously. My mother looked away, on the edge of tears, waiting for my father to do what he had to do. He was bundled, as always, against the cold in the purple scarf and hat she had knitted for him. She had a runny nose, which she frequently dabbed with her handkerchief. Not the one I had given her, with the pink flowers. Another one. He told me they had faked their death.

"Why, why?" I asked. I looked back and forth between them. I tried smiling, hoping it was a joke.

My mother turned her body toward me, stepped closer to my father, and pushed her head slightly in my direction. "We were ashamed of you."

I woke up in a panic. It was still before dawn. My heart beat violently. I felt like throwing up. *It's only a dream,* I tried to tell myself; *it's not real.* I lay down again in my sleeping bag. Sleep would not return. My parents died years ago. They loved me, in their own way.

I felt as though a piece of decayed meat were stuck in one of my many digestive tubes. I pressed down on my belly with my hand. It was like a rock. My spine was aching, my body sweating, but very cold. The pillow was cold; the wall behind my head was cold; the sleeping bag was cold. I tried to keep totally still in the darkness, seeking desperately for the gentle oblivion of sleep. Somewhere, I knew there was a door, somewhere within the confusing corridors of my memory and mania, a door that would lead me back to soft sheets, to the caress of forgiveness, the grace of a fresh start. But there was no returning for me. It was cold. I was alone.

"Think of something nice, dear. Think of all your blessings." My mother would console me as a child. Just her caring could send me back to sleep after a bad dream.

"Mummy," I whispered into the darkness, into the silence. I closed my eyes, my mind racing to try to remember how to get home, how to feel safe again. I tried relaxing my body, little by little. The big toe of the left foot, the underneath of the left foot. Some bright and confident woman with flashing earrings, perfume smelling like polyurethane varnish, had assured me this would work, on the radio years before. But here in my cold attic, before I could even reach the knee, an image would flash, a thought of money, or Dominic, or Sarah, and my belly would clench again.

I could feel in my chest the longing to scream, the desperation for release, like trying to break free from under a heavy blanket.

I sat up in the bed. Turned my head as far as I could to the left, to look at the wall behind me, stretching my spine. Then the other way. Better. Do not get pulled in. Swim. Fight. Be strong. It was getting lighter in the room. I could see the grapes, washed and in Paul's cracked bowl on my makeshift table. This was the morning of day eight. Three whole days more. I could breathe again. Three days, new lessons, new insights. Joey seemed pleased enough with my progress. "Just trust him," Sam had said. I breathed.

The night before had been easy. The grapes were on sale, left over from Christmas feasting. I got five pounds for a few dollars. I joked with the cashier, flirted even. Paul was home, bless him. Engrossed in his slow zooms of nuclear reactors. I gave him a vase I had made with Cheryl. He asked me no questions, for once. Perhaps he sensed he was sparing me the need to lie. I left the keys on the dresser. Paul had bought me a small picture for my attic room, an Ansel Adams print. As I climbed the stairs, I had a spring in my step. I folded all my clothes neatly onto the makeshift shelves, preparing for my appointment with grace.

The clothes were still folded now, behind the grapes. The light was enough to see everything as gray in the room. It was no use. Don't meditate, he said, and don't write. What the fuck do you expect me to do then?

It was no use.

I'd never had a chance anyway. My father was a weak man, my mother withdrawn. They had loved me, their only son, and then they died. My whole life I had been desperately swimming in turbulent waters, using all my energy to avoid drowning. Never a fighting chance.

I stared at the wall ahead of me. Be careful not to meditate. Fight for some mood of optimism. But it was all in vain.

When I was a child, we found a small bird one day, my mother and I. It had probably been attacked by a cat or a raccoon, she said, but abandoned before the killing was fully done. I was only six at the time. I begged to take it in. One wing was broken, useless, one leg was gone. I fed the bird milk by the fireplace from a medicine dropper. It could not move. I made it a bed in a shoe box, out of cotton wool. It had tiny insects crawling in and out of the feathers. It was starting to smell strange.

By the time my father came home, we had developed an understanding, that bird and me. I was its lifeline, its only hope. I would not give up, I would be there no matter what. I talked to it, whispered affirmations and Bible quotes. My parents huddled in the kitchen, obviously in some kind of a dispute. I could hear their terse whispers as I sang to my bird. Finally my father called my name, "Matthew." I knew when he called me "Matthew" it was serious. His somber voice carried tidings of disappointment or death. He chose his words carefully, treading with caution on my love affair.

"Sometimes we have to do things we don't like, Matthew," he began cautiously. Not the bird. "You've done a kind thing here, my boy. You have shown caring to a hurt creature." Not the bird, please not the bird. "But sometimes we have to end suffering to be kind, Matt. We have to be cruel to be kind." Not the bird, anything but my bird, Dad. "Matt, when a creature is weak and has no defenses, it cannot survive." I did not watch as he did something brutal to my bird in the garage, or as my mother gave him a small plastic bag to put the body in the garbage. Later that evening, he told me about Darwin and evolution, by the fire, in my pajamas.

When a creature is small and has no more defenses, it cannot survive. And what defenses do I have left now, Father? All gone. You are dead now. I have never made any real contribution. Even the radio show, just riding on others' greatness and gifts. A parasite hiding in the wings of people with nobility and mission. I have never even made enough to support the family. We got by with Mafia-funded hand-me-downs.

I got lost in mental arithmetic. If I could persuade Becca and the kids to come home, how much would I need to make to rent a small apartment? Could the kids share a room? Would they? They never have had to before. Food. Four hundred. Three-fifty, if we relax the organic thing. Eat simply. I could work anywhere. Drive a bus. What do they pay? Does it give dental? Remember *American Beauty* . . . Kevin Spacey got a job at a burger place. I could do that. Live simply. We can. The kids' activities. Soccer. Could I still afford the soccer? How would Dom take it if I couldn't? My mind was spinning. My world was collapsing again.

Thoughts. These are all thoughts. These are not real. Just remember that. It was full daylight now. Sunshine through the window. I was sitting in an attic room thinking thoughts. Crazy thoughts. My mind, that's all. It's not reality.

I stood up. I'm 34 years old. I have a degree. I stretched from one side to the other, felt the aching in the muscles. I made a mistake, that's all. A simple mistake. Born more of benevolence than malice. A deep breath into the belly.

There are clean clothes on the shelf. Another breath into the belly. I changed into fresh jeans, T-shirt, sweater. I brushed my hair. Straightened out the bag on the mattress, sat down, and ate some grapes. All thoughts. I smiled. Amazing that I can get caught like that. I remembered being sick when I was a child. My mother gave me grapes. We'd watch Mr. Rogers on TV. Things will be all right. There's a meeting tonight. Still two more lessons to go. I'll see Cheryl and Sam and Maryanne. They'll help me. Maybe one of them can even give me a job. I never asked. There's hope. Now I'm back in the yurt again at that meeting. I never shared. Only gave feedback. I need a job, so I can get my family back. I should have shared. They would have given suggestions. I missed the boat. That chance will never come again. All ruined now. Thoughts.

Don't give in. These are thoughts. Just remember. Thoughts, not reality. Feel this moment now.

The day passed. Sitting, lying, stretching, waiting. Thinking, getting lost, coming back. I ate grapes now and then, trying to remember that they had to last. Lonely meandering visits into hell, hating myself as much as my life. Desperate plans for restitution. And every now and then stepping back from the madness, all thought, only my mind. A moment of peace. A moment of just the room.

I tried to remember all Joey's lessons. There were so many. I felt lost. I remembered "Just like me." I tried to think of people I hated. Pushar, dominating, stupid, greedy, just like me. My father-in-law, angry, frustrating, untrusting, just like me. I tried closing my eyes and throwing a ball of socks into the air, to see if I could catch it with my eyes closed. Time passed. I kept trying to remember.

It must have been mid-afternoon when I started to get excited about going out. Like a child before a treat. I ate grapes greedily, planning the questions I would ask Joey. Surely he would call me in afterward. I thought up elaborate questions about destiny and free will, about collective consciousness. Some became burningly urgent. Write them down. Where's a pen, where's paper? No. Not allowed. So if we are really just this consciousness, then who is making all this happen? What about God, is that the way that the unmanifest, undifferentiated source of creation becomes manifest when it—

A knock on the door. It was dark outside already. I was sitting thinking, lost in my questions. It was Paul. He handed me a note, in his spidery handwriting, and stared at the ground. "I am your driver tonight. I will take you to the meeting."

Paul was taking his role very seriously. He pursed his lips and gestured to my jacket. I wanted to kiss him, tell him what a wonderful man, a wonderful friend he was. I squeezed his arm. He looked apologetically into my eyes for just a split second, and then took a step, very soberly, toward the staircase, like a policeman in Stalinist Russia obliged to arrest his brother. He descended ahead of me, his great weight swaying from one leg to another. I could hear his heavy breathing, as I followed him down. To me, he was my emancipator.

"But Paul, you've got to tell me, I mean how did this happen? How do you know where to go, what time? Just tell me that." We weaved our way through the evening traffic. His great frame was packed into the Honda's modest accommodations as though he were sitting in an infant car seat. He made a noise on the exhale each time he changed gears. Finally, when we stopped at the light on Channon and Broad, with more grunts he rescued a paper and pen from his pocket, and scribbled a few words. Eyes still averted, he handed it to me. "He called me on the phone today." The light changed, another grunt and we were on our way.

"But Paul, you've got to tell me, I mean you were so down on him. Told me not to go see him." Paul looked pained at my disobedience of the rules. "Just tell me Paul, I mean what happened?" I was laughing, we were almost at Alan's now. Who cared about rules? I was with my old friend, driving to my new friends. I felt good. "Just tell me that Pauly, and I'll shut up, I promise."

Paul parked the car. Another growl. He slowly maneuvered himself, with great effort, out of the seat and onto the street. Still avoiding my eyes, he stopped at the entrance to Joey's alley. Looked around for street numbers. Under the streetlamp he struggled again for pencil and paper. More laborious huffing and puffing as he wrote another note. He passed it to me as one might give a cigarette to an addict, and waddled off down the alley. I read it before following him: "He knows Coppola."

I followed Paul up the faded staircase. Alan was doing his best to embrace Paul at the top landing, his arms barely reaching around Paul's body, like one of those postcards of someone trying to hug an old growth redwood tree, just to show you how big it is. Paul was all smiles and pleasantries, now that his mission was complete. I waited my turn for Alan's embrace, but as soon as Paul had been separated from his shoes and ushered into the room, Alan's manner changed completely. He looked at me without a flicker of recognition, turned abruptly, and was gone. I felt a sudden searing sensation in my chest. I looked around desperately for a friendly face but found none. Things didn't get any easier as I stepped into the room. I felt like a picket breaker at a union meeting, or a snitch in jail. Those who didn't have their eyes closed when I walked in closed them immediately as soon as I tried to make eye contact. I took a seat and closed my own eyes, hoping my calm demeanor would hide the chaos in my heart.

After some minutes Joey came into the room, and everyone and everything became silent, except for the questions in my mind. What evil had I done? I could not keep my eyes closed for very long; involuntarily they opened every minute or so, to check on what was happening in the room. I shifted my position from cross-legged to kneeling to straight out in front. Joey began speaking. Sam was sitting against the other wall, wearing a soft pink woolen sweater. Any hopes that I still had an ally there were soon dashed. She refused to meet my eyes.

As the meeting drew to a close, all became clear to me. They were jealous. Joey had probably given me more attention in the last few days than any of them had in years. Perhaps ever. It was so obvious now. They had talked among themselves, since we got back from the farm. I was the new upstart, stealing the show. Perhaps his chosen heir. What do they call that? Lineage holder. People are so petty, so transparent. Couldn't they understand that this is about love and freedom, not just satisfying their petty desires to be in the teacher's good graces? Once the meeting was over, Joey would usher me into the back room, and give me some deeper dimensions of the teaching. They would have to go home with his mere public appearance.

Finally Joey stood up. He grinned at Paul, and slowly left the room. His eyes never met mine. That was all the confirmation I needed. He didn't want to make their jealousy any worse than it was. I sat quite calmly and waited for the cue that I knew would come. Any moment now Alan would reluctantly call me in.

Sure enough, he left the room; and sure enough he poked his head back in a couple minutes later. I was ready, just getting to my feet. "Paul," he said, in his amiable British voice, raising his eyebrows and his chin just a little. "He'd love a word, if you have the time." Paul struggled to his feet, looking surprised. He started across the room; I stood up to follow him. So it was to be the two of us. I was looking forward to this.

"Not you, Matt. He just asked for Paul." Hot tears welled behind my eyes. He's interfering. Alan's jealousy is actually interfering and distorting.

I know how easy Joey is to manipulate, he'll say yes to anything. So I followed Paul anyway. "Matt," said Alan sternly. "Did you hear me, mate?" His voice was crisp now. "Just. Paul."

I glared at him. My lips quivered. I swallowed hard. Alan partially blocked my way. Paul turned for a moment and hesitated. He leaned forward slightly toward me, as though there was something he really wanted to say but was afraid to be overheard. He wore his discomfort like a straightjacket for all to see. But Alan just tightened his grip on the situation. Feigning a pleasant exterior, he smiled at Paul.

"C'mon then, lad, let's not keep him waiting." Alan glared at me again. Paul was gone, back into Joey's room, and I was left with my opponent. He raised his eyebrows slightly, closed his eyes for a moment, and breathed out through his nose. He started picking up cushions from the floor and stacking them. The room was empty, except for the two of us.

My mouth trembled with emotion. I stared at the carpet as Alan cleaned the room. Without looking up at him, I made a last appeal. "Alan, I really need to see Joey." I waited. My heart pounded. I wanted to cry or vomit. Alan was still busy. I noticed that the flowers in the corner of the room were not evenly distributed in the vase, and went over to straighten them, on my hands and knees. I would win my favors through servitude, if that was what was needed. I lifted out some of the flowers, long slender orchids. The stem of the longest caught the tip of the vase. The vase fell and broke. Water everywhere. Alan stopped, turned and looked at me, on my hands and knees, water and flowers and pieces of vase all around me. "I need to see Joey," was all I could find by way of explanation, as though my ineptitude at flower arranging was the proof he had been waiting for.

Alan said nothing. He went to Joey's door, I followed. He knocked. I could hear Paul laughing inside the room. "Sorry, guv," said Alan, poking his head through the opening, "but Matt is hoping for a word."

"Eh?" I heard Joey's voice from inside. "He's still here? Tell him to go home, tell him to do what I told him." Alan turned to me, widened his eyes, raised his eyebrows and pursed his lips.

I turned away, knowing only hatred. I could have waited. I thought about it. But my whole body was electric; I could not keep still for a moment.

As I ventured into the alley, the door closed hard behind me. Call it a slam. I didn't care. It was a cool night but dry. I began to walk fast, breathing deeply. As I turned the corner of West Broad Street I passed a Coke can someone had thrown there. I crushed it with my foot. "Hate. Fuck. Hate," I chanted as I splashed through the gutters. I saw only dirt and rotten things. A dead cat next to a garbage bin. "Leave me alone," repeated itself, like a hammer on stone, for blocks. "I hate you." Three youths were sauntering toward me on Clarindon Street. Black jackets, chains, menacingly short hair. One spoke, out of my earshot. The others laughed. A rush through my body. Fear and hate. I'm ready to die, bring it on. I walked directly toward them, staring ahead. They parted to let me through.

I could feel the tightness in my jaw as I clutched the hand rail of the bus. The driver smiled this time, and I tossed coins into his cold money machine. "Fuck you, you miserable loser," I said with my eyes. He withered.

As I climbed the stairs to my attic room, more than grapes and a sleeping bag and pictures of Peru awaited me. It came in waves. I desperately tried to block it in my chest.

I lay in the cold darkness, my body innocent like a baby, craving rest. Give me comfort. Give me breast milk. The horror sent spasms through my tortured belly. The clenching left me on the edge of retching the whole night. I would feel pulled for a few minutes into welcome oblivion, and then an image would come, just a fleeting thought, sending spasms of pain back through all of me. It was not as I had thought. One could only laugh now, or better, weep at my delusions of grandeur. They were not jealous. They saw through my trumped-up self-importance. Nothing, nothing, I was left with nothing. Children, wife, best friend, the man I had trusted these days as a teacher, all gone, all dust. All quicksand upon which I had been building my house. My body finally dropped into sleep, and threw me into a toxic dream, wild parties, hundreds of writhing naked bodies, rubbing against each other, but not for me, the outcast. I woke up in a cold sweat.

It must be morning. Tortured long enough. Switch on the light, find something to do. 2 A.M. It had come down to this. Nothing. Fooled by a madman, his shallow tricks just thimbles offered in cruel jest to bail out my sinking boat. I sat. I tried to retch. It had always been this way. I remembered interviewing a biologist on the radio. It's all in the genes. The DNA. Nothing you can do. Predetermined from birth, the hand you are dealt. Mine, all low cards. The two of clubs for weakness of resolution. The three of hearts for an endless destiny of betrayal. The two of spades, all effort just digging a deeper grave. Genes. Biology. I am the product of biology. Hopeless.

When my parents died it made the headline news in every country, suspected terrorism. They never knew for sure. They were flying back from burying my grandfather. A weak man, the death certificate said he died of heart failure; those who knew him would call it a more generic habit of failure, an oblivion to all passion. My parents carried back the urn as hand luggage, together with their inheritance of mutually supported weakness. My mother was asthmatic. Always wanted a bigger family, but the strain on her frail body of giving birth to me had almost killed her. I would have had a brother, Philip, but she had a miscarriage at seven months and almost died. The doctors told her she was playing Russian roulette to try again. So it was, she lived out her life in timid resignation to the limits of her body and her fear.

My father was an engineer, worked for a big airplane manufacturer. Gave my mother just the formula of security and regular routine that would allow her to survive the day, but nothing more than that, no direction, no mission, no higher purpose to admire. He wore sensible thermal underwear under his button-down shirts and long-sleeved cardigans. His wire-rimmed glasses were the only bridge he had to the outside world. They were as fragile as his self-confidence. A hearty slap on the back would shatter them into a thousand pieces. But he worked hard, did what he was told to do, eventually designing high-tech killing machines under a cloak of government secrecy. My mother could finally find some pride in her man, bringing in huge sums of money, serving his country. I called it organized genocide and wanted no part of it.

I left home at 18, when I went to college. I purposely chose a campus far from home. I was ashamed by the flag they hung over the front door, a token of their obedience to organized cruelty and imperialism. I refused my father's offers of financial help through college, preferring to work in bookstores and late-night cafés. They were heartbroken, and asked me again and again why I didn't come home. One Christmas, about a year before they died, I did go back. My hair was long by then; I smoked ostentatiously on the porch. See, I have my little stubborn spots, too. My mother baked and cleaned and fussed, and silently pleaded with drooping eyes for the return of the son she'd raised. But I was adamant. The war machines or me, choose. You can't have both.

The night before I left, after my mother went to bed, I sat out on the porch, smoking in the cold night air. My father must have been working late in his study. To my surprise, he came out and sat beside me. And to my even greater surprise, asked me to roll him a cigarette.

"I know you don't like the work I do," he offered. Silence. "And, honestly, Matt, neither do I. But your mother is frail; we need the income, and this is what came my way. You don't always have the free choice to do things exactly the way you'd like to. Sometimes you have to compromise." Yes, buddy, but you can't make compromise a way of life.

We talked for a while that night, my father and I. I argued a little, he defended himself. As I look back, he was pleading for my approval. Pleading for me to forgive his crippled life. He offered me a hand to shake, smiled a little tensely, and went to bed. After they died, they left me money, plenty of it. But I was angry. It all smelled to me of the machines my father was building to wipe out entire villages in Asia or the Middle East. Children mowed down in their sleep, women widowed, life hardly begun. For what?

I donated the entire amount, under the heavy influence of marijuana, to the Save Tibet Fund and Amnesty International. I figured I could make it on my own.

Genes. Biology. What more can I hope for than what I'm made of, this legacy of embarrassed compromise, of failure to stick to one's course? But it's so much bigger than that. I'm not only shackled to a family of mediocrity, but to a species that's bent on consuming its way to destruction. This is the legacy I pass on to my children, this legacy and this example. I come from a long line of weak-willed men, generation after generation, whose ideals are so faintly conceived and asserted that they are washed away in the current of the status quo.

I conceived my children like Nero did, when the culture was already beyond the point of no return. Just last week I read somewhere that global temperatures are averaging three degrees above normal. The signs are everywhere, but like lemmings, we rush, following power-crazed self-righteous leaders over the cliff. Give me a bigger house, an upgrade to my airline seat and my RAM, and I'll turn a blind eye to the madness.

It's all dying. Not dying in a natural way: dust to dust, ashes to ashes. The very system that supports a healthy life and death is itself dying. Every year more species are wiped from the globe by this collective trance of greed. A huge machine smashing everything in its path, chomping everything greedily down its gullet. Bigger and better SUVs blindly adding to the burning of fossil fuels and forests and simple values, the assuring of an uninhabitable planet for our grandchildren. What possible difference would it make anyway if I bailed myself out of my current crisis? Even if I did bring myself back into alignment with the great machine, where is it going? What nobility is there in participating in mass stupidity? Ours is an economic system so out of balance that more than two billion people live on less than a dollar a day, while puppet politicians and their corporate friends and sponsors gamble with stakes beyond our capacity to understand.

What's the very best that I could do? Write a book? Make a movie? What's the very best that I'm capable of—and who would listen? And if they did, how quickly would it be forgotten? What kind of books do people read? The daily journal of a golf celebrity, the interior decorating of your favorite film star. Guide books on how to fiddle more successfully while Rome burns all around you. Corporations corrupt, governments corrupt, the very fabric of our living corrupt. I'm really no different from the rotten machine to which I belong. My failure, my greed, my mistakes, no different than the rest of the lemming pack.

It was getting light, but it made no difference to me. There was no point to any of it, only a pit where my belly used to be, an empty hole with my spine aching. Even to undertake the almost impossible task of bringing a life back into balance, to what end? What possible nobility would we find there?

I once read a story in the paper about a man, quite well-to-do, good job, worked for one of the long-distance phone companies, with a wife and three children, all doing well. One day he shot them all and then committed suicide. The question we all ask ourselves is "Why?" When all is going well, why? In my attic at dawn, cold, alone, I knew why. Perhaps that poor crazy man was saner than the rest of us, perhaps he saw through the futility of trying to make something right that is plunging, out of control, into something wrong. Perhaps he saw the future he was raising his children for; one with polluted water, polluted hearts. One in which love and nobility are insidiously turned into products to sell.

It was light now. I ate the grapes greedily. I didn't care how long they had to last. I didn't care about anything. I lay back on the bed and masturbated fiercely, fantasizing about women with black lipstick and spiky hair. I needed to feel something. Anything. I came quickly, before I was even hard. I wiped myself with a sock I found lying on the floor. I lay back exhausted. I hadn't slept. I wondered if masturbating was against the rules. There was still nothing. I was empty. I thought again of the bridge. If I were there in this moment, I would jump, but just the process of getting there seemed like too much effort. All Joey's advice seemed pathetic, infantile even. A cruel joke at my expense.

So the day went on. Every now and then I did what I could to pull myself out of the hole, but with every hour the motivation grew less. What point was there? For whose benefit would I try to find some energy, some motivation to continue? Hour upon hour went on in this way, and by the time the sun was going down, the world was already gray and dismal. I could not remember one single thing to give me reason to continue.

Paul knocked at my door, looking sheepish. I didn't even bother to try connecting with him. I followed him down the stairs, the way people walk after receiving electric shock therapy, mechanically, lacking the energy to do anything else. We drove in silence. We walked from the car, one behind the other up the stairs. I didn't even try to connect with anyone, just left my shoes, stepped through the door into the room, sat down, and closed my eyes. Joey must have come in at some point; I didn't look to see. He began to speak; I didn't try to listen.

Then something else began to creep over me, slowly, barely noticed. It was a silence, a nothingness. It wasn't blissful; it wasn't mystical; it wasn't ecstatic. It was just empty, devoid of anything, devoid of desire, devoid of any energy or motivation to change anything anywhere. Utterly empty. Utterly still. Devoid of enthusiasm, devoid of despair. It was really as though Joey, and his meeting, and the people, and my family, and the whole human drama, and even Matt Thomson himself were in another room. Here it was silent; there was nothing happening nor had there ever been. It felt neither good nor bad.

Joey stood up to leave. I didn't even open my eyes. I sat there as though dead, and in a way I was, for everything I had called human life had ceased to operate. He left the room. No one tried to connect with me, and I left them alone, too.

After a few minutes, a hand lightly touched my shoulder. Alan. He didn't speak, just motioned for me to follow. He ushered me in to Joey and left the room.

"Sit down," Joey said.

I felt nothing. I was neither happy to see him nor resistant. I just sat. He looked at me. In a certain way he was also dead, but somehow with a difference. He had some humor; I had none.

"How's the retreat been?" he asked.

"Hell," I spoke without emotion. "Just hell. Nothing you've taught me makes any sense now. I find no reason to live but also no particular reason to kill myself. It's just empty, dull, and lifeless."

I sat looking at him, aware that I was expressionless. He didn't react in the slightest, just looked back at me, very still. Finally, after some minutes, he left the room for a moment and returned with a very old leather-bound book.

"I was given this book in Istanbul," he said. "By a Sufi named Ishmael Bul-Jamal." It meant nothing to me and I didn't care. "This book is very old," he went on. "It contains many secrets."

I just looked. He laid the book on his knee and thumbed through the pages until he found an elaborate colored print, covered by thin tissue. When he lifted it, the colors were bright and luminous. It showed many symbols, and an arrow, like a snake, weaving through them all.

"The Sufi map of the human soul. See here, down at the bottom, death. Just above it is apathy. Then comes anger, hate, and destruction." I assumed he must be talking about my state, but I really didn't care. "And so it winds its way up; above hatred and destruction comes restlessness, desire, then greed, and creativity.

"In the middle of the diagram is Love, the heart open. Many people think that's where it ends. But look where it continues."

He pointed. I couldn't read the script; it was in Arabic.

"Beyond Love, there is Clarity, the capacity to see things and speak of them clearly. Beyond Clarity there is Intuition, knowing without the need for perception. But look here. Before the final open sky of freedom, there is this. Despair, complete despair. It's what the Christians call the dark night of the soul. It precedes freedom. You must pass through where you are now, and no one can go there with you. That's why I gave instructions to everyone to ignore you, to give you no support. Everyone has to come to this place of absolute nothingness, sooner or later. To this place where there is neither fear nor desire, neither attraction nor repulsion, just a clear seeing of the futility of all of it, and the lack of motivation for it to be any different.

"It's not finished yet, but you've reached here on your own. You have to become friends with the darkness. The Zen poet Bunan said once, 'Die while still alive, be absolutely dead. Then do whatever you want; it's all good.'"

I heard him; I saw him. I felt no flicker of anything in particular. He was clearly done. I stood up, and without any formal acknowledgement, I left the room.

Paul was waiting for me outside, with head still bowed. I now knew why, but it made no difference. He drove me home. I climbed the stairs and went to bed. Not with happiness, not with sadness, not with anger, not even with peace. I lay down in the darkness and didn't sleep.

CHAPTER 23

FREEDOM

Where was I? I looked around. Slowly I recognized the pictures of Peru, the clothes, and the sleeping bag. I sat up and stretched. The last day. One more lesson, if the restaurant tasks were eight and the darkness thing was number nine. This was Wednesday. There would be no meeting.

I had no arrangement to meet with Joey. It felt suddenly absurdly unimportant. I remembered that my children were living with their grandparents; my wife would obviously still give me a chance. My world might be going down the tubes, but I could still make a small difference today. I was still feeling empty, but now it was different. The day before I had no motivation to do anything. Now it had expanded, I had no motivation to do anything, but equally no motivation to resist what obviously needed to be done. The impulses to action were no longer coming from me, they were commands I was bound to obey.

I rose from the bed and took a few deep breaths. I wanted to write a to-do list, start aligning jobs, get my hair cut. Still, I felt a certain obligation to complete this time with Joey. He'd given me a lot, and I would see this tenth day out, even if the tenth lesson eluded me, and even if I never reached the giddy heights that he offered.

I spread my sleeping bag out on the floor, did some of the yoga postures I could remember from Sam's class. I did them very slowly, breathing deeply down into my belly all the while. I must have passed a good hour and a half in this way. There were still a few grapes in the bowl. I knelt on the bed, spine erect, and ate them slowly.

No desire, only readiness.

It was Wednesday; Paul would be working the whole day. Around noon I went down and let myself into his apartment. I showered, washed my hair, and put on the clean clothes I had brought with me. I spent a few minutes cleaning up his mess and then went back upstairs. My movements were all slow. I figured if I saw the day through until evening, I would have given Joey's assignment at least a fair shot.

For the afternoon, there was really nothing that I could do, so I just sat there. My spine was straight. I just sat and waited. I noticed the way thoughts would drift into a variety of different directions and then come back again. I really didn't care. The tools Joey had given me at the farm seemed ludicrous, self-indulgent, the preoccupation of New Agers with too much time on their hands. I was just sitting, waiting, until I was free to get on with my life, until I could take action. It really didn't matter now whether these actions would succeed or fail. It made no difference; that was not the point. I knew for sure a response was being called forth from me. There were things that needed to be done. Not to do them would be an act of defiance.

Finally, around six o'clock, I put on my jacket and shoes; I made the room as immaculate as I could, and stepped back down the stairs into the evening. It was still cold, a little damp, but no rain. I decided to walk across the town and find Joey. My steps were brisk, pulled forward more from my belly than my head. I could feel the contact my feet made with the sidewalk. I said good evening to almost everybody I passed; it seemed like the right thing to do. By 6:45 P.M., there I was, back again on the Donahue Bridge, 11 days later, everything the same as it had been. The smells of Asian food, Indian food, mixing with that of American diners. Neither disgusting nor attractive. Just smells. I breathed deeply and looked into the water below.

Eleven days before I had stood in this spot and considered jumping; I had wanted to end my life. I could do it tonight, too. The difference between living and dying seemed almost a technicality. There was no clear reason to jump, so I didn't. There was not much greater reason to stay alive. The moment stretched out forever. I stood on the bridge, looked into the water.

A car approached the bridge. It slowed down as it passed me. I turned. Out of the corner of my eye, I saw someone standing there. A dark figure in a hood, in the shadows, watching me. It appeared to be holding a staff, divided into three barbed points at the top. I shuddered. It was the same figure that had stood there 11 nights before. An electric ripple of fear, no one would hear me shout. It was fully in the shadows of the bridge's tower, just a silhouette. I looked away, back into the water, but I could feel those eyes still on me. It stepped out of the shadows onto the bridge itself. I didn't look up. Footsteps moved down the bridge toward me. My heart, pounding. Footsteps moving straight toward me. Where could I run?

"This is the evening of your last day," said the voice.

I looked up. Skin bleached white under the neon light, glistening with the moisture of the evening. Eyes bore into me, unwavering. He came close, stood still, not a muscle of his face moved. He waited. I felt compelled to offer some defense on my behalf. It would only be a testament to my failure. I looked back down at the water, not at him. So we stood in silence, each of us waiting.

I had no idea how or why he was here, how or why he knew I would be here. I had to speak.

"I know it's the tenth day," I said. "I know there must be a tenth lesson, but really . . . " I struggled for the right words. "To be honest, I've lost interest. All day I've been feeling restless. I'm grateful for your help, I really am; but I don't think I need a teacher or a teaching. I need to live my life."

I turned and looked into Joey's eyes. They were absolutely expressionless, absolutely still.

"I have two children. I realized today that if I don't take some kind of action, they will suffer more than they have. More than they need to. I have a wife. You were witness; you helped me connect with her. You spoke with her on the phone. She's waiting for me to take action, so she too can get on with her life. Everybody is waiting. I feel, in a certain way, like I have just been playing around with you these last days."

He said not a word; not a muscle moved in his body.

"There may be all kinds of higher states of freedom and enlightenment," I went on. "And maybe one day I'll find out about them. But right now . . ." I paused and felt strong, like the iron of the bridge. "Right now, I just need to live my life. I need to take care of the things I've already started. I may not do it perfectly; I may not do it the way other people would, but I will bring all of me to it. I will do the best that I can."

Still he waited; still no reaction; still not a flicker of response.

"I want to thank you. I know you've done your very best to pull me out of my predicament, and maybe, in a way, you have. Maybe, in a way different than either of us expected. I really find not a shred of interest left within me in being spiritual or learning anything or passing any test. It's up to me. I have to do it. Me, Matt. I have to take action, and I'm fully responsible for the consequences."

His eyes widened a little, his mouth remained soft and still. Finally, he spoke.

"Our work is complete," he said. "You have, in your own way, stepped into and owned your own freedom. You are free. You are free even of the need to be free. You are free of me, free of any work, free of any teaching. It is done. Come, I want to take you somewhere."

I slowly followed him off the bridge. It had a railing along the side. Around the tower, each post cumulated at the top in three barbed points.

"But what about the last lesson? You said there were ten lessons. We only did nine."

He looked at me from the corner of his eye. His face showed a tinge of boredom, frustration even, like trying to tell a good joke to a serious German scientist.

"Matt, Matt. This ain't some celestial prophecy. This is real life."

He led me off the bridge in silence, in the direction of the café where I had first met Sam. He walked right up to the door; it was dark inside. "Closed," said the sign. He produced a key from his pocket, slipped it into the lock, and opened the door. I followed him into the darkness.

The moment my foot touched the café's linoleum floor, lights came on. The sound of cheering. Streamers, balloons, bright colors everywhere. Somebody activated the jukebox, the place was filled with Fleetwood Mac encouraging us not to stop thinking about tomorrow, that it will soon be here.

My eyes roamed the room in disbelief. There, at the table closest to me, were Becca and our two children, sitting with Will Thurston and Paul. At the next table were Alan, June, Maryanne, and Cheryl. In my peripheral vision I could see there were at least 50 or 60 people here. Sam and Tim, even Carlos. Everyone from Joey's meetings, everyone from the farm. Even friends of Becca's and mine I hadn't seen since before we separated, who had nothing at all to do with this crazy world. Almost the entire staff of the radio station was there. Joey evaporated immediately and joined Katie and Jesse at a booth in the far corner.

The kids jumped up and climbed on me with cries of "Daddy!" Becca stood up and threw her arms around me, too.

They ushered me to their table. Food and drink were produced; cake, bubbly wine. I looked at my kids and my wife. I looked around the room. How strange, only a hair's difference from jumping to my death. It's just another movie.

They talked and laughed and tried to unravel the intricate web Joey had spun us all into. I ate the cake, slowly. I sipped the wine. I pulled my children toward me.

"Would someone for pity's sake explain to me what on earth is going on here?" Becca wasn't angry; she was playing. From the way she was looking at me I knew I was Captain Fantastic again in her secret velvet world. "I got the strangest call yesterday. Matt's friend, same one who had him over for Christmas. Said he'd really love to show me his Bresson prints, but he was leaving town. Wanted me to come with the kids the same day. From Chicago, mind you, not round the corner. I thought he was a crackpot. Then you call," she looked at Thurston, "telling me you could vouch for it all, offering me three prepaid tickets. So what gives? I thought you moved to Hawaii, Will. How'd you end up in all this?"

"It was me," announced Paul, with an affable smile, wiping cake from his face with his sleeve. Paul had always regarded Becca's indifference to him as a huge misunderstanding, and hence completely ignored every cold shoulder she had offered him. "Matt's been going to these meetings, see. Tried to get me along, told me he was seeing God. I thought it was all hooey," he shoveled in some more cake, and continued his story while chewing, "until, that is, I found out that Matt's friend knows Coppola. I was ready to sign up after that, that's my kind of a cult. So I went along to a meeting, and had quite a talk with the guy afterward. Cartier-Bresson, Olivier, he's known everyone. Joey wanted to know how to reach you," he looked over at Thurston, "and all the details I knew about that deal with the bike and all that."

Sarah had fallen asleep in my lap. Like nothing had ever happened. Dom was finding a number of very convincing arguments why I should let him try my wine. Out of the corner of my eye I saw Joey walk from his table toward the door. He motioned to Alan, and they left.

"Joey called me that same night," Thurston picked up. "It was quite late, he called Annie first in Hawaii and got the hotel room number from her. Now mind you, I had no idea Matt had lost all his money to that swindler Harmer, or lost his house, or any of the rest of it. And Becca and the kids! Dom's my godchild you know. I was mortified. I felt so badly to have been out of touch with everyone. I'd only just found out you were no longer with the station." I was only half listening; Dom was telling me the rules for Diablo. "But I did know how to track down Harmer. Pushar had only just gotten through with trying to persuade me to invest, seems they were in cahoots.

"We tracked Harmer down to a hotel room in Detroit yesterday morning. He was still merrily raising funds. I got my lawyer onto it right away. They have an office in Detroit, so they sent someone over. Made him an offer he could not refuse. Return all the money Matt lent him, with the promised interest, or face immediate prosecution. I've got you a cashier's check back at the office, Matt." Dom had just got as far as how to raise your life shield significantly by attacking the druid forces with elves and drinking purple potion. I mumbled thanks to Will. Cashier's check. Why not?

"So all that was left was to send you the tickets, and here we are! I'm sorry Annie couldn't join us. Tai Chi weekend in Kauai. Oh, by the way, I checked with the bank about your house. It hasn't sold. Had the lawyer look into that, too. They took repossession a full six days before they were allowed to by state law. You should have been given six months clear with no payments. They took advantage of your situation. We've negotiated; you can have your house back tomorrow. You simply have to make the payments for the last six months, and the loan is reestablished."

I looked from Becca to Paul to Thurston. It was all I'd ever wished for and a lot more, but strangely I couldn't even muster happiness. It was just fine like this, but really only a rearrangement of the same pieces from a few days before. I felt extraordinarily still, as though I had died, and this was borrowed time. Sarah asleep in my lap. Dom wrapped up in his virtual war with dark cyber forces. It all felt liquid.

"So," said Thurston. "I've grown to love Hawaii, can't stay away too long. Annie's all alone there, you know. I made a very poor choice with that Pushar character, think I let my head overrule my heart. Turns out there's been some funny business at the station. I met him yesterday. He was actually getting paid by Harmer to solicit investors, including me. I fired him on the spot.

"I've got to get back in a few days and I'm gonna need someone to look after the station, someone I can trust this time. Someone who'll keep the kind of quality and integrity we've had for decades. I'd like to offer you a job, Matt."

I looked at him. Sarah had just woken up. She was burying her head into my belly. All these explanations made no more sense to her than they did to me. She ate some cake off my plate with her fingers and then wiped them on my pants. I took another sip of wine; it tasted good, a little sweet. My breath reached down to the lowest part of my belly.

"Okay," I said. "That would be okay."

They laughed.

"I like this new Matt," said Becca as she kissed my neck. "He's, you know, cool."

CHAPTER 24

TIME RELEASE

"Gooood morning, matey, Alan here." The last two words were unnecessary; who else began a phone call like that? "Just calling to let you know that a good friend of yours and mine will be back in town and was hoping to see you."

It had been more than 18 months since I had seen Joey. He left town the day after the party. True to reputation, once the meetings hit 15, he was gone. Becca and I got settled into the old house, and within weeks we were back in our old routine. The kids returned to school, I got busy running the radio station, Becca seemed to take her responsibilities as a graphic artist much more seriously now and kept the money she made in a separate account. I didn't blame her.

I willingly put on the hats of father, radio interviewer, manager, husband. It all worked fine, better in fact than it ever had before. But in my heart I was in a bigger room, I was with Joey and his horses. I was playing on the beach, surrounded by a feeling of invisible protection. Not a day, not an hour passed without the need to return to Joey's lessons. I used them not out of choice, more from a sense of preserving sanity. When judgments came to visit, it felt dangerous, wild, and destructive, until I remembered those magic words, "just like me." When powerful feelings took me over like monsters out of the deep, some instinct in my heart demanded they be met, fully met, just as a skillful animal trainer might bring an unruly beast back into submission, lest someone get hurt. Even the depths of despair I had felt at the end of our time together revisited me regularly. The darkness would show up uninvited at breakfast, lunch, or dinner, oblivious to any sense of appropriate timing. Only in embracing it, was it transformed.

Days and weeks turned into months. I spoke to almost no one about the continuous practice in which I was now engaged. I rarely even reflected on it; it became as inevitable as breathing or the beating of my heart. I stayed in contact with Alan and June and the others. I even called Cheryl from time to time. Paul once again became a frequent visitor to our house and freezer. One night, we invited him to dinner with some other Joey friends, including Sam. That was it. They married within a month. We visited Katie on the farm now and then. I heard fragments of Joey stories from South America, China. I'd heard he came back to the farm once, just the same time we were visiting Becca's family. And now Joey was back in town and wanted to see me.

"Well, of course," I answered Alan. "It's been quite a while. I mean, where? When?"

"Same as usual. We've given him the apartment above the café. Tomorrow, seven-thirty. Oh, and bring your wife."

I looked out of the window at the early spring flowers. Daffodils, all in a row. The front lawn, neatly cut, the bushes trimmed. Our life was working now, a well-oiled machine painted in bright, happy colors. My days were filled with kids' soccer matches and ballet lessons, work and friends. Much as I had thought of Joey this last year, now I had a queasy feeling in the pit of my stomach. On the way to work I went through angry scenarios in my head with him. No, you can't drive my car, it's an almost new BMW, and look what happened last time. No, blind man's baseball on the edge of a cliff is just not responsible when you have a wife and two children dependent on you. No, Joey, I'm not accosting strangers in a restaurant for your amusement. But later in the day I pictured a great reunion, Joey taking me into his private room, looking deeply into my eyes, and telling me I had reached the final stages of enlightenment.

Becca got a sitter. We went to the café on West Broad Street early, and had monster sandwiches for dinner before climbing the faded stairs. Joey seemed quite unchanged, greeted me and everyone else as though there had been no break at all. He chuckled when he saw me, but more as a private joke he was remembering than a greeting. He looked a little older, suntanned from some adventure somewhere. He laughed a lot more than I remembered, but seemed distant, like an atheist showing up at a Baptist meeting, along for the ride. Many of the old faces were there, Maryanne, Jack, even Carlos. Sam held Paul's big hand throughout; she was visibly pregnant. At the end of the meeting, Maryanne was called in to speak with him, then Sam and Paul. Becca was loving every minute, talking to everyone afterward, like she'd been doing this all her life. I waited nervously.

We drove home together, to our floral print wallpaper, our neat rows of flowers, our sleeping children. I spent the ride home explaining to my wife how unaffected I was by not being called into Joey's room. Totally, totally cool. Appropriate. I shared my theory with her, from a number of different angles, that our work together was done. He needed to give his attention to the new people, the people who still needed him. She smiled at me and rubbed my knee.

I saw him one last time, a couple of days later. I went over alone after work, met Paul and Sam at the café. The room was fuller by now, some old faces, some new. One newcomer stood out. Despite his open white shirt, casual and spotless, his faded jeans, shoulder-length hair, and stud earring, he had the unmistakable air of a man with private means. He couldn't hide the relaxed amusement that only those born wealthy can pull off convincingly. He was probably in his early 40s. He was doing his best to sit cross-legged, but looked very uncomfortable. Alan offered him a chair, but he refused in an Ivy League accent.

Joey was shining that night. From the moment he came in I noticed it, as if his skin were emitting a luminous glow. Once he began speaking, he cracked up frequently, and closed his eyes, relishing some feeling, as though he were being tickled or massaged in a particularly pleasurable spot. Despite his shaggy white beard, he seemed half-feminine, extraordinarily sensual. He laughed, as if to say, "I've tried to control myself but it's no good. I'm hopelessly gone." Someone read a Rumi poem, and he wept. He looked at me with transparent, empty eyes. I felt I was looking at someone in rapture, but on a TV screen. His ecstasy was unmistakable, but he was no longer really with us. He had moved on.

This was the time that George Bush was creating the Department of Homeland Security and the Patriot Act was still quite new. A man I did not know, wearing a serious tie, serious glasses and a very serious expression told us that he was a member of a local group that met weekly to discuss citizens' rights. They had recently been infiltrated by a plainclothes police officer. When he made a blunder and the group found out, it made the news. He asked Joey for comment. Joey looked right back at him, closed his eyes for a moment, and was gone again. I felt embarrassed for the people meeting him for the first time; it was as though he had taken laughing gas.

"Everyone needs someone to make into the enemy. That's how we get by. Just now everyone has it in for this Saddam fella in Iraq. He is the problem. Looks like you've got it in for the president. 'Get rid of Mad King George, and we will all be okay.' The undercover cop had it in for you. 'Get rid of the lefties, and we will all feel safe again.' The most revolutionary act is to relax the urge to revolt. We are all the same, fighting ghosts of our own choosing. I'd say that the most revolutionary thing you could possibly do would be to see how similar you are to George Bush. Another chip off the old block."

The questioner looked shocked, surprised, and speechless. The Ivy League visitor seemed to relish Joey's political observation, however, and laughed with glee. Joey was delighted. They were looking at each other, tears now streaming down their faces. I tried to laugh, too, but it was forced. I didn't get the joke.

"So who are you, sir?"

"Oh, I'm sorry. I'm Charles. Charles Dee."

"Pleased to meet you," said Joey. "And where do you hail from?"

"I live up in Bellingham."

"You a sailor?" The question seemed disjointed.

"No, actually, chocolates." He said the word with relish, as one might say it to a child to convey the sense of a special treat. "I'm in the chocolate business."

"A chocolate salesman, eh? Brought any samples?" Joey's eyes lit up.

"Well, I'm not a salesman. I stumbled into the business from my family. Not much good at anything else, actually. We have a little business up there."

"A little business" was modest indeed. Dee's chocolates are the Rolls Royce of confectionary. Sold in gold boxes with ribbons, and a price tag to match.

"Ah," said Joey. He stopped laughing, straightened his back, and paid much closer attention to Charles, in a caricature of "If I'm a good boy, can I . . . ?" He glanced around the rest of the room, as if on the lookout for competition, then turned back. "I've been waiting for you forever," he whispered. The more serious he got about his chocolate heir, the more the rest of us laughed.

He looked affronted by our laughter and suddenly sobered. "So what are you doing here?"

"Not on chocolate business, I'm afraid. Been taking part in a little skydiving event."

"Skydiving?" Joey leaned forward in his chair again. "Now that's something I've never tried. That's jumping out of planes and stuff, isn't it?" Charlie nodded. "Is there an age limit, do you suppose?"

Charles looked a little embarrassed. He was straining to satisfy. "Don't think so. You need to be fairly fit though. Requires some strength in the upper body."

Joey pulled up his shirtsleeve to expose a fairly impressive bicep.

"Yes," Charlie laughed. "That will do fine."

"Good," said Joey. "We'll talk afterward."

Not long after, Joey rose, mumbled his "KYSH," and left the room, back in his private rapture. I was first up, and on my way to the door. Becca would be waiting. I had my shoes on, and was halfway down the stairs, when Alan called me back.

"Matt," he called. "Could he have a word?"

I turned back. Was my heart pounding from the increased exercise?

I took a couple of deep breaths, trying to regain the calm I had felt as I was leaving. I stood for a moment and looked at Alan, lost.

"You know where to go," he smiled, and went back into the meeting room.

The door was not fully closed, so I pushed it open. Joey was sitting bent over a yellow pad, covered in his scrawl. Next to it on the low table was his glass of chocolate milk. He carefully dipped his finger into the glass, then wiped it across the bottom corner of the pad, as though finger painting. I cleared my throat; he jumped.

"Eh!" he exclaimed, and squinted at me, not so much to ask, Who are you?, more like, Which planet is this?

"Wait outside till I'm ready." I did as I was told.

When I heard him grunt again, I entered, tentatively. Joey was sprawled in his chair, eyes closed. The satiated look on his face made him appear drunk, or otherwise intoxicated. The yellow pad was empty now, and on top of it was an envelope, with more of his writing across it.

"You've done well," he said, not even opening his eyes. "You've done well. The seeds are sown. The fascination with yourself is almost gone now. Everything else will happen on its own. You have reached the end of the futile attempt to improve yourself, and only from here can real evolution begin." He opened his eyes and looked into me. They had never seemed so brilliantly blue. Nor had he ever before seemed so strong and fragile at the same time. He was older, and at the same time much younger, like a small child. He was speaking to me from a threshold, already leaning backward over the edge of the abyss. I glanced at the envelope, wondering if it was for me. He scowled, and immediately turned it over.

"There are no more questions," he said. It was halfway between a statement and a plea. I shook my head, no. "All that remains now is to give it away," he went on. "You will never be the human being people want you to be. You will never live up to their standards, or even those which you impose on yourself. But you can offer yourself as a vehicle for the great gift. You know what that means now, don't you?" I nodded. "Even a cracked cup can be used to serve the best champagne."

He closed his eyes again. I knew he was gone. I didn't know where.

I stood there, arms limp by my sides. Inside, I was bursting with feeling. "Thank you," I whispered into the silence. His eyes opened suddenly, as if I'd woken him from a dream. "Give thanks by all means," he said, "but not to me. The thanks you give is in service, and only in that service can you really find the core of all you give thanks for." He closed his eyes again. "Our work is done. Go now." As I reached for the door handle, I waited, and looked back at him. I wanted so many things in that moment, yet I knew not one of them was real. I looked at his feet in their white woolen socks, resting one upon the other. I wanted to kneel before him in respect.

"Go," he snapped, with eyes closed. "It's done." I turned again to the door. I knew, and I knew that he knew, we would not meet again.

"Only in giving it away," he whispered, more as if speaking in a dream than to me, "can the gift be fully received."

Our house was about 15 minutes from the university district, on a route that I had taken perhaps thousands of times in my life. But I managed to take two wrong turns. It took 45 minutes to get home. I parked across the street and sat in the car, staring at the dashboard. I was churning. I felt I had watched a train pull out of the station. My beloved was traveling with a one-way ticket.

CHAPTER 25

CHOCOLATE-COVERED FRIEND

Two days later I came home from work early. It was a sunny summer day. The kids were in after school care, Becca was down in the basement meeting someone's advertising deadline. The cleaner had been there that day, the carpet was perfectly vacuumed, the cushions on the sofa freshly pumped up, not a speck of dust anywhere. Better not mess it up before Becca could enjoy the pristine vision. I took a Coke from the fridge and went out on the deck, taking the phone out with me. The kids would get a ride to a friend's house around the corner and would need to be picked up; the call would come any minute. I looked at Becca's neat rows of flowers in the beds below. I looked out over the valley at the houses, the routine, the predictability.

When the phone did ring a few minutes later, it startled me. I had sunk into a reverie, repeating Joey's last words, like a refrain, for the umpteenth time.

"He's gone, Matt," said a flat British voice.

"Excuse me?"

"He's gone, Matt. He's left us."

"What do you mean, Alan? Gone where?"

"There was an accident, Matt, this morning. He's dead." I had never heard Alan speak in a monotone before. I hardly recognized him.

"What happened?" I sat with the news. A part of me had been waiting for this since I left him two days before.

"After he talked to you that last night, he called Charles in. About fifteen minutes later he emerged with a bag packed and told me he'd be gone for a few days. Charles took him up to Bellingham. The family has quite a place up there; the chocolate factory is on an estate, where they also have a big old house—and an airstrip." I breathed deeply. "Joey went up for the first time yesterday and took a jump with Charles. They were harnessed together."

"And?"

"All went well; they landed safely. Charles told me they spent the rest of the day and the evening talking. Joey had, apparently, told Charles that he had one day to learn everything Joey had to offer, so they were up late into the night. Today Joey was very insistent about doing a jump alone. Charles was guilt stricken when he called me at lunchtime, said he should never have let him jump alone so quickly, but he felt unable to refuse Joey's insistence. We all know that one.

"Normally they would fly right over the chocolate factory and then jump out of the plane into a field about three miles farther on. But Joey jumped out early, without warning, right above the factory. Charles jumped out immediately behind him, trying to steer him safely down. Charles told me Joey was lost in a state of complete rapture, free falling in space. Joey's chute opened fine, then he kept steering himself toward the chocolate factory. Charles said he was shouting out to Joey the whole time, to pull on this rope or that, but Joey just looked back at him, laughing, doing the very opposite of what Charles was saying. Tears were streaming down his face, he was letting go of the pull ropes and waving his arms to the side like a bird. 'This is it, this is it,' he was calling out. Charles said he'd never seen a face like that in his life, he said it was as though everything was pouring through Joey's eyes.

"The factory has a big glass sunroof covering most of it. Joey went straight through the glass. He dropped into a large vat of cooling chocolate."

"He drowned in chocolate?"

"It's strange," Alan went on. "The ambulance was there in a few minutes. They're going to do an autopsy, of course, but they say it seems he was dead before he landed. His heart had stopped beating before he hit the chocolate. He hadn't inhaled any of it. He must have died in the air, just seconds before he hit the roof, or he wouldn't have been able to steer himself.

"They pulled him out, and he was dead. Charlie told me Joey still had a look of utter ecstasy on his face."

I waited. There was a pause as we tried our best to feel it all. Joey had died covered in chocolate.

"A chocolate-covered . . . " I spoke my thought aloud.

"Yes, a chocolate-covered Joey."

There was a long somber silence.

I don't remember who laughed first. It seemed like the wrong thing to do. But once we started, it went on and on. We laughed, and we laughed, and we laughed. I looked out at Becca's orderly rows of flowers. They seemed to be laughing, too. The sky was laughing, the birds were laughing. It was the same laugh I could still hear from the last night I had seen him. When I breathed in, it was him, laughing. When I drank my Coke, the bubbles were him laughing, too. As much as the story indicated the contrary, I knew he was not gone. He was more present than he had ever been.

I picked up the kids. I didn't tell the family about Joey's death for a day or two. I did not want to fabricate a tragedy where I knew there wasn't one. That night Alan called again.

"How are you making out?" he asked.

"I'm fine," I replied with an inquiring tone. "I'm fine. I'm fine." The last time I said it like I actually meant it.

"Well listen. There's a new lad turned up tonight. Name of Ben. Can't be more than twenty years old. Joey told me if anyone new came, to send them over to you."

"What?" I asked.

"Yep. That's what he said. He's on his way."

"He's on his what?"

The doorbell brought the answer. I went to the door, with Alan still in my ear on the phone.

"Come in. Why don't you . . . uh . . ." I was fumbling here, "wait in my office."

It was really a storage room: boxes, discarded kids' toys, a makeshift bookshelf, and a computer in the corner. He sat in the only chair.

"What am I supposed to do with him?" I whispered to Alan once I could escape to the kitchen.

"I imagine Joey thought you would know the answer to that question, or he wouldn't have had me send the lad to you." He hung up.

I went back in to the room again. Ben was certainly young. He tried to offer me the chair, but I persuaded him that I always prefer to conduct such interviews while sitting on the desk. His hair was tied back in a ponytail, a wispy beard was probably original growth. He seemed ill at ease, like he thought he had come at a bad time. He glanced at the door now and then, as if to see if it were locked. I tried to think of something to say to reassure him he was welcome.

"I've been waiting for you," finally came to mind.

He brightened. "I'm sorry, I got lost." He had taken my welcome as a reprimand for keeping me waiting.

"You are not late; you are right on time," I offered. I wanted to say that I was totally here, that I had all the time in the world. Eternity.

"No, I've been waiting for you . . . ," how to put this, "forever."

I could feel his discomfort as if from the inside. He seemed like a younger but otherwise identical version of me only the year before. He glanced at the door again, and then fumbled with his watch. I knew that if he kept still for more than 30 seconds he would cry. And that just now every cell of his body was bent on resisting that. He wanted to run away from everything, just like I had.

"You cannot run away anymore," I said, feeling my belly relax now. He had ended up in my storage room, just as I had ended up at Joey's. "Something has brought you to this place; there is nowhere left for you to run."

And sure enough, he started to cry. And then it all came pouring out. His parents were getting a divorce, his father had been drinking.

His grades at school had gone downhill the last year, and he finally dropped out of college. His girlfriend left him, after calling him a loser, and took up with the football captain. And to cap it all, he developed a skin rash that had resisted all treatment. He had moved out from his home, now his mother's house, just a few weeks before, and was staying with a friend on the floor.

The skin rash was an extra touch, but otherwise I could empathize to a T. "You are lucky; you have no idea how fortunate you are to face all this at your age." I was feeling very relaxed, as totally sure of anything as I had ever been. "You have to pass through this kind of a death for a new life to come. It may be hard to see it right now, but if you can stay with it, you will find blessing in all that you speak of."

A tiny spark came into the boy's eyes. He seemed to me to be hardly older than Dom, asleep upstairs. He leaned forward . . . and slightly knitted his brows.

"It's time to let things die now, things as they have been, but it is a death you can learn to welcome. There is life on the other side of despair. I have been just where you are, not long ago."

"What do I need to do?" He looked at me with a trust that seemed almost unnatural. The fact that we were surrounded by empty computer boxes and cleaning supplies did not apparently detract from the sacredness of the moment for Ben.

"Okay," I said, taking a breath and a dive into the unknown. "You have told me your story. You talked about 'my life,' 'my parents,' 'my school,' 'my girlfriend,' 'my pain,' 'my problems.' But who is the 'I'? What is the 'I' you talk about? Have you ever seen this thing you call 'me'? See if you can find it for real now."

He looked confused, but unperturbed. "I am me," he said, with a rise at the end of the sentence that made it sound more of a question than a statement. He waited, innocently. "I am Ben."

"Yes, that's right. Me. I am me. I am Ben. But these are words. Very familiar words. Every word points to something. What does the word *I* point to?"

I looked around for something to make my point. There was a Mr. Potato Head, in a box Becca must have been keeping for the thrift store.

"See this?" I asked, tapping it on the brow.

"Yes, I believe that is a Mr. Potato Head," Ben replied, looking serious and focused now. If his salvation was to be found in broken plastic toys, then he was all in.

"Mr. Potato Head. That's a name, isn't it? And there is a plastic thing here, to which the name is pointing."

"It is missing one ear and one arm," he quickly pointed out.

"And do you see this?" I asked, holding up a broken grey screen with a red frame.

"Etch A Sketch," he replied in dead earnest.

"We say a word, and it points to something. Each name has an object that it labels, like a signpost pointing to a city. The signpost is not the city. The city is not the signpost. One points to the other."

He started to look a little impatient.

"Now can you see this toy airplane?" I asked, miming the act of flying an airplane through empty space.

"Nothing there," he replied.

"Good. Now try to find this 'I', this 'me,' that you talk about."

The whole thing was over in about 15 minutes. Ben ended up as wide-eyed and legless as I had been a year and a half before.

He moved into our house ten days later, and occupied that same storage room where we had our first meeting. Every few weeks Alan would send along someone new, and we would meet on the patio or in the kitchen, or go for a walk in the park nearby. After a few months we began to meet, all of us, now and then, for an evening. And so it was, without really noticing, that I came to earn all that Joey had given to me.

In giving it all away, I learned how to receive the gift I had been given.

Epilogue

"I was sleeping every night under a bench in the west wing of the Buenos Aires central railway station." The short, stocky Argentinean woman speaks in a high-pitched South American accent. Gray curls hang in a chaotic mop loosely on her shoulders, huge colorful earrings like peacock feathers droop from her ears. The bright sequins covering her dress turn her into a loud human firework.

"He found me one night. He saved me. I was only fifteen." Her mouth quivers. She pulls out an ornate handkerchief and fingers it nervously. "He saved me from myself. I used to go to restaurants and cafés to sing to earn a little money. He heard me one of those nights. Only two years later I was singing in the Argentinean National Opera." She dabs her eyes, then flashes them at a balding man in a dark gray suit, doing all he can to appear fascinated. She takes a deep breath.

"And who would have thought that I, Fernanda Zapiola," she straightens her posture, "would become one of the most sought-after opera singers in South America?"

I whisper an "excuse me" as I step around her there, in the doorway. The main reception room of the Pendleton County Country Club is already looking full; 60 or 70 people are gathered into small clusters. The colonial building, with its ornate paneling rising halfway up the walls, its dark hardwood floors, mahogany furniture, hyacinths, exudes old-world stability. Trophies and photographs around the room commemorate the athletic achievements of muscular young men, almost certainly all dead now, or at least long forgotten. One photograph, larger than the rest, has been added just for today. The black-and-white picture, mounted onto hardboard, sits on the mantelpiece above the marble fireplace. Joey's deep penetrating eyes seem to overshadow everything else in the room.

On a table below the photograph sits the largest chocolate cake the club has probably ever served, four feet in diameter.

I take a breath and feel the room. It is bubbling, animated. Not exactly what I expected. Some of the people I already know: an evening of relaxed reminiscence. But the others, from all over the world, are a surprise, many only familiar from magazines or television.

"Matt, you made it!" says a familiar English voice.

"Al!" I reply, with a smile. "I'm sorry; I tried to get here earlier to help you set up. It's been madness at the station."

"What do you think?"

I say nothing, just breathing out through my nose and widening my eyes.

"Yes, isn't it something?" he goes on. "Now I am glad that Joey set things up this way. Not too many people want their memorial held ten years after they have died. He said there was something special about this time. Astrological. It took years to gather them all together. Four address books spanning forty years. Of course we had names, but almost everyone had moved. We invited more than a thousand, we're expecting five or six hundred will be here today."

"Five hundred people? There's no room!"

"Oh, we're just starting in here. We'll spill out onto the lawn, there's a tent set up, and a stage."

"For what?"

"Wait and see! There's going to be some reveling tonight all right, my lad. A party you'll never forget. All according to his instructions. But how are you?"

I have to stop and check. "Okay," I breathe deeply. "I just got off work not long ago. Stressed."

"Tell me about it!" He grins. Our eyes meet again, silently for a few seconds. A momentary sitting back in the saddle, a remembering of what we share.

"I saw something strange on the way here," I break the silence. "I had to stop on the way over. In the middle of nowhere. Went to look for a discreet tree a little ways from the road. Then I saw a miraculous thing. The tree was like the burning bush in the Bible. It had a scarlet hue; it was shimmering. The bark was alive and crawling, shifting, and changing color. I looked down; the rocks were shimmering too, red and alive. I blinked, thinking I was hallucinating. But as I peered a little closer I found that almost the entire tree and the rocks, and then other trees too, were covered with ladybugs. Hundreds, thousands of them, maybe millions, gathered together in that one spot."

Alan makes a soft murmur.

"I have no idea how many ladybugs were there in that little glade. I wanted to ask them. I wanted to know how and why they all came to be there together at the same time in that way. Were they mating? And why that place? Did they know that together they made the trees alive; did they realize they were creating living art? People say that seeing just one is good luck, and here was a good part of the world's population. Must be bonanza blessing."

He laughs and nods.

"One ladybug is a beautiful sight, but this many, it created a fabric, it changed the texture of the trees and the rocks; it changed reality."

"You eaten?" he asks.

"God, no, I didn't even have lunch."

"Go grab some of the goodies before they're all gone." He motions to the corner. "And get yourself a drink, too." I continue my obstacle course through the room. Every little cluster of people offers a different array of accents, another species of humanity. I step right up to a threesome, politely waiting for them to finish their exchange before maneuvering around them.

"Helped us write a lot of our lyrics in the early days, 'e did," says a man in a thick Cockney accent. Shoulder-length hair, lined face, I recognize him from the cover of an album I used to play very loudly in college while under the influence of various substances. He is talking to a bald elderly priest, complete with black suit and dog collar, and to a middle-aged woman in a business suit.

"'E were a wild one, aw right. 'E could outdrink any of us, out-smoke us, 'e were always the last one to leave the party. Weren't 'e jus!"

The priest is staring in fascination, as if hypnotized, at the gold medallion exposed by the aging rock singer's half-unbuttoned crimson shirt.

"What year was that?" The priest has gentle eyes, a gentle accent, could be Spanish.

"Dat were sixty-free, werenit?" The rocker sniffs sharply through one nostril, looks quickly around the room, as he chews his gum. "And what brings you 'ere, Farder?" He hardly bothers to soften his sarcasm, as though he assumes the priest has gotten lost on his way to an ecclesiastical convention.

"Oh, he was very kind to us," replies the priest softly, looking for a moment at the ground. I look down, too. The priest's somber black lace-up shoes are eyeing the rock singer's crocodile skin boots with suspicion, like old domestic cats who want no trouble, faced with unknown exotic and wild animals. "He and his family spent several months with us at the seminary near Barcelona. He made generous contributions, allowing us to start an orphanage, which still thrives in his name to this day. I remember he encouraged his own children to play with the orphans, making no distinction."

"What year were dat, den?" The rock singer swaggers a little onto one hip, sticks out his jaw and sniffs again. The priest seems confused for a moment. He looks into the far distance, narrowing his eyes, calculating. "It was the summer of," he pauses, "the year of our Lord nineteen-hundred and sixty-three."

I laugh out loud. They all look at me, startled. "Excuse me," I say, and wind my way closer to the drinks and the food. Almost there, but not quite.

"Matt, darling. Wonderful you are here."

Katie's long, gray hair is pulled back into a broach on top of her head. She kisses me on both cheeks. "I want you to meet Vanessa, she writes for a magazine."

A well-dressed woman with dark wavy hair and blue amused eyes, looking very East Coast, is wearing pearls and a cream Ralph Lauren outfit. She holds her wineglass gracefully in one hand, while brandishing an elegant leather-bound notebook in the other. She cocks her head to one side a little, and smiles at me discreetly, offering me a very manicured and jeweled hand. "Vanessa Hinds, *New Yorker* magazine. I really feel I missed out on something," she continues, exposing a set of extremely white teeth. She flashes that special cultured look, ever so slightly enlarging her eyes. She obviously expects some response from me, but nothing comes, so I just look back at her and wait. "I came here with our managing editor, who knew him in New York decades ago. I hear he worked quite secretly and that he refused for his name ever to be made public . . . " She trails into a reflective silence.

Katie proceeds to point out to her new friend actors, writers, musicians, as well as hippies, office workers, and mechanics, the rock musician, the anchor of a late-night TV show, politicians, a plumber, a hairdresser, and a marijuana dealer from the backwoods of Mendocino County.

"This is all very . . . intriguing," comments Vanessa. "I feel I've seen half of the room on the pages of *Time* magazine." She swallows, and returns to her subdued New York sophistication. I glance at Katie. I smile. She winks. We both know it is pointless to explain. There is a secret here that cannot be told, much as we might want to. I look around at this strange minestrone soup of humanity, eyeing one another with interest, like bemused animals from far-off corners of the world, brought together in this makeshift petting zoo.

The reporter fixes her eyes on me again as she smiles calmly. She carefully and quickly scans my eyes, then my mouth, then does a quick check on how I am dressed. I am being evaluated by a refined eye. She cannot hide the fact that she gives me low points for shopping off the rack rather than on Fifth Avenue. A tinge of condescension, a cultured sarcasm, is waiting in the wings, ready to be activated at a moment's notice. I still find nothing to say to her, so I just look back and relax, waiting. Silence wins out over any potential words, she softens a little, the space between us becoming its own communion.

"Matt got to know him very well, dear," Katie says. "He often spoke of him like a son." Vanessa cocks her head at a different angle. I can see my rating changing with each new piece of information she is offered, like the Dow on a volatile day.

"Excuse me," I force a smile. "I'm on my way to the drinks. See you later."

On I go, through this forest of humanity. It is overwhelming. I take the glass of wine and assemble a little plate: sushi, small carrots, doll-sized biscuits. Finger food, my mother called it, at the socials after church. I find a place in the corner between two plants and look back at the room. People are still coming in, sidling around the Argentinean opera singer, delivering her own praises to another unsuspecting middle-aged man. They are pressing more tightly into the room; no one has yet caught on to the "spilling into the garden" concept.

From low in my belly I can feel the pull, like a child dragging on my hand asking for attention. It is yearning for the wide-open spaces, for a depth beyond these exchanged scrapbooks of memory. The French window behind the plants is ajar. One small step out, with my little plate and wineglass, into the sweet rich smells of a late September afternoon, and I am free.

The sun is coming through the dappled leaves still on the trees, sending a patchwork of light and shadow onto the lawn, past the ornate gardens: geraniums, orchids, roses, sticky close fruity smells merging into an intoxicating brew. It all makes me want to sit in a deck chair and stare at a plant or a tree for hours, a heavy satiated smile in the middle of my brain. At the far end of the manicured lawn I can see a gazebo next to a large pond. I head for it in the hope of quiet. Even just a few minutes will be enough to prepare myself for the rest of this event. Miraculously, none of the other guests have had the same idea.

A weeping willow broods over the pond where swans and ducks share the late afternoon. The lawn is bordered by the edge of a small forest. I look back to the clubhouse, a magnificent turn-of-the-century colonial structure, perfectly maintained, with a full covered porch all the way around. A few clusters of people are starting to spill out of the building, holding bounty from the snack table. The medley of laughter and low-level conversation buzzes around the building like an orchestra tuning up for the main event. Hopefully no one will find me here. I close my eyes in relief.

Minutes float over one another, as I rest my legs on the bench opposite the one on which I am sitting.

"May I disturb you?" A voice beckons me back into the world of name and event. And here, standing before me, is Vanessa, the journalist from New York. She looks shy and hesitant now; it must have taken her some gathering of courage to follow me here. The tense muscles in her neck and jaw make it quite clear she is prepared to beat a hasty retreat at the slightest hint of rejection.

"Of course, there's plenty of room here, please join me," I reply. My moment of quiet was enough; I feel ready for people again.

"You know, I am intrigued by this whole . . . " she hesitates, looks at the bushes for a cue, "reunion." She raises her eyebrows with the last word, and cocks her head to one side. Then she looks to the ground and knits her brow. She has the look of someone contemplating statistics for infant mortality and trying to generate some appropriate feeling. "Charlie brought me along in the hope I would write a story, but frankly I find myself at something of a loss to know what to make of it all."

"Yes, it's hard for me, too," I laugh. "And it must be even harder if you had never met him."

She falters. "I was wondering," and glances at the ground again, "would you be comfortable if I asked you a few questions about him? I know this may be a very personal and emotional day for you, so if you'd rather just . . . " and her voice trails away into a sophisticated breed of embarrassment.

I rest my gaze on her for a moment. She is torn between a journalistic assignment and a genuinely open heart. She has been touched by something unknown she has felt here. I don't even know if she knows it, but it is spoken in the imploring in her eyes.

Out of nowhere comes the answer. "Yes, I'll tell you anything you like."

Like a child finally allowed a ride in the car after a long wait, she steps briskly up into the gazebo and pulls out a very sophisticated form of voice recorder. I smile; this could be fun, as she relaxes even more.

"Let's start with you." Her professional confidence is returning. "You do seem to have an extraordinary presence. You seem so totally . . . " She hesitates and flashes another coquettish smile. "Relaxed. Sort of really present and not involved."

I find no response forthcoming to her words. It is like she is talking about someone else; I feel as though I am eavesdropping. "There's really nothing to say," I begin.

"Tell me about when you first met him." She leans toward me and smiles quizzically.

"It was more than twelve years ago, I came upon him by chance," I reply.

"What led you to him? What were you doing the night before you met him? Let's start there."

I have to stop to recall. It seems so long ago now, not only in time, but almost like someone else's life.

"The night before I met him," I begin, "I was walking through the city at night. It was just before Christmas, and I remember at one point I was standing on the Donahue Bridge, trying to make up my mind about whether or not to jump off."

My interviewer stiffens in surprise. She eyes me cautiously, as if to see if I am making fun of her. "Why on earth were you thinking of killing yourself at Christmastime? The woman who introduced us told me you have a family, and you're in broadcasting."

"Well, that was the year when everything fell apart. In that year I lost my job, my house, my wife and children, and all my money." I pause to see if I have forgotten anything. "And on that particular night, my front door key."

Vanessa looks horrified, and leans forward involuntarily in consolation. "That sounds terrible . . . you poor man." She regains her self-composure. "What happened to you?"

Okay, I think to myself, *I might as well tell her the whole story.* I look over to the building, people are still coming. We have plenty of time till the long-awaited announcement.

"I've heard it said that when a body hits water from a great height, it is like hitting concrete. . . . "

It is starting to get dark. The lawn is lit up now and crowded. Still holding her small voice recorder, Vanessa has hardly moved for more than an hour.

"Extraordinary," she says, finally. "I was looking for a good angle for an article, but this is more like a whole book. Listen, I'd love to stay in touch." She gives me a card. "I know people in New York who might be really interested in your story. I am sure you have heard of Hay House. Very good people. But I think it may be best to pitch it to them as fiction."

"Hey, Dad, we've been looking for you." We are interrupted by Dom, who saunters up, hands in his pockets.

"Dominic, this is Vanessa Hinds, she writes for the *New Yorker*. Vanessa, this is Dominic, my son. He just graduated from Stanford."

Here come Becca and Sarah bringing up the rear. "So sorry we are late, darling," Becca kisses me, "the traffic was terrible getting out of the city." I wait for the request for an explanation as to why I am sitting here with a woman neither of us know, but no one asks for any, so I offer none.

"Friends, please gather now on the lawn," comes Alan's voice. "We will read a message from Joey in five minutes."

We step down together from the gazebo. Paul waves at us, absorbed in filming a group of Tibetan monks, who are absorbed in photographing him. Sam is close by with Violet, their daughter. She must be almost ten. And there is Carlos with his Carla, his wife. I swear she looks like she is pregnant again. They have four already.

Katie walks toward us, holding the hand of a balding middle-aged man in a sharp business suit and natty tie. Introduces him as her and Joey's oldest son. She points out the other son to me in the crowd. And there, to my disbelief, is Diana Milton Jones, the voice of God herself. But a transformed Diana. Her hair is no longer permed, but tied back. It is streaked with gray, she is wearing jeans. I look for her assistants, but there are none.

"Friends, please gather round," says Alan, now up on the stage. "Our mutual beloved friend wrote a message for you all before he died." He speaks slowly and theatrically, overcompensating for the fact that some of the guests are not English speakers. "He left this envelope," Alan waves it in the air, "with instructions that I should open it and read the message inside to you all tonight, almost exactly ten years since his death."

Alan opens the envelope with a flourish, as though about to announce an Oscar winner. We are close enough that I can see Joey's scrawl all over it. Looks oddly familiar.

"'My beloveds,'" Alan begins. "'I kiss your sweet hearts. I wish I could be with you to watch you meet each other. I know there will be some raised eyebrows. But as you can understand, I am prevented, due to another engagement which I am unable to get out of.

"'As I write these words, I can feel it is soon time for me to go. This earth and its people and dramas that I have enjoyed so much for so long are losing their grip on me. Every day there is less pull to stay. During my life I have met many people, all over the world. It's all been one-on-one, that's how I like it. I've seen things change. Over the years it's getting easier for people to get the joke, to wake up. At the same time, the grip of fear and greed gets stronger in our world and threatens to destroy this precious earth.

"'You are living through the end of the dinosaur mind. It lives in borrowed beliefs, in an endless variety of fundamentalism. All mental, not much fun. In the next years I'd say you'll see these fundamentalist dinosaurs at war with each other. The reptile mind lives in black and white, fear and greed, they all think that anyone who disagrees with their particular brand of righteousness is evil and needs to be destroyed. The dinosaur mind is not so much wrong, it's just stupid.

"'Dinosaurs lumber ahead, unaware of the destruction they create in their path. All that's left of the real dinosaurs is fossils, oil. And today's dinosaur mind is obsessed with oil.

"'You are part of a new mankind. You, and many people like you, people who have learned to live outside of belief, outside of fear and greed, to live in the present moment. The new humanity has the capacity to be conscious of the consequences of its actions. You are the new man, the new woman.

"'You can't save this earth and its living beings from fundamentalism by being right or angry. That just adds to the chaos. The antidote to fundamentalism is being aware, present, living life with humor. When you see the dinosaurs ready to drop their bombs on each other, by all means march, protest, stand up to stupidity, but make sure you wear a clown nose and a flower that squirts water.

"'When I was alive I never asked anything of you. We have had no organization, no membership. Most of you didn't even know each other. Or how many you are. But now you all have a part to play, a destiny. So I have something to ask of all of you. I want you to . . .'"

Alan pauses. He peers more closely at the paper.

"'I want you to . . .'" He turns the paper toward the setting sun. "'I want you to . . .

"I'm so sorry, I can't read this word." Alan looks embarrassed. "But it goes on. 'Do it with totality, and keep going until the day you die. I kiss your sweet hearts. Joey.'"

Alan looks up at the crowd, apologetically. I look around. Uneasy confusion. A few people are murmuring among themselves.

"'E wants us to what?" shouts out the rock musician, standing quite close to me, now holding a beer bottle. "'Ere, let's have a look." He strides up toward the low stage, hoists himself up, and takes the paper from Al. "Where is it then, Al? Oh yeah, 'ere it is." He looks up at the audience with relaxed authority. He scans quickly, "'But now you 'av a part to play, a destiny.'" He slows down for "'So I 'av sumfin to ask of all of you. I want you to . . .' What's this, Al? Looks like it's been smeared in something. Woz 'appened to it?"

"It was like that," said Al. "I opened the envelope just now. Look." He holds up the torn envelope, which indeed looks quite clean.

Cheryl has made it up onto the stage by now. She plucks the paper out of the rocker's hand with disdain. "I know his writing quite well. Thank you very much. Now where is it? Here. 'I want you to . . .'" she also trails away.

"Chocolate. It's had chocolate spilled on it. Or chocolate milk. Why didn't he give it to me to type? I was always telling him. Dear me, now we'll never know what it is we all have to do. Here, Katie, you try."

Katie shrugs, advances to the stage, and takes the paper.

The sound of a child's laughter. It is Violet, standing there between Paul and Sam. She is looking down at her shirt, where three or four ladybugs have landed. "Look, Mama," she calls out. "It means good luck." Now Sam is laughing too, then Paul, even Cheryl. Labybugs everywhere, on noses, on shirts and elbows.

It becomes infectious, ladybugs and laughter, spreading through the whole crowd.

Katie's voice carries over the laughter on the PA system. "Well, dear friends, it is quite simple. It looks like Joey spilled some chocolate milk on his last message to you." Katie's tone makes it clear that she sees this as quite normal, predictable even. Nothing to get upset about. This only seems to amplify everyone's amusement. "So I suggest you simply fill in the blank. Joey has something to ask of all of you. He wants you to . . . " She pauses dramatically. "So you decide for yourself. Anyway, whatever it is, he wants you to do it with totality, and keep going until the day you die." She folds the paper in a businesslike way, winks at Al, and jumps down from the stage. The laughter intensifies.

The rock musician has found himself a guitar by now, and has been joined by a drummer, a bassist, an electric violin. As Katie finishes her last words, the music starts. Earthy, zesty music. Sounds Celtic.

I look around, a sea of laughter, ladybugs, and movement. There is Paul dancing with Sam, with their daughter between them; he is still holding the video camera. There is Diana, the Voice of God, dancing with an elderly Tibetan monk. Carlos is surrounded by children, all wanting to be picked up by their papa. The lawyers from Philly, the chief of police with his wife. Jesse with a very adoring girl. The music goes on and on.

We're dancing still; we're laughing still.

Put that book down now, my beautiful friend. You must be nearly done with it.

Come join the dance.

Thank Yous

So many people have influenced me with their kindness and wisdom, in so many ways that have contributed to this book, that it would be impossible to mention them all here. But here are a few highlights.

I have been blessed with great teachers. Really, out of the box, extraordinary, wonderful teachers. OMG.

Twenty-one years ago I met a man in northern India who changed my life forever. His name is H.W.L. Poonja. He was the one who pointed my attention back to the ocean in which the waves are dancing, to the space in which form is arising and dissolving. He is the One for me. His teacher was Ramana Maharshi, the renowned sage who lived in South India in the first part of the 20th century. I bow in gratitude to both of them. I have also been greatly blessed by my Tibetan teacher Urgyen Tulku Rimpoche, and his son Chokyi Nyima Rimpoche.

The insights in this book are also influenced by my friends and teachers Byron Katie, Gay and Kathlyn Hendricks, Brad Blanton, Ken Wilber, Osho, Barbara Marx Hubbard, and so many more.

The original manuscript was lovingly midwifed by my lifelong friend and the world's greatest editor, bar none, Tinker Lindsay.

Since I much prefer to talk than type (even today, after a lifetime as a writer, I still type with two fingers!) I am grateful to Connie Kishbaugh,

Pamela Bryant, and Kate Bishop for transcribing the fruits of long hikes with a voice recorder.

The folks at Hay House have been a dream team. If you are reading the acknowledgments section 'coz you are thinking about working with Hay House, the answer is "Just Do It." Thanks Laura Gray, not only for great copyediting, but also for many inspiring phone calls. Thanks to Erin Dupree for talking to the press about this wacky tale, as well as having such an elegant name. Thank you Sally Mason for proofreading and unbridled enthusiasm, and to Celeste Phillips for final proofing of unimagined accuracy: next time I get a new *Where's Waldo?* book, I'm calling you in. Thanks to Heather Tate and Darcy Duval for honest marketing (a revolutionary concept!). Huge thanks to Amy Rose Grigoriou for a great cover design, and to Christy Salinas for creative direction. Thanks to Stacey Smith, Shannon Baum, Quressa Robinson, and Johanne Mahaffey for general having-your-sh*t-togetherness. I aspire to your level of functionality. Thanks to Patty Gift and Reid Tracy for welcoming me into the Hay House family, and of course to Louise Hay for being the incomparable Louise Hay!

Above all, I want to thank my family. The original draft of the manuscript was written when my sons, Abhi and Shuba were still little boys, and they were patient and kind while Daddy shut himself away in the garden shed to write. Again. And again. Most of all, thanks to my beloved wife, Chameli, for always calling forth the best in me, and laughing again and again at the same old jokes!

About the Author

Arjuna Ardagh is an Awakening Coach, and he trains others to be facilitators of Awakening, a process he developed which focuses on how to integrate spiritual awakening with discovering and giving your unique gift to the world.

Ardagh was educated in England, at Kings School, Canterbury, and later at Cambridge University, where he earned a master's degree in literature. He is the author of seven books, including the number one national bestseller *The Translucent Revolution,* which was featured in *O, The Oprah Magazine.* He speaks at conferences all over the world, and has appeared on TV, on the radio, and in print media in 12 countries. Ardagh is also a member of the Transformational Leadership Council.

Website: arjunaardagh.com

HAY HOUSE TITLES OF RELATED INTEREST

YOU CAN HEAL YOUR LIFE, the movie,
starring Louise L. Hay & Friends
(available as a 1-DVD program and an expanded 2-DVD set)
Watch the trailer at: **www.LouiseHayMovie.com**

THE SHIFT, the movie,
starring Dr. Wayne W. Dyer
(available as a 1-DVD program and an expanded 2-DVD set)
Watch the trailer at: **www.DyerMovie.com**

. . . . .

THE DALAI LAMA'S CAT, by David Michie

THE MAN WHO WANTED TO BE HAPPY, by Laurent Gounelle

PUSHING UPWARD, by Andrea Adler

All of the above are available at your local bookstore,
or may be ordered by contacting Hay House (see next page).

. . . . .

We hope you enjoyed this Hay House Visions book. If you'd like to receive our online catalog featuring additional information on Hay House books and products, or if you'd like to find out more about the Hay Foundation, please contact:

VISIONS

(760) 431-7695 or (800) 654-5126
(760) 431-6948 (fax) or (800) 650-5115 (fax)
www.hayhouse.com® • **www.hayfoundation.org**

* * * * *

Published and distributed in Australia by: Hay House Australia Pty. Ltd., 18/36 Ralph St., Alexandria NSW 2015 • *Phone:* 612-9669-4299 • *Fax:* 612-9669-4144 www.hayhouse.com.au

Published and distributed in the United Kingdom by: Hay House UK, Ltd., Astley House, 33 Notting Hill Gate, London, W11 3JQ • *Phone:* 44-20-3675-2450 *Fax:* 44-20-3675-2451 • www.hayhouse.co.uk

Published and distributed in the Republic of South Africa by: Hay House SA (Pty), Ltd., P.O. Box 990, Witkoppen 2068 • *Phone/Fax:* 27-11-467-8904 • www.hayhouse.co.za

Published in India by: Hay House Publishers India, Muskaan Complex, Plot No. 3, B-2, Vasant Kunj, New Delhi 110 070 • *Phone:* 91-11-4176-1620 • *Fax:* 91-11-4176-1630 www.hayhouse.co.in

Distributed in Canada by: Raincoast, 9050 Shaughnessy St., Vancouver, B.C. V6P 6E5 *Phone:* (604) 323-7100 • *Fax:* (604) 323-2600 • www.raincoast.com

* * * * *

Take Your Soul on a Vacation

Visit **www.HealYourLife.com®** to regroup, recharge, and reconnect with your own magnificence. Featuring blogs, mind-body-spirit news, and life-changing wisdom from Louise Hay and friends.

Visit **www.HealYourLife.com** today!

JOIN THE HAY HOUSE FAMILY

As the leading self-help, mind, body and spirit publisher in the UK, we'd like to welcome you to our family so that you can enjoy all the benefits our website has to offer.

 **EXTRACTS** from a selection of your favourite author titles

 **COMPETITIONS, PRIZES & SPECIAL OFFERS** Win extracts, money off, downloads and so much more

 **LISTEN** to a range of radio interviews and our latest audio publications

 **CELEBRATE YOUR BIRTHDAY** An inspiring gift will be sent your way

 **LATEST NEWS** Keep up with the latest news from and about our authors

 **ATTEND OUR AUTHOR EVENTS** Be the first to hear about our author events

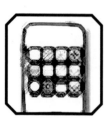 **iPHONE APPS** Download your favourite app for your iPhone

 **HAY HOUSE INFORMATION** Ask us anything, all enquiries answered

join us online at **www.hayhouse.co.uk**

  Astley House, 33 Notting Hill Gate
London W11 3JQ
T: 020 3675 2450 E: info@hayhouse.co.uk